SHOAL CREEK

LANNY BLEDSOE

BLEDSOE PUBLISHING

1

PRELUDE

John Watt pushed his wooden bateau away from the landing at River Bluff, paddled across the Chattahoochee River to Big Island and beached in a small inlet. He tied to a willow tree, grabbed his shotgun, and started in a trot down the island. He was running late to his favorite hunting place. The crisp Fall leaves blanketing the ground rustled and cracked as he ran. He reached Back Slough and as he turned downstream, a bright reflection from the water below caught his eye.

Curious, he stopped and peered down at a raft of logs washed up against the bank. The glint caught his eye again, the afternoon sun reflecting from a dead limb in the debris below. But looking closer, he saw it was not a limb but a boot with a silver star on the side sticking out of the water. He grabbed a tree limb and leaned out for a better look and saw the boot was attached to a leg and the leg to a man's body half-submerged in the water, a rope tied around his neck. His eyes were open staring toward the sky.

"Good God Almighty," muttered John as he fell back on the steep bank. "Them Shoal Creek people done killed Harold Hobb." Leaving his shotgun where it lay, he headed in a gallop across the island toward his boat.

2

Rep Doe was born in South Georgia into a third-generation share-cropper family. His father, mother, Rep and four younger siblings -- lived in a dilapidated two-room, roach-infested shack on a dirt road far away from town. The house belonged to the farmer whose land they worked. His mother, who grew up in a share-cropper family some miles away, had birthed five children, the first at age fourteen. She was the daughter of her husband's second cousin.

There was no electricity to the house. Plumbing consisted of a two-hole outhouse in the back yard and a well in the side yard. The only heat was a small wood stove used for cooking. The roof leaked, so buckets were placed throughout the house to catch rainwater.

A barn, which sadly matched the house in appearance, stood in the backyard adjoined by a corral for their one mule and a milk cow. The family owned neither of these animals. Both were paid for along with the land rent at the end of the crop year. After all the ongoing costs were calculated by the landowner, the family ended up with little, if any, money.

Chickens of various breeds roamed the yard, fending for themselves. There wasn't a house for them to nest, so each day, the children would search around the house for eggs. Occasionally one of the roosters would end up as supper. Rep's mother would grab it by the head, sling the flailing bird around several times, then toss the headless carcass to the ground where it would thrash about and then lie still. It was special to have meat with any meal. The normal menu was cornbread and a potato.

His parents slept in the one bed in the house. Rep slept with his two younger brothers on a quilt pallet on the floor, as did his sisters. They were accustomed to the patter of mice running across the floor during the night. Various other kinds of walking and flying critters infested the house.

His two sisters wore homemade dresses. The flour they used in cooking came in cloth sacks, the thin cloth printed with a pattern of small flowers. His mother used this cloth to make dresses for the girls. They'd never had any store-bought dresses.

Both his mother and father had little schooling. It was accepted in the family that children went to work in the field at an early age. Rep was intelligent and learned quickly in school when allowed to attend, which was sporadic at best since he wasn't allowed to attend during planting or harvest time. During the years up to the sixth grade, his attendance hadn't been more than three months in any year. Education of children wasn't a priority for sharecropper families struggling to survive.

He was twelve when his father took him out of school and put him to work in the field fulltime. He said the boy didn't need schooling to know how to plow a mule and without him helping fulltime they would lose their land. Rep didn't understand this concern. He wondered how could losing the land make their life any worse than it was? Month after month, the family worked from daylight till dark. After decades of working this same way, the Doe family owned nothing.

Their location was far out in the country with no neighbors nearby, except for the farmer who owned the land. The farmer's house, painted white with flowers planted all around, sat on a hill above them. The farmer had a truck and a bright red barn with cows and horses in the pasture, so Rep knew it was possible to have more than his family had. It could be done but he decided you had to own land. Hard work alone wouldn't do it. He thought that might be the main reason none of the grownups in his family had been more successful,--they didn't own the land. Based on their present situation, his family had no hope to ever own any land and faced a bleak future.

There was little food in the house and hopelessness pervaded the home. More and more, Rep's father got drunk and vented his frustrations out on him. The beatings became more frequent and more violent. His mother tried to protect him, but with little effect. He came to equate his father's violent temper to alcohol.

He tried to stay out of his father's way and do his work, but the situation got no better. This year's crop in the fall hadn't been good and the farmer took almost all the revenue from what they'd sold to pay the year's rent. After the farmer left with the bad news, his daddy started drinking. He was drunk for three days. Rep and the children hid under the house. His mother took most of the punishment during this time.

After one violent evening his daddy passed out on the kitchen floor. Without prior thought or planning, Rep, now almost sixteen, awoke early before daylight, gathered up his clothes, slipped quietly out the backdoor in pitch-black darkness and started running down the path and up the road away from the house. Barefooted, all he had were the clothes he wore, and a piece of salt pork left over from supper the night before.

He had no plan, no thought about tomorrow, except to get as far away from his miserable existence as he could. He ran up the dirt road in front of the house and when he got to another road heading north, he took it. He had no idea where the road led. He walked in the darkness with no thought or concern about the danger he might face.

Finally, the sun broke over the trees toward the eastern sky and lighted his way. He'd never been on this road before. In the early daylight the world was waking up. Birds were singing, squirrels in the trees along the road were beginning their day and a chipmunk scurried across the road ahead of him. He noticed none of this, just kept walking.

Later in the morning, he saw two men in a wagon coming down the road towards him. He hid in the bushes until they passed, afraid he would be caught and sent back to his family. His concern seemed baseless since they didn't know him and even if he'd been seen, they wouldn't have cared about a white-trash young'un wandering up the road. Regardless that it made no sense, this would be his strategy for the next several days -- avoid contact with anyone.

The morning sun turned blazing hot and the salt pork was soon gone. Apple and plum trees were plentiful on the road, so he filled his pockets and munched on them as he walked. Walking barefoot on the rock-filled dirt road wasn't a problem; he'd shed his shoes the first warm day in the spring, as all the children did. The soles of his feet were like leather. Creek water or smaller running branches quenched his thirst throughout the day and cooled his burning feet when he stopped and sat on the bank.

This part of the country was sparsely settled. He hadn't passed a single house or seen another person other than the two men on the wagon early that morning. As the hours passed and the miles went by, the concern about getting caught began to fade. He felt, for the first time in his young life, that he was free.

Later in the evening the sky darkened, a light rain started falling, and he realized he couldn't go in his house, as miserable as it had been, to find shelter from the weather. This was his first taste of reality. Just before dark he found a deserted barn on the side of the road and crawled into a pile of hay for the night. He was alone for the first time in his life. His two younger brothers weren't on the floor pallet beside him as they usually were, and a touch of loneliness brushed over him. Then he thought about not having to go to the field with his father tomorrow and walk behind a farting mule, and he savored the feeling.

When darkness settled in, strange noises disturbed the night as an owl hooted, the wind howled, and the tin roof rattled as the rain pelted down. These strange sounds made him afraid and lying in the hay he began to think that maybe he should consider turning back. But then he remembered the reasons he'd ran away and the concern disappeared. After a time, the tiredness of the long day took over and he slept.

He woke up at daylight and it took him a minute to realize where he was. When he got up, he realized he had nothing to eat or drink, so he started looking as he went up the road. He found a horse apple tree and then a stand of blackberry bushes. The combination filled his stomach for the time being. He was thirsty and it was almost noon before he found a small branch along the road and got water. He was beginning to understand how unprepared he was to be on the road.

That night he didn't find a barn, or any other shelter, so he had to spend the night beside the road under an oak tree lying on the bare ground. The ground was covered with sticks and rocks and there was no way to get comfortable. He was at the mercy of mosquitoes and other critters that walked and crawled. He had no cover and during the night the temperature dropped. He had a cold miserable night and the following day and night was no better.

By the third day of eating plums and apples, his stomach ached, and he had to run to the woods several times to squat and get relief. He knew he couldn't continue to sleep on the ground along the road and had to find some real food to eat soon.

Later in the afternoon he came to a small peach farm and saw a man and woman and two small boys in the orchard picking fruit. His situation had overcome his usual shyness, so he climbed over the fence and went looking for help. When he found the farmer and asked him for work, the man didn't question his age or situation.

"What's your name, son?" he asked as they walked through the trees.

The question caught Rep unprepared. "My name be Jim," he said. His brother's name was the first thing he thought of.

"Well, we're glad to have you with us, Jim," replied the farmer.

There would be no pay for working, but he'd get fed and have a place to stay so long as the picking lasted. The wife took one look at him so dirty and ragged and figured he was hungry. She gave him a chicken leg and a biscuit from her lunch sack. Rep thought he'd never tasted anything so good. Everybody worked till dark and the farmer told him to wash up at the faucet in the yard and come in the house for supper.

He'd never been inside a house other than the one where he'd grown up, so he had no idea what went on in a normal household. He could tell the people who owned the orchard weren't rich, but he thought of them as being so. When he entered their small frame house, he quickly saw the difference from the world he'd come from. The house was clean and neat, the two sons had a room of their own with individual beds and they had electric lights in every room. The bathroom was inside the house with running water, both hot and cold. He walked through each room marveling at things the family took for granted.

For the next weeks he slept in the barn. The farmer set up a small cot for him and the wife put sheets and a blanket on it with a down pillow. That night was the first time he'd ever slept in a bed and not on a floor pallet.

He ate meals with the family. They ate breakfast at daylight, then a quick midday lunch in the orchard and supper after work was finished. The farmer and his wife talked and laughed together as they shared the work. The boys minded their parents and were never yelled at by their father; all he had to do was speak and they responded. It was all so different from the homelife he'd known. He'd never imagined there were families where everyone could eat all they wanted during the meal and there was food left on the table after everyone was fed. Cookies and fruit were left on the table after supper and anyone could help themselves.

The family had another custom unknown to him. Before each meal began the family would get seated, then bow their heads and be quiet. The father would bow his head and say some words in a calm, quiet voice. Rep had never seen this done before a meal; his family never had. Rep's teacher in school had said words like this each morning after they said the Pledge of Allegiance, so he figured this was the same thing. Nobody had ever talked to him about it but he bowed like everyone else until the farmer was finished talking and they could eat. He never asked because he didn't want to seem stupid.

The farmer's wife was concerned about him, had been since she first saw him walk into the orchard. She asked about his family and what he was doing on the road alone and so unprepared. He only had the shirt and pants he had on and no shoes so she gave him a pair of the famer's old overalls to wear so she could wash his clothes. He told her he was out of school for the summer and was going to his uncle's house to stay until school started. He had seen them picking peaches and thought it would be fun to stop and rest for a while. He hated to tell such a lie, but he was afraid to tell the truth, for fear he'd be sent back to his family. This fear would remain with him throughout his wanderings.

The wife asked a few more questions, got fewer answers, then looked at her husband with raised eyebrows and said no more. She knew he was alone and obviously on his own. They had no idea how this had come about, and they didn't quiz him more. They would help him temporally, but wouldn't be able to help long term, they had their own challenges. As a mother her heart went out to him. In the following days she would make sure he got plenty of food and always gave him the best piece of fried chicken and the biggest piece of pie.

The farm wasn't large, mainly the orchard and a pasture for the bull and a few cows, but together with a vegetable garden, a pen full of chickens and a hog pen the family fared well, but they all worked hard every day. Rep had been accustomed to working hard every day and had no problem with it, but unlike his family, this one had something to show for it. The boys' outlook was positive; they told him they went to school and were looking forward to starting in the fall. Rep didn't mention anything about his schooling.

After he'd been there several days, the farmer took him to the small pond on the edge of the pasture. He showed him how to dig worms around the hog pen and taught him to fish for brim and catfish. Afterwards, he showed him how to dress the fish they caught. Later he took him to the pond at night with a light and showed him how to gig and dress bullfrogs. The family supplemented their meals with fried fish and frog legs, a break from ham and fried chicken.

After several days of fishing with the farmer, he began getting up earlier each morning and fishing in the pond alone. He would catch fish, have them dressed before breakfast and take them to the kitchen. He felt this was a way to repay the family for their kindness. This was a new feeling for him, thinking he was beholden to someone for their kindness. He'd never thought of such before, but then he'd never experienced much kindness from anyone in the past.

After four weeks, the picking was finished, and the family returned to their regular life. They were able to handle the daily chores themselves and didn't need any outside help. Since there was no more work for him on the farm, he understood it was time to leave, and he was ready. For some unknown reason the road was still pulling him to continue the trek north. But he was sad to leave these kind people, another feeling new to him. He realized how fortunate he'd been to find this family at the outset of his journey. Later, in the future he would appreciate what they'd done even more.

The taste he'd had in the first days on the road of having nothing to eat and sleeping on the bare ground was stamped in his memory. He knew he had to be better prepared in the future if he was to survive. He hadn't yet figured out how he was going to do this. But at least he had some idea of what he needed to do.

He still owned nothing but the clothes on his back, and they were threadbare. The farmer gave him some of his older clothes, including a jacket he could use to ward off the rain. He also donated a cane pole with extra hooks, a frog gig, an old pair of shoes and a blanket. The wife donated a small skillet, a sack of potatoes, a cured ham, a can of lard and salt. Most important, they gave him a box of wooden matches.

He put his meager possessions in a croker sack, looped a rope around it for a make-shift backpack and threw it over his shoulder. He felt with these supplies and the experience he'd had with the family; he was better equipped to feed himself. He had learned to fish and gig frogs and had cooking gear.

He hugged everyone, thanked them for being so good to him and again headed north. The farmer's wife stood on the porch wiping her eyes with a dish towel and watched until he was out of sight. She couldn't help but think that but for the grace of God, there went her son. She vowed to pray for Jim every night.

On the road he still had no idea where he was going, had no specific objectives in mind and wasn't equipped to deal with any serious challenges he might face. Fortunately, he'd never been seriously sick, so he never gave that possibility a thought. The only positive aspect of his trip north was he could get up each morning and decide for himself what he would do that day, even if it made no sense. So, he continued north as if he knew what he was doing.

In an abandoned barn where he spent the night, he found a piece of tarp used to cover baled hay, so he had a ground cloth to use when he camped and something waterproof to put over him in case of rain. He always tried to camp near a running branch or creek where he could fish and get frogs. He usually had enough to eat, although his menu was limited, sometimes supplemented with corn or tomatoes he borrowed from an adjacent field. On occasion he would borrow a watermelon from a field of many, put it in a swift creek to cool it and then eat until he was gorged.

There were few cars and trucks on the road but when he heard one coming, he headed for the woods. He still had the fear of being caught and sent back home and he also knew there could be people on the road that were dangerous and needed to be avoided. He carried the long stick in case a dog came at him, but he had no other defense. He knew he should arm himself in some way at the first opportunity. He didn't know exactly what that meant since he'd never fired a rifle or pistol of any type. However, at the present time, he didn't have a cent to his name, so it was a moot question. His only defense was to stay out of people's way.

❧

everal days later he came to a farm where people were cutting and baling hay. He had been alone for a while and was tired of eating his own cooking, so he felt the need to stop. While he could get by with a meal of whatever he had, it didn't taste the same as a home-cooked meal prepared by a real cook. He especially missed cornbread and homemade biscuits sopped in sorghum syrup plus all the vegetables he'd had at the last farm. The food the farmer's wife gave him was about gone and he had no money to purchase more.

He approached the farmer and was quickly hired. Handling hay required a strong back and the more the merrier as far as the farmer was concerned. Again, the pay was meals and a place to sleep. This farm was much larger than the peach farm. In addition to the hay fields, there were acres of fenced pasture for the herd of beef cattle to graze. The stored hay was to get them through the winter months. After a day of loading bales on a wagon and then stacking them in the barn, he went to bed at night sore and totally exhausted.

Everybody was up early each morning and worked hard all day. There were no days off, the hay had to be cut and in the barn before the weather changed. Rain was their main concern. This family, like the one he'd been with earlier, were kind and helpful to him. They also asked few questions, but they knew his situation, although he was much better off now than when he'd been with the first family.

He now understood there were many people in the world who were different from his unhappy and destitute family. The thing he noticed was that all of them worked hard with a purpose, were fiercely independent, they looked after their personal business and wanted no interference from outsiders. Within each family the parents made the decisions and children did as directed.

The farm was located on the north side of the Flint River and the farmer, like most of the men in the area, was an avid fisherman. He wasn't only a sport fisherman, for bass and such, he also fished for catfish, which he sold. At the end of the first week Rep had impressed the farmer with his hard work and positive attitude, so he asked him to go with him to fish the trotlines and set hooks he'd put out for catfish in the river. This was a new experience for Rep. He had no idea what they were about to do, but he was eager to go.

That afternoon the farmer gave him a cane pole and a bucket of wigglers and led him to the river where they fished along the bank until they had about twenty live brim in a bucket. They boarded a wooden bateau and paddled downstream to the first set hook, which was a piece of line with a hook on the end. This line was tied to a limb of a willow tree leaning out over the water. The limb would serve the same purpose as a pole, giving when the fish pulled but keeping him from breaking away. The farmer put one of the live bream on the hook, dropped the end in the water and made sure the brim was swimming well. Then he paddled on down the bank to the next limb.

As they approached the fifth set hook Rep could see the limb slowly going down into the water. At times half the tree would be submerged.

"Got a good one here," said the farmer as he paddled closer, "you can tell the big fish, they pull down steady without jerkin'." He eased the boat to the limb, took hold of the line and when he pulled, a huge fish boiled to the surface. Rep had never seen a catfish so large. The fish saw the boat and bolted down, pulling the large limb far into the water. The farmer held on for several minutes until the fish tired and came to the surface. He grabbed it under the gills and hoisted it into the boat.

Rep was amazed at the size. "What is that?" he asked.

"Flathead, best eatin' catfish there is."

"I ain't never seen one before. How big is it?"

The farmer eyed the fish for a moment. "Probably about twenty pounds, they get a lot bigger". The farmer explained that flathead catfish live in deep holes in the river but come into shallow water at night to feed. They will only bite live bait, such as the live brim they used. They're not bottom feeders like most catfish, so other baits aren't effective for them. So, most people haven't used the proper bait, haven't caught any flatheads and don't know they're in the river.

He fished with the farmer for the next few days, watching what he did. Then he baited several hooks with the farmer watching. The next week the farmer allowed him to go alone in late afternoon, catch brim and bait all the hooks. He went back at daylight to check them. He found he enjoyed fishing, had a special talent for it, and he tucked that knowledge in the back of his mind.

When all the hay was cut and stored in the barn, that job was finished. The farmer talked to him about staying with him on through the winter, which wasn't far away. Rep studied on that for a while but decided it was time to leave. He couldn't explain why he wouldn't stay and didn't try. He'd begun this odyssey with no definite plan and still didn't have one, but he didn't feel it was here.

With his pack filled with cured ham and bacon which the farmer's wife gave him, he again headed north, living in the woods along the way. He still owned little, had no money and the warm summer weather was about to end in a few weeks

3

September wasn't far away; the weather was getting cooler and he knew in a few weeks would get colder. Muscadines, one of his favorite fruits, were ripening on vines hanging from trees along the creek banks. He would shake the vines and pick up fruit until his pockets were filled and then savor the sweetness as he walked up the road. Leaves on the hardwood trees were beginning to turn red and yellow so he knew it would get much colder soon and he couldn't survive the cold weather without proper equipment, and he didn't have it. Soon afterward, he awoke with a white layer of frost covering the ground and knew he had to find a place to spend the winter. He also knew harvesting was over so jobs would be hard to find, and he had no choice but to find something soon. He thought about having turned down the job at the last farm and if he didn't find something quickly, he might have to go back.

Several days passed, the weather continued to get colder, he'd found nothing, and he saw few houses as he walked. All those he saw seemed to be small family homes with nothing to offer. He was running out of time and beginning to have concerns about what he could do. For two days he'd been walking in a forest of pine and hardwood trees and hadn't seen a single building along the road of any kind.

About midmorning he topped a hill and ahead was a crew of loggers cutting in the woods off the road. It looked like a large operation, with much equipment and people. He saw ten or more men near the road and others were cutting trees farther back in the woods, but he couldn't tell how many. He thought there might be a job there, at least it was a chance. He'd have to get a job here or head south.

The men were using mules to drag the logs from the woods to load on wagons pulled by mules. He'd had experience with mules, although behind a plow, so he thought that might be in his favor. He walked off the road and approached a young man, not much older than himself, sitting on a stump near the wagons eating a raw sweet potato. He asked him who was in charge. The boy pointed at a tall man wearing a big black hat who was talking to the driver of the lead wagon. "That's Jake. He be the boss."

Rep, his insides churning, walked alongside the line of wagons and stopped behind the man in the black hat. He was nervous. This was different from asking a farmer for a job, he'd been around farms but had no idea what these people were doing except cutting down trees. The men standing in the area around the wagons were older, rough looking and unkempt bearded men. Two of the men standing near him reeked of the odor he remembered from being around a wet mule. None of the men, except for the boy eating the sweet potato, seemed to be very friendly. To this point none had paid any attention to him.

The tall man, who the boy said was named Jake, was obviously displeased with something the driver of the lead wagon had done or hadn't done and they were involved in a loud, profanity-filled argument. Rep nervously stood off to the side. He'd only been here for a few minutes and he'd already heard more cuss words than he'd heard in his entire life, some he'd never heard. Jake had a holster on his hip with a pistol in it. Rep stared at the ivory handle and wondered why he would be armed.

The argument continued with loud shouting and arm waving by both participants. Suddenly, without any warning, Jake wheeled about while stepping away from the wagon and walked into Rep, sending him crashing to the ground. Jake struggled to avoid falling and when he regained his balance, he stood staring down at Rep with great displeasure. "What the hell are you doing boy, standing there in my way?" he shouted. Some of the men saw what happened and were laughing but one glance from Jake stopped that.

Rep struggled to his feet, brushing dirt off the back of his pants. "I'm sorry, I be lookin' for a job." he replied, stammering with every word.

"A job?" Jake shouted, his face getting redder by the minute. All the men standing around were watching. "You want a damn job? The hell you say. How old are you boy?" he asked, peering down over his glasses.

"I be seventeen." Rep replied, trying to stand as tall as he could.

"Damned if you are," Jake said as he glanced toward the road and then back at Rep. "Where the hell did you come from anyway? I ain't never seen you around here before. You live around here?"

Rep shook his head. He could think of nothing to say.

"If you don't live around here, where do you live?"

"Down south a bit."

"What the hell does that mean, down south a bit? You done run away from home?"

"Yes, suh."

"Anybody lookin' for you?"

"I doubt it."

"How long you been gone?"

"I don't know. Pretty good while, we be plowin' fore plantin' when I left."

Jake shook his head. "How'd you get way up here?"

"Walked."

"You been livin' on the road all summer all by yourself?"

"Yes, suh."

"Why'd you leave home?"

Rep looked at the ground again without answering; he didn't know what to say.

"Bad, huh? Your old man beat the hell out of you?"

"Yes, suh."

"So, you just been wanderin' up the damn road, with no place to go, and not a pot to pee in. Right?"

"Yes, suh."

Jake looked up at the sky and held up his arms. "And then you decide to come down here and ruin my day," he said this loudly and pointed at the driver, still sitting on the wagon, looking like a whipped dog. "I already got enough idiots here to deal with. There's one right there on that damn wagon, ain't got shit for brains. I don't need no more idiots and specially don't need no snot-nosed runaways." All the men around had stopped working and were watching and laughing. The wagon driver bowed his head and wished he was somewhere else.

Rep glanced at the red-faced driver, then up at Jake who was towering over him.

"Damn it, boy. Why'd you show up here, today of all days? I ain't got time for you, I got enough problems already." He pointed toward the road. "You need to get back on that road and get the hell away from me." Shaking his head, he turned and walked away, disappearing around the first wagon.

Rep didn't move, unsure what to do. He felt this was his only chance to get a job and get out of the cold weather, so he had to stay and wait it out. He had no other choice. He could see Jake talking to a group of men on the other side of the wagons. Then he walked away and disappeared from his sight. All the men went back to work, business seemed to be getting back to normal. Rep stood by the wagon, his head down, not knowing what he could do now.

Suddenly Jake came around the front of the first wagon and stared down at him. "Boy, you look like a damn lost-ass, pitiful puppy." Then his voice softened. "Hell, come on with me, boy. Don't just stand there like a bottle of piss."

Rep followed him to a small shed which functioned as his office.

He sat behind a desk and motioned for him to sit in the chair facing him. He took out pad and pencil and looked at him. "What's yo' name, boy?"

"Rep Doe."

"Where'd you say you from?"

"Down south a bit."

He stared at him over his glasses. "Damn boy, that ain't no place. What town?"

"Weren't no town, just country. Twas on the other side of the Flint River, I know that fir sure."

Jake laughed. "By God, I'm glad you know some'un. How old are you?"

"I thank I be sixteen by now."

"How long you been on the road?"

"I left home when we be plowin', gittin' ready to plant."

He stopped and looked at him, a questioning look on his face. "You been on the road by yo'self all this time? That's over four months. What you been doin'?"

"I picked peaches one time and I baled hay for some folks. All them folk be real nice to me. I catch fish and gig frogs to eat on the road."

He chuckled. "Damn boy, it's a wonder something ain't done ate you. Come on, let me git you settled."

Rep found out the tall man's name was Jake Mott. He owned the logging company and was the on-site ramrod who tolerated no nonsense from those who worked for him nor anybody else he happened to meet. The men cursed him among themselves but never to his face; they were scared of him. He was fair but demanding and everybody, even if they didn't like him, respected him. He had a scar on his face from his left ear to his chin and a tattoo on his left forearm that Rep saw but didn't understand. One of the men told him later that Jake had been a Marine and fought in a war somewhere at a place called Belleau Wood and the tattoo had something to do with that. Rep never asked about it and Jake never mentioned it.

Rep was told the crew would be cutting timber in the area until spring and then they were scheduled to move to another job to the south. He was glad they would be there throughout the cold months. That would allow him to survive the winter and he'd have a place to stay and hopefully get some warm clothes.

He found his experience plowing mules didn't mean much in the logging business and he had to learn from the ground up doing menial jobs. Jake seemed to take a liking to him and brought him along slowly, probably because he felt sorry for him. He spent his time cleaning up behind the crew as they moved through the forest.

Jake scrounged up a pair of boots and a heavy coat for him and gave him a bunk in the house where the crew stayed. Logging was a tough and dangerous job. The equipment they used was dangerous, capable of killing or maiming a person in seconds if they were careless. As they moved through the forest, a lot was going on in all directions. Trees were constantly falling, logs were being dragged out, wagons were being loaded and moving from one place to another. Everyone had to be aware of their surroundings all the time. In warmer weather rattlesnakes were killed almost every day and cutting around creekbanks had everybody looking for water moccasins. It was good the cold weather was driving the snakes to ground.

The men in Jake's crew were profane, irreverent, and prone to violence. A couple were just mean as hell. Logging sometimes attracted these type people. Several days into the job Rep wandered in one man's space and was head-slapped to the ground. He lay there with his head spinning and blood pouring from his nose, unsure what he had done to deserve such treatment. Jake saw the hit and came after the man with his pistol drawn and cocked. For a minute Rep thought he was surely going to shoot the man, but thankfully he didn't. After that incident Rep had no more problems with the men. They knew where he stood with Jake and didn't want to test him.

The work was hard, and the days were long. The weather grew colder, usually wet and uncomfortable and they never took days off. Jake was a tough task master and took no pity on Rep, requiring him to carry his weight as did the other men. He was growing taller and the heavy physical work was changing his body, getting rid of the baby fat. Mealtime was mostly meat and potatoes. This type work burned up the calories that needed to be replaced.

There were other young men in the crew, all older than Rep and if he got into a confrontation with any of them, Jake let him work it out. After one altercation where he ended up with a black eye and bloody nose, one of the older men, Hoke Holt, who had once boxed as a semi-pro, took him aside and offered to train him to defend himself. Some of the other young men heard Hoke make this offer and wanted to take part. Hoke set up training sessions in the evenings and worked with the entire group.

Later, after Rep and the other young men had trained for several weeks, they wanted to show off what they had learned. Jake announced he'd allow boxing matches between the younger men on Saturday night, the entire crew could watch the matches and there'd be no work on Sunday. This news was met with great enthusiasm. They built a makeshift ring outside in the yard and made rough benches for the spectators. Jake bought a keg of beer for the crowd. Beer was flowing freely and as the matches continued, the crowd got more and more rambunctious and several arguments started outside the ring. Soon there was more action among the spectators than in the ring. Jake had to step in and order two of the men to sit on opposite sides of the crowd so the matches could continue.

These were the first real bouts for the younger men and the action was mostly dancing around and swinging wildly. Nobody was in danger of getting hurt but the crowd, most about half drunk, enjoyed it anyway. Rep was judged to have won one bout and tied another. He was proud of himself.

When the bouts between the younger men were over, two of the spectators, who had no love for each other and were feeling no pain by now, went into the ring to settle their differences. This match, unlike the younger men's bouts, was for real. They battered each other for several minutes, both men were covered in blood and the fight lasted until one man, totally exhausted and drunk, passed out. During this bout, two fights broke out outside the ring and Jake finally had to fire his pistol into the air to stop the melee and establish order. He then decided he had to shut it all down if he was going to have anybody able to work on Monday.

Sunday was a very quiet day; most everybody was hungover and slept to noon. Everybody agreed the boxing matches was the best outing they'd ever had and wanted to have another one right away. Jake said that would never happen and swore he'd never buy another keg of beer for the crew.

After that, Rep held his own with the younger men and didn't have to prove himself to anybody. As the months passed, he was accepted by the crew, but he still stayed mostly to himself. He wanted no part in the nightly drinking and card games. Sometimes the card games ended in fights, especially when one or both players had too much to drink. He'd suffered firsthand the effects alcohol had on his father and he knew what it could do to innocent people around him. These memories were still fresh in his mind. At times, especially at night when he thought of his father, he would think of his two brothers and sisters and wonder how they were doing. He felt some guilt in leaving them alone but that soon passed.

The logging job was winding down as spring approached. He was operating some equipment on his own by this time and was earning his keep. Jake talked to him several times about staying with him and going to the next job. Since he wasn't married, and had no children, if Rep would stay, he could have a good future. When he asked Rep to tell him his objective in going on the road again, what he thought he would accomplish alone doing that, Rep had no answer.

He appreciated Jake's offer. He felt closer to him than anyone he'd ever known but still felt drawn to continue alone to the north. He knew it made little sense to Jake and Rep was sad about leaving him and the other men. For the first time he felt a bond that he'd never felt before, not even with his family. When Jake paid him his wages, he had more money than he'd ever seen in his life and felt he had the wherewithal to survive going forward. Jake gave him the address where he was going and told him if things didn't work out, he would always be welcome to come join him.

Rep stayed with the crew until they loaded up and went south, then he put his pack on his back and headed north. The weather was warm, but nights were still cool. He was glad to get out of a house and on the road. He'd enjoyed the experience with the loggers, and he missed Jake, but he looked forward being on his own again.

He'd been gone from home almost a year now. He'd learned a lot and felt more confident about the future although he had no idea what that future was.

4

Rep now had money for the first time in his life. He knew what items he needed to be better prepared on the road and when he came to a town several days later, he immediately went searching for a general store. He'd gone to town with Jake to buy supplies a couple of times, so he knew how things worked. But this was his first time alone, making his own decisions about what to buy. He went through the store getting the smaller necessities on his list and then bought a breech-loading .22 caliber rifle and a small pistol. He'd never shot a gun of any kind. The rifle was for squirrels to eat and the second in case he ran into someone on the road that wanted to take what he had. He knew it would take practice before he was able to use either gun effectively. He felt he was now set for whatever he faced.

For the next two years, he headed north. Most of the time he lived in the woods along the roads, usually camping on a creek, sometimes for weeks at a time. He especially enjoyed these times while alone, talking to no one, living off the land. He had become proficient with both the rifle and pistol. Thankfully, he'd never had to use the pistol for protection.

Sometimes he would venture into a small town or stop at a country store at a crossroads along the way to buy necessities such as coffee or salt, but never stayed long. He still didn't like towns and didn't like townspeople. There was no reason for him feeling this way; no one from a town had ever treated him badly. He felt more comfortable around farm people, he understood them. In all that time he'd never had a conversation with a single person in any town, other than storekeepers. He thought living in a town would be like living in an ant hill, with people running in every direction, all in a great hurry. He had no idea what all the people did and had no interest in finding out.

Despite having been on the road for over two years, he was still concerned about being caught and sent back to his parents. He was especially careful when he saw a policeman or any other law enforcement officer. He felt that way despite the fact that no one, in a town or on the road, had ever questioned him in any way as to who he was. He didn't carry any identification, not one slip of paper to prove who he was or where he came from. So, there was no actual reason to worry, but he always left town before the sun went down and was in the woods before dark.

He required nothing from the world. He still had most of the money Jake had paid him because he required little. He had accumulated the equipment necessary to live and survive outdoors. Everything he owned was in the pack on his back.

While he could have lived in the woods all the time, he would feel a need to be around people at times, but this was always farm people, not townspeople. While working in different places with different people he learned how to deal with the good and the bad. Anytime he joined a new farm he had to deal with some young man who was the top dog of the local pack who felt he had to prove to the newcomer who was in charge. Rep never started the trouble, but he never backed down. As the years passed, he had grown up and filled out and at a new place the other young men quickly found out he wasn't a man to fool with. Most didn't bother to test him. He was tall and larger now and his outfit set him as someone different.

As he matured, he started noticing the girls on the farms. He knew they were different from boys physically and he could see the obvious differences. Their bodies stuck out in places and had shapes that interested him and drew his attention and he was attracted to them. If they bared a part of their body usually covered, it would immediately get his attention. When he was around girls, they affected him positively, he liked to be with them, but he wasn't sure why. He knew they smelled good, but not only with perfume, there was something more. They were smaller and weaker. He could whip anyone he knew, but when he was around a girl, she seemed to be in charge. That made no sense to him and he resented it.

They also noticed him; he was a good-looking young man. Clueless about women, and how to deal with them, he was frustrated about his feelings. He knew about sex, having seen the carrying on of bulls and roosters and ducks in the barnyard and he knew his feelings had something to do with that.

He knew farmers in general were very protective of their daughters so he was hesitant to take any actions that might get him run off the farm or even get him shot. He'd had one encounter with a girl at the last farm, initiated by her, not by him. He'd noticed her and she him when he arrived and that led to talking, then to meetings in the barn and hugging and kissing. He found out she not only smelled good, she tasted good and she was soft in various places. Holding her body against his also caused reactions by his body that were new and stirred up strong feelings. He knew there was more to this, but he had no idea how to proceed. She was as clueless as he was so nothing more happened. However, these short physical encounters stoked his interest and appetite for more while increasing his frustration.

This changed when he signed on at a new farm and met Tish. He'd only been there for two days when he saw her walk by and was totally smitten. She was the oldest of the farmer's four daughters, tall and tanned with long blond hair. She was older than he was, more mature physically and more experienced in worldly ways. Although he felt an attraction toward her, his shyness made him hesitant to approach her. He felt she was out of his league since she was older, and he was a newcomer. During the next week he tried to put himself in her path when possible He had spoken to her a couple of times in passing but had no real conversations, nothing he felt was constructive. He didn't realize it, but she'd also noticed him and had put herself in his path several times and was frustrated he hadn't been more aggressive in approaching her. She wasn't accustomed to men seeming to ignore her. The opposite was usually the case.

One afternoon she saw him enter the barn, so she positioned herself outside the door and when he came out, they collided. While they were trying to regain their balance and Rep was clutching her all over thinking the meeting was accidental, he found the nerve to ask her to go back in the barn with him. That first rendezvous led to talking, then touching and kissing. He had no idea she was choreographing every step.

After several days of passion at an in-between level, he was over his head and had no idea what to do next. She had grown tired of the delay and made the next move without warning. That evening after supper, she met him in the yard, took him by the arm and led him to a room in the rear of the stable. Without any discussion she pushed their affair to the next level. Shortly they were both partially undressed, then she took off everything and told him to do the same. Then she led him to a pile of feed sacks and taught him all he needed to know. After it was over, she let him believe he'd been the aggressor.

This situation worked out perfectly for Rep. He was looking for a place to spend the winter, so having a warm bed and Tish in it was perfect. At times she would slip out of the house late at night and come to the barn with him. Other times he would sneak into her room, slipping out in the middle of the night. He wasn't concerned about her father; she seemed to be in charge and handled everything. This went on throughout the winter.

He thought he was in love. That seemed to be the logical conclusion since he was having feelings he'd never felt before. He started thinking about settling down, getting married and becoming a farmer. He had never broached this subject to her, and she had never mentioned marriage at all, but he thought it was the next logical step. It seemed obvious she loved him, why else would she sleep with him? Perhaps this was why he had come north. He was satisfied and content.

Spring came, the dogwoods were in full bloom and life was good. He walked out of the barn early one morning and Tish was waiting for him outside. She quickly came to the point, saying she had enjoyed her time with him, but their connection was over. He should leave the farm that day or her daddy would want to talk with him about his molesting her. Rep, completely surprised by her words and the threat she'd voiced, stared wall-eyed at her. He wasn't sure what molesting meant but he knew it wasn't good, especially if her daddy was going to talk with him about it. He tried to think of a suitable reply, but nothing came. Her ultimatum had been plain and direct; she wanted him gone. Although he knew he was innocent and knew she had been a willing participant, that wasn't a valid defense under these circumstances.

He turned away, went into the barn, gathered his belongings and left without speaking to or seeing her again. He felt grateful for having known her. She had taught him a lot. He would later find this last lesson about the wiles of women was the most valuable.

He'd thought Tish was special, unique in every way, made just for him, the only one for him and he'd lost his chance at happiness. Later he would find out the truth. He would learn that all women have the same equipment; physically they are the same. They come in various sizes, some are fatter and some skinnier, some shorter or taller. Some are packaged more attractively than others and have larger equipment, but mechanically they all operate the same way. They all will use their attributes to make a man in heat act like a complete fool.

After this unhappy but worthwhile encounter with Tish, he vowed to handle himself differently in the future. He had no intention of making any permanent connections with the women he met, and he would make no promises. He would take what they offered and walk away when he chose to do so. He pledged to be his own man.

He'd been on the road for over two years and worked at several farms during that time. The experience had been good for the most part. He'd learned skills he could use for the rest of his life, given the right opportunity. He'd also been in homes where he learned about morality and civility and learned how happy families get along. His early life at home in his miserable family hadn't taught him any of these lessons he found civilized people take for granted. The people in the functioning families hadn't taken him aside and told him how he should act. He learned by watching them.

For the most part the farm families were all very similar in the way they approached life. They learned from their parents who had learned from their parents and so it went down through the years. Farming was a tough life. If the family didn't do the work, the work didn't get done. Weeds flourish in untilled soil.

Sometimes their best effort wasn't enough. The weather, which nobody could control, could wipe out a year's work in a matter of days. The fields could be prepared properly, plowed properly and planted properly but too little or too much rain controlled the harvest. That was the way it was. Complaining did no good. You just hiked up your britches and went back to work.

For the next two years he continued north, interspersed with periods working. He spent time on a dairy farm, on a pecan farm and on a cattle farm. He learned at each stop, especially about people.

During these years he'd worn out and outgrown his original clothing, had grown several inches and gained pounds of mostly muscle. His attire was a hodgepodge of various styles. Brown leather work boots, denim trousers and a plaid lumberjack shirt covered by a black leather jacket. His head was covered with a fur skin cap he'd bought at a general store some years back. Around his waist was a large bowie knife in a scabbard attached to a wide leather belt. The pack on his back was store bought brown leather with a tarp tied on top with his .22 caliber rifle hanging from the side. His brown hair touched his shoulders. His face was tanned and smooth, yet untouched by a razor.

The nomadic life began to lose its appeal for him, and he thought of getting settled in a job with more future. The farms where he had been stopping were smaller and while they could provide jobs for a spell, especially during harvesting, there was nothing long-term. He decided to look for something permanent.

5

Rep Doe was twenty years old when he arrived in Shoal County, Georgia. Now three inches over six feet tall and weighing a rock-hard two hundred pounds, he was an imposing young man. Tanned from the outdoor life with shoulder length brown hair, and outfitted with his pack and rifle, he looked like a mountain man on the frontier. He had been on the road for over four years, survived four winters and walked all the way.

As he stared at the Shoal County sign, he thought of all the different places he'd seen in the years since he ran away from home with nothing but the clothes on his back and a piece of fatback. He seldom thought of those times. The memories of his drunken father hitting him and the sadness of his homelife were best put far back in the recesses of his mind and allowed to remain there.

At times he would think of his mother and his brothers and sisters he had left in that ramshackle sharecropper's house. Sometimes a touch of guilt about leaving them would brush over him, but at fifteen there was little he could have done. His concern was what to do for the future. The last four years had led him to this place.

He stopped at a country store at a crossroads just inside the county line to replenish his supplies and get information. The store, while not large, was typical of other stores he'd seen. This one looked to have everything a person could want in the way of merchandise and served as the town's post office. On the right side as he walked in was a long marble-topped counter lined with jars containing various kinds of candy and a large hoop-cheese on the end. Behind this counter were shelves filled with every kind of canned goods a person might want. The opposite side of the building was lined with clothing, both for men and women. In the rear were stacks of feed sacks of various kinds. To the side were coops with all varieties of biddies and pullets.

The proprietor, a bearded white-headed man of unknown age, was glad to see any living person and as soon as Rep walked in, he started talking and gave no indication he would ever stop. Rep, who hadn't talked to anyone in several days, gathered the few items he needed, found a seat, sat quietly and listened. He was looking for information and this seemed to be a good place to find out what he wanted. The old man rambled on for several minutes about his ailments, the weather, and various local happenings. Rep understood the old man was lonely and just making conversation, so he bided his time.

The front door opened, and a young boy entered, walked straight to the counter lined with candy jars, reached in and took out a large sucker on a stick. The old man watched him, then walked to the front, had a brief conversation with the boy and watched him walk out the door. He turned and came back toward Rep. "Grandboy," he said smiling, "don't ever pay for nothin'."

Rep got up quickly and met the old man at the counter before he had a chance to begin talking again. "I'm new here and wanted to ask if there be any jobs around?"

The old man peered over his glasses. "Don't know 'bout that. What can you do?"

"Most anythin' around a farm. Been workin' on little family farms for a spell and hoped to get with a bigger farm and stay in one place for a while."

The old man shook his head. "Ain't no big farms around here, just little jack-leg outfits. I don't know nobody hirin'." He turned away, then peered back over his shoulder, his glasses low on his nose. "If you set on a big outfit, there be a big farm up north on Shoal Creek, sho-nuff big, but I damn well wouldn't work up there."

Rep was taken aback by his negative tone. "Why you say that?"

The old man hesitated, seeming to choose his words carefully. "Bad people, that Hogan family." He looked at Rep. "You ever heard of 'em?"

Rep shook his head.

"They be liquor runners, make shine liquor and sell it. Got stills right there on their land and don't try to hide it, haul liquor all over the state. Damn well run the county too, all the way to Atlanta." He paused to catch his breath and gather his thoughts. "Mean folks. You cross 'em and they'll kill yo' dog and burn yo' house down. They be mean folks."

"You had dealings with 'em?"

"Not the old man, not Red Hogan, he be the head man, but I've heard enough 'bout 'im. Had a run-in with one of his sons, young red-headed smart-ass. He came ridin' in here one day in one of them brand new Ford A-model coupes with a rumble seat in the back. He had three other boys with him. They been dranking and they seen one of the young girls from up the road come out of the store and they give her a hard time. They said thangs to her decent folks don't say to a young girl. They put their hands on her, feeling her all over and sent her home cryin'. I was standin' by the door and seen and heard it all. Then they barged in the front door yellin' and raisin' hell and I met them right there with a twelve-gauge shotgun and told them to get the hell out. I knew they be gonna give me a lot of grief if they stayed."

Rep smiled. He could just picture the old man standing there with his shotgun. "What did they do?"

"That red-headed boy asked me if I knew who his daddy was? Thought that would scare me. I told him I damn well knew who his daddy was, but I didn't give a damn, and if he didn't get the hell out of my store, his daddy might have to bury him."

"What did he do then?"

"Cussed and threatened me some more about what his daddy was gonna do to me. I kept the shotgun on them the whole time. I could see meanness in his eyes and hate fur me stoppin' him. Them other boys feared he was gonna get them all shot so they pulled him back and finally they walked out the door."

"Did you ever hear anythin' about it?"

"Never did. I reckon the boy didn't want his daddy to know about it, especially after I run him off. Old Red Hogan is mean as hell and he's got a crowd of mean people workin' for him too. They do all the dirty work for him. If he wants somebody beat up and all, they do it. Did worry about them comin' after me for a while though, slept here in the store with my gun for a week. Thought they might burn the store down. Like I said they be mean folk up on Shoal Creek."

Rep shook the old man's hand, thanked him for everything and walked out the door. When he left the store, he knew where he was headed. According to the old man, to the north on Shoal Creek was a large farm owned by the Hogan family and that was his destination. The concern about the Hogan family's reputation didn't bother him at all. He figured he could handle whatever came.

His last winter with the loggers had tempered him as fire tempers steel. Surviving those months working with that profane and irreverent crowd of ruffians had convinced him he could deal with anybody. Only time would tell if that sentiment was true.

Some days later he stood in front of a large metal gate staring at a sign that read, "Shoal Creek Farm". For some reason he felt this was where he'd been heading all the time.

He had never heard of the word 'destiny.'

6

The Farm

Rep looked over the Shoal Creek Farm sign toward the late afternoon sun. A dirt road led straight away from the gate to a red barn about one hundred yards away. Cornfields lined both sides of this road. On a hill some hundred yards past the barn was a large two-story white house, with large columns on the porch. Magnolia trees lined the drive up the hill to the house. Dogwoods were in bloom across the hillside. Beds of colorful flowers dotted the yard. He'd never seen such a house in his life, certainly not anything to match it in his recent travels. If Red Hogan was the owner of this farm, Rep thought that had to be his house.

Looking back to the south where he came from was a large cotton field with several people, both black and white, cotton sacks over their shoulders, picking cotton. To his right, as far as he could see were cornfields. Looking straight ahead over the barn were fields and then tall trees as far as he could see. The old man at the store had been right, he thought, this is a big farm.

A large Negro man was standing across the road by the fence to his right, eyeing him with concern. He didn't seem to be a guard since he was holding a shovel, but he hadn't taken his eyes off him since he arrived. Rep had no idea what his function was, but he was the only person in sight. He walked across the road to the fence and stopped directly in front of him. The man was tall and huge and his facial expression didn't look friendly. Rep had to look straight up to look in the man's eyes. "I'm lookin' for work," he said, watching the man's face for a reaction.

The huge black man leaned forward on the shovel handle and stared down at him. He seemed to be deciding if he was going to reply or hit him with the shovel, in any case he didn't look interested in replying. "Ain't no work here," he said in a raspy voice, "ain't been no work here for what be a long time." He leaned forward as if wanting to make sure Rep heard him. "Folks here don't never hire no new folks." The reply was stated matter-of-factly, with no emotion. His tone showed he didn't care to talk to him.

Rep's journey had been too long and tough to be put off so easily. Obviously, this man wasn't involved in hiring so he had to get to someone who did. "How do you know that? You ain't in charge of hirin' folks, are you?"

The man straightened up and his face tightened. He wasn't accustomed to people arguing with him and didn't like it. He looked at Rep as if he was a bug he was about to squash. "Mr. Red, he do what hirin' be done and he don't like folk comin' round here a'tall." He leaned back over him and looked down. "It be best you be gittin' on yo way. I done tolt you there ain't no work here."

Rep knew the man wasn't accustomed to people talking back to him. His size usually quieted any discussion. He looked in his eyes and shook his head. "Then they might need help if they ain't hired nobody in a long time," he replied. "It be best I go down there and see for myself." He turned and started walking along the fence toward the gate.

The Negro followed him step-for-step, staring at Rep as if he must be stupid or deaf. "I done tolt you there ain't no jobs. Why cum you still be here?" He was getting more irritated.

Rep turned and faced him. "Do you be the guard here to keep people out?" he said, as he stared up at him. "All you got is a shovel. That ain't much to stop nobody."

This statement stopped the black man in his tracks. He straightened up and looked flustered. It was obvious he had no authority to stop anybody, but his size and threats were usually enough to deter visitors. He didn't know how to deal with Rep.

Rep pushed it further as he saw his hesitation. "I reckon I'll just go down there and find out for myself." He put one foot on a rung of the gate and watched the man's reaction, knowing he was big enough to break him in two if he wanted.

The huge black man stepped back, the look on his face changed. It was obvious he was out of options and completely frustrated. "Mr. Red, he do all the hirin', what be done he do hisself." He pointed down the road toward the red barn. "Mr. Red, he be to that red barn. You jest go on down there and talk to Mr. Red if you want to. But I done told you they ain't no work here."

Keeping an eye on the man to make sure he wasn't going to grab him, Rep crawled through the gate and started walking down the dirt road toward the barn. He glanced over his shoulder. The black man was still standing at the fence watching him.

Looking down the road as he walked, there were two men digging post holes beside the fence on the far side of the road in front of the barn. They were the only people he saw anywhere. Both were dressed in work clothes and were tough looking, bearded and muscular men. Based on what the old man at the store had said, he expected to meet these type people at Shoal Creek. Men that handled the dirty work.

He was halfway to the barn when they noticed him. They both stopped digging, propped on their hole-diggers and watched him approach. When he was about ten yards away one of the men left the fence, walked to the middle of the road and faced him, hands on his hips. "Where the hell do you thank you goin'?" he said.

Rep stopped several feet away. "I be lookin' for work. The man at the gate said come down here and see Mr. Red."

The man standing in the road looked back at the other man then back at Rep. "Big'un told you that? Why the hell would he tell you that when he knows ain't nobody supposed to come down here?"

"I don't know why he said it but that be what he said."

"Do you know where the hell you are?"

"The sign said this was the Hogan farm and that's what I be lookin' for."

"Where the hell did you come from?"

"Down south a bit."

The other man spoke for the first time. "They must raise some stupid bastards down south if you come through that fence and walked down here like you own the place." He stepped to the edge of the road. "You need to get your dumb ass back on the road and keep on goin' north or wherever. We don't want you here."

"Why would I do that?" Rep replied. "I'm lookin' for a job. I just got here."

The second man dropped the post hole digger and stepped toward Rep. "Well, smart ass," he said in a loud voice, "you either move or I'll move your ass myself."

The man in the middle of the road put up his hand. "Hold up now. This son of a bitch is mine." He turned toward Rep. "I done told you to get yo' ass back over the fence or I'm gonna whip yo ass right here and put you on the road."

Before Rep could reply he heard another voice from the barn. "What's the trouble here, Joe?"

Rep turned to see a large red-headed man standing in the barn door.

"Ain't no trouble, Mr. Red. This dumb ass done wandered down here and I'm gonna put him back on the road and on his way. Big'un done let him come down here. It won't take me but a minute to get rid of 'im."

The red-headed man walked toward Rep, his eyes looking him up and down. "You sure you want to tackle that, Joe? Dan'l Boone here don't really look like or talk like he wants to leave, no matter what you say." He motioned them back. "You boys just wait a minute and let me talk to him. Then maybe you can put him back on the road." He took out tobacco and paper, slowly rolled a cigarette, licked the paper and turned to Rep. "Who the hell are you boy and what rock did you crawl out from under?"

"Name's Rep Doe and I be lookin' for work."

The man lit the cigarette and took a puff as he looked at Rep. "Where you from?"

"Down south a bit."

"Do you know who I am?"

"No, suh."

"I'm Red Hogan and I own this farm."

"Yes, suh, I heared 'bout you."

"Where did you hear about me?"

"Talk in some of the towns comin' up the road."

He chuckled. "I bet you did hear some talk. So why did you stop here?"

"Like I said, I be lookin' for work."

"Do you know what we do here?"

"Folks say you farm and make liquor."

He smiled. "That's about it. You know anybody from Shoal County around here?"

"No, suh. Not a soul."

"People say anything else about me except we make liquor?"

"Most said you was tough, and it was best to stay away from you unless you wanted trouble."

"But you didn't do that, you came here anyway."

"Yes, suh."

"So, do you want trouble?"

"No, suh, I just want a job."

"Joe don't like you coming here and said he's gonna put your dumb ass back on the road. What do you think of that?"

Rep looked at Joe, who was three or four inches shorter but heavier. "I ain't got no fuss with 'im."

"That's got nothing to do with it, boy. Joe don't want you here, so you have a choice. It's Joe's business that he don't want you here and I'm gonna step back out of the way and let him settle it. So now you can either stay here and face Joe or get back on the road and leave. That's the choice and it's up to you to decide what you're gonna do. But let me warn you, Joe is one mean bastard and he won't stop till he's hurt you bad. My advice to you would be to get back on the road while you can still walk."

Rep stared at the red-headed man for a moment, remembering the times on the road when he'd got to a new farm and had to face some young man that was the top dog in the local pack. When younger he had taken whippings but then as he got older and grew, it was a different story. Then, while he was with the loggers one of the men, an ex-boxer, took him aside and gave him some pointers. After that, the other young men gave him a wide berth.

He glanced at Joe standing in the middle of the road. Then he slowly and deliberately removed his pack and rifle and set them on the ground. He unbuckled his belt with knife and scabbard and placed them beside the pack. He glanced at the red-headed man and then turned to face Joe, arms by his side.

"Well Joe, looks like you done got yo' wish," said the red headed man. He smiled and seemed to be enjoying the moment. "This boy ain't gonna leave. Now let's see if you can really put his ass back on the road like you said you would."

Joe looked at the red-headed man, then he started to move toward Rep.

Rep watched Joe's eyes. The ex-boxer had told him during training, "If you get in a fight, watch the eyes. The eyes will tell you when they're about to move. Most people are just brawlers and will rush forward to get you in a bearhug. Don't ever let a big man get a hold of you. Slide to the side to avoid the charge and hit him in the face with a right as he goes by and then when he's off-balance, rush in and bust him good."

Joe was a brawler. He rushed forward, swung wildly at Rep with a right hand but missed. The force of the swing put him off balance and staggering. Rep's right hand hit him flush in the shorter man's right eye and stunned him. As he tried to regain his balance Rep moved in with a left and right to his face and followed with a right to the mid-section. This last blow hurt him. Joe staggered back gasping for breath but stayed on his feet. He was stunned, surprised by what had happened. His right eye was already swelling, and blood poured from his broken nose. The front of his shirt was covered in red. He shook his head, having trouble locating Rep, who stood with his arms at his side, waiting to see what he would do.

Joe finally focused his good eye on Rep and again charged, although this time he was moving slower. He again swung wildly and again Rep slipped to the side and hit him in the swollen right eye as he went past.

The two bull rushes had sapped Joe's energy and he stood with both hands on his knees as he gasped for breath. His eye was almost swelled shut and blood poured from his nose and mouth. He stared at Rep as he breathed and then charged again. Rep didn't move to the side but stood his ground and pounded Joe's face with a right and left, stopping him and putting him back on his heels. He stepped in quickly and hit him flush in the nose. This last blow put Joe on his back on the ground. He lay there for a moment, then struggled to get up but only got to one knee. He stayed there on his knees trying to breathe and get his eyes focused, then slowly toppled back on his butt in the dirt. Blood seeped from his busted mouth and nose and his right eye was completely closed. He made one last effort to get to his feet but finally gave up. He was beat.

The red-headed man looked at him with disgust as he wallowed in the dirt. Shaking his head, he motioned to the other man. "Get his ass up and help him to the bunkhouse," he said. "Damn! That was pitiful." The other man helped the dazed Joe to his feet and led him away.

Rep picked up his belt and buckled it around his waist, then swung the pack onto his back and turned toward the red-headed man who was staring intently at him.

"You surprised me, boy. I thought Joe'd beat the shit out of you."
He turned toward the barn and yelled, "Mose!"

Immediately a slender black man appeared in the barn door. "Yes,
suh, Mr. Red."

"You see what happened?"

"Yes, suh, I seen it."

Red looked at Rep, brow furrowed as he thought about what to do
next. Finally, he motioned to him. "Come in the barn." He turned and
walked through the door.

Rep followed, not certain what was about to happen. Mose
followed behind him, walked to the far wall and stood with his arms
crossed.

Red walked around a desk just inside the door, sat down, opened
a desk drawer, and took out a fruit jar filled with a colorless liquid. He
unscrewed the lid, took a drink, then screwed the lid back on and put
the jar back in the drawer. Then he looked up at Rep.

"You bother me boy. You come wandering in here looking like
Dan'l Boone and beat the hell out of one of my toughest men like it
was nothing. Tell me again who you are and where you're from."

"Name's Rep Doe and I be from down south a ways."

"What town?"

"Weren't no town. Just country."

"How old are you?"

"Bout twenty, I thank."

"What you been doing before now?"

"Workin' on farms and some with loggers."

"And you don't know nobody in Shoal County?"

"No, suh, not a soul."

"You've never talked to the sheriff here or any other law people in
this county?"

"No, suh."

"One time, some years back, a boy about like you come in here
looking for work. Later we found out he was with the law in Atlanta.
Nobody has found that boy to this day." He stared at Rep. "You
understand what I'm saying, boy?"

Rep nodded. "Yes, suh, I know what you sayin'."

"Anyway, I'm gonna check up on you. Does that bother you?"

Rep shook his head. "Don't bother me none, I don't know no law."

"You've had some fight training. You handled yourself good."

"One of the loggers had boxed and he showed me some stuff."

Red nodded toward the rifle hanging on the pack. "What's with the rifle?"

Rep smiled. "Ain't much. Just shoot squirrels"

"You any good with it?"

"I get by."

"You wait outside," Red said as he turned to the tall black man. "I need to talk to Mose."

Rep walked out the door and stood waiting on the porch.

"Something about this don't seem right," Red said to Mose. "This boy bothers me, and I've got to think about it more. I'm think I'm gonna see what else he can do except fight. He might just leave if I push him, and my problem will be gone. But again, he is impressive and might be good to have around, if everything checks out right."

"I don't know what you gonna do," replied Mose, "but that boy ain't about to leave. Leavin' ain't in him, I seen that right off." He shook his head. "If he be gonna leave, he don't fight Joe. He done fought him to stay here so be plannin' to stay awhile."

"You might be right, but we'll see," said Red as he got up and walked out the door, Mose followed close behind.

"Tell you what," Red said to Rep as he got outside. "You talk a good game, but I want to see if you're worth a damn at anything else except fightin'. Straight behind the barn a piece is Shoal Creek. Plenty of squirrels down there in the oak trees. You kill me a mess before dark and I'll talk to you about a job. You understand what I'm saying?"

"Yes, suh."

"If you don't have at least ten by dark, you hit the road and keep on your way. Don't you show up here again because we won't talk no more. We won't fool with you next time." He turned to Mose. "You go show him where the kitchen is before he leaves, so if he comes back, he'll know where to go. Then you wait for him till dark, so if he does come back, you show him to the bunkhouse."

Mose nodded and started walking down the dirt road. Rep fell in behind him. He cut his eyes at Rep as they walked, studying him. "Why you be here?" he asked, watching Rep's face.

"Lookin' for work, like I say."

"Be best you take yo' stuff right now and keep on walkin' north. That be the smart thang for you to do."

"Why do you say that?"

"You stay round here you find out." He kept walking. "You done made a mean enemy today, maybe more than one. That Joe is a mean man and he's sneaky. You beat him in front of everbody and he won't forget. He ain't gonna' fight you fair next time, cause you done beat 'im. He might cut yo' throat tonight if you be here."

Rep didn't comment but he knew what Mose said was true. He followed him to a group of buildings where he showed him the kitchen.

"I be here till dark, if you do come back," said Mose. "But you oughta thank about goin'." He walked away without any other comment.

Rep watched him for a moment then headed to the rear of the barn. He had no concern about killing a mess of squirrels. In the years on the road, sometimes living for weeks alone on a creek bank, squirrels and rabbits had been his supper many times.

He found the creek as Red had told him. Squirrels were plentiful in the oak trees on both sides of the creek and he killed ten in a short while. He dressed them and headed back to the kitchen where he found Mose, who took the squirrels into the kitchen without comment.

Rep had no intention of staying the night in the bunkhouse or any other place where he could be found. He intended to follow Mose's advice. He took his pack and headed for the woods. He stopped in the edge of the trees and watched to make sure he wasn't followed, then went deeper and set up a cold camp.

He was up at daylight. He wanted to have some time alone to look over the farm. Behind the bunkhouse were two groups of houses. One group was to his right on the hill and to the left was another group at the bottom of the hill towards the river. Between these two groups was a single house sitting alone, at least a hundred yards from the nearest neighbor. He thought this lonely house between the other houses was very strange. He didn't know for sure, but he figured the separation between the two groups of houses was because one group was for whites and the other group was for colored. He figured this was true because he'd seen it in the towns on his way north. Where he grew up as a boy there had been only white people on the farms around him, so he'd had no dealings with colored people. The people at the school where he went were all white. He didn't know where the colored people went to school.

He had seen and met colored people on some of the farms where he worked, in fact worked with them in the fields and their houses were always separate from white houses. That was the way it was.

Looking at the houses down toward the bottom of the hill he saw colored children in the yards, so he knew that was their section. Past these houses toward the west were fields all the way to the trees along the river. Up the hill from the colored section toward the white houses was the single house off to itself. As he watched, Mose came out the front door of this house and headed toward the barn. Rep wondered what Mose was doing at that house and watched until he was out of sight, then turned and walked to the bunkhouse, sat on the porch and waited.

7

R ed Hogan came out the front door of the house and was headed to the barn when he saw Mose walking rapidly up the road toward him. He took out paper and a can of Prince Albert smoking tobacco, rolled a cigarette and stood smoking as he waited.

Mose had to catch his breath before he could speak. "That white boy you done sent to kill 'em squirrels done come back. I told you he ain't gonna leave."

"So, he's back. So what?" Red puffed and waited for him to continue.

"He kilt ten squirrels, ever one shot in the head."

"Then what did you do?"

"I took him to the bunkhouse, but he weren't gonna stay there. He took his pack and went to the woods. I don't know where he stay. He sittin' on the bunkhouse porch right now, been there since daylight. That boy got some smarts. Ain't nobody gonna fool that boy."

Red nodded. "Don't blame him for staying in the woods. That was smart."

Mose grunted. "Hunh! -- It be smart Joe didn't go in the woods huntin' for 'im. That boy be done cut Joe's throat before he ever saw 'im. I sho' wouldn't do it. That boy been livin' in the woods by hisself for years. He be like a snake."

Red laughed. "Damn, Mose, you talk like a old woman." He thought for a moment. "You go tell him to come to the barn."

Mose went to the bunkhouse where he found Rep. "Mr. Red say you to come with me and see him at the barn." He turned without another word and started up the road. Rep trotted to catch up.

Mose stopped and looked around at him. "You know 'bout fishin'?"

Rep was puzzled. He nodded. "I know 'bout fishin'."

"I talkin' 'bout in the river for catfish and such."

"I've fished trot-lines and set-hooks before. I know how to fish for catfish."

"It be best you get down on the river and away for a while till some folks settle down. That be the way to do it."

Without another comment Mose turned and headed toward the barn. Rep followed but was unsure what had just happened.

At the barn Mose entered with Rep trailing. Red was sitting behind the desk with his feet propped up, a large cigar in his mouth. Mose walked to the far wall and stood with his arms crossed. That seemed to be his usual position. Red puffed on the cigar and ignored Rep.

Rep looked around the office. Except for the desk and chair Red was sitting in, there was no other furniture. There were no pictures or signs of any sort on the walls. Then he noticed a young man sitting in a chair in the back of the room and was surprised. The young man was a younger version of Red Hogan, red hair and all. He was glaring at him, which was puzzling because he'd never seen the boy before.

Then he remembered his conversation with the white-headed man at the general store some days earlier, about Red Hogan's red-headed son giving him grief. The boy in the chair had to be him.

Red set the cigar on the desk and looked up. "Tell me again where you came from, boy."

"I was born down south and left home when I was fifteen."

"How old are you now?"

"Like I said before, 'bout twenty, I thank."

Red picked up the cigar and puffed as he stared at the ceiling. "So, since you left home you been doing what?"

"Headin' north, workin' different places"

"You don't know a soul in Shoal County, never been here before but you just show up here and walk right in looking for work."

"Yes, suh. I was told you had the biggest farm around so I figured there might be work here and I wanted a job I could count on."

"Do you have any idea what happens if someone comes in here and tries to cause problems with our business?"

"No, suh, but I can guess."

"The last time the people in Atlanta sent somebody in to spy on us he was never heard of again, like I told you before. Do you understand what I'm saying?"

Rep nodded. "I know what you're sayin'."

"You damn well better know." Red looked at Mose. "You think this boy is telling the truth?"

Mose didn't hesitate. "It sho' sound like the truth."

The young man in the rear spoke for the first time. "Why don't I just take the bastard outside and beat the truth out of him. That'll save a lot of time and then we'll throw his ass in the creek."

Red spoke without turning around. "Shut the hell up, Brit. This ain't your business."

"Well, the son of a bitch busted the face of my friend so I might make it my business."

Red laughed, turned and stared at the young man. "Damn it Brit, you ain't got a smidgin of sense, not one damn bit. I ain't got no doubt this boy could stomp your ass in a minute, I done seen him in action. He beat the hell out of Joe and Joe's a damn sight tougher than you are. You keep running your mouth, I just might let you see if you can back up yo' big talk, but I don't want you to get half killed." He pointed at the rear door. "I've heard enough out of you. Get the hell out of here."

Brit got up slowly and pointed his finger at Rep. "You ain't heard the last from me, boy. You remember that." He turned and walked out the door.

Red watched Brit go out the door, then turned to Mose. "That damn boy ain't got shit for sense."

Mose chuckled. "Who fault he be like that?"

Red ignored this comment and looked back at Rep. "What else can you do besides fight and kill squirrels?"

"I 'spect whatever you want, 'cept I ain't havin' nothin' to do with no liquor."

Red, surprised at this comment, leaned forward, his face questioning. "What the hell does that mean?"

"My daddy beat the hell outta me when he drank, "replied Rep. "I ain't got nothin' for it."

Red shrugged his shoulders. "I don't reckon that matters." He looked at Mose. "What do you think he might be worth a damn at?"

Mose paused, as if he was thinking about the question. "That boy you got fishin' on the river ain't much good and I speck this boy can fish. It'll help to get him on the river till Joe gets settled down. If he gonna stay here, it be best he stay where we don't have no trouble."

Red looked at Rep. "Can you fish?"

Rep nodded. He now understood why Mose had asked him about fishing; he was trying to protect him. He wondered why he was doing that. "I can fish."

Red nodded. "That might work. Let's do that till things settle down. Mose will take you to the river and show you where the boats are. You just stay away from the farm for a few days. He can get whatever you'll need, most of it should be in the shed anyway. We'll try this for a few days and see if you do as good as you talk. Any questions or problems you go see him." He looked back at Mose. "I got some things I need to say to this boy. You go to the bunkhouse and wait." Mose nodded and walked out.

Red got up, his eyes on Rep. "I don't know you, so I don't trust you much. I'll be watching you, everything you do. You've done good so far, but something about you don't seem just right, but I don't know exactly why. You came in here too smooth for me and that bothers me. You mess up and I'll have your ass. Am I clear?"

Rep nodded. "It be clear."

"Until I'm sure about you, you stay on the river and fish and don't be wandering all over the farm. Stay away from any of the houses. We got colored living down below the bunkhouse. You stay the hell away from them, that'll get you in lot of trouble."

He looked at Rep for an answer.

Rep nodded.

"We have lots of women here on the farm, white and colored. Every one of them is somebody's wife or daughter. You done come in here like a damn stray tom cat and you get to tomcatting around you better watch out. You mess around with any woman and stir up trouble, if they don't shoot you, I will. We just don't put up with that."

Suddenly Red stood up and pointed to the back of the barn, toward the river. "You listen to me now. Across the river is a town called River Bluff. It's in Alabama. You don't ever go over there or ever talk to any of them Alabama people. If you're on the river you might run into one, but you don't ever talk to them. If they try to come close to you, you get the hell away. Some of them do come over here and buy liquor, but they don't hang around. We don't want them hanging around. They just get their liquor and get the hell back across the river." As Red talked his face darkened and his voice got louder. "They have churches in that town and the Baptist preacher over there calls us heathens. I'm told he preaches sermons about me on Sunday and says I'm going to Hell because I sell liquor. I might go to Hell but it's not any of his damn business." He stared at Rep. "You ever go to church?"

"Ain't never been to no church."

"That's good. You just be sure and stay away from them damn Alabama people."

Rep didn't move, wondering if there was more coming.

Red motioned toward the door. "That's all, get the hell out of here. Go find Mose."

Rep walked outside, his mind trying to understand all Red had told him. Some things he'd said, like messing with the women, he understood, but all that about people from Alabama and what the preacher said about Red had him confused. He wondered what the Alabama people had done to get Red disliking them so.

Mose was waiting for him outside.

"Who was that red-headed boy sittin' in the back of the barn doin' all that big talk?" Rep asked.

"That's Brit, Red's boy. Best you stay away from 'im. He be sho-nuf sneaky mean and he don't like you."

"Figured that must be who he be, but I ain't never seen him before. What does he do here?"

"He live here on the farm in Red's big house. Ain't never been worth a damn at much of nothin' but raisin' hell and causin' trouble. Red let him do what he want to so he be like he is."

Rep put that information in his head for the future. He hadn't been here hardly a day and already had a passel of folks that didn't like him. He was carrying all he owned with him and since he wasn't staying in the bunk house, there was no reason to delay going to the river.

Mose led him down the trail to the river about a quarter- mile away. The path followed a small flowing branch and the way was lined with tall pines and oaks and sweetgums. Rep saw schools of branch minnows in deeper holes in the water along the trail so he knew bait would be plentiful and should be easy to get.

At the boat landing, which was little more than a small cleared spot, were two wooden bateaus tied to willow trees hanging low over the river. On the back of each boat was a small Johnson outboard motor. A rough table covered with fish scales and obviously used for cleaning fish was on the bank below the landing.

A small shack sat off the bank nearby. He walked inside and saw several shelves along the wall holding a supply of hooks, sinkers, small set hook cord and heavier trotline. In the rear was a bunk, a table and a wood stove. He was surprised that most of what he would need for fishing was already here.

"You be knowin' how to use this?" Mose asked, pointing at the shelves.

Rep nodded. "Looks like 'bout everthang I'll need."

"If you need somethin' else let me know," said Mose. "We mostly eat meat we raise, but Red likes fish and sometimes squirrels and rabbits. So, you do good with the fishin' and huntin', there won't be no problem."

"I ain't worried about fishin' and huntin'," replied Rep. "I be fine and ain't gonna look for no trouble."

Mose stared across the river for several seconds before he replied. "You be lucky you be down here on the river. That way you be outa da way and not be round where the trouble be."

"You don't think they'll let go of what happened in a day or two? They started it. I didn't want to fight."

Mose shook his head. "You just do yo' huntin' and fishin'. Best you stay down here much as you can." With that Mose turned to leave.

"Ya'll ever catch flatheads here?" Rep asked.

Mose stopped and looked back, a puzzled look on his face. "What that be?"

"Flathead catfish."

Mose shook his head. "We ain't got 'em here."

Rep nodded and smiled. "That's what he thought." As he watched Mose walk up the path back toward the farm, a plan was already forming.

8

Rep stood at the Shoal Creek boat landing looking out across the river. This was his first time seeing the Chattahoochee. He knew the river was the state line between Georgia and Alabama. About a hundred yards away to his left in the middle of the river, he could see the tip of a large island. This island divided the river. The main river flowed to the right or west side and the smaller stream flowed to the left or east side of the island. Mose said this smaller stream was called Back Slough. The Georgia bank of this slough was Shoal Creek land. He figured to do most fishing in this narrow slough and stay away from the wider part of the river toward Alabama. After Red's warning about Alabama people, he intended to stay far away from them.

To his right upriver was set after set of shoals with large boulders protruding out of the water as far as he could see. Shallow swift water flowing over rocks was dangerous so going up the river in a boat with the water level as it was now was out of the question.

He understood his main priority was to supply fish to the farm kitchen. He wasn't sure about fishing this time of year or what bait would be best since he'd never fished the Chattahoochee. However, he'd have no choice but to go with what was quickly available and what he'd used with success in the past on the Flint. Directly in front of the landing about fifty yards away was a small island about an acre in size. He decided to run a trotline from the landing to this island and see what happened. A trotline was a long heavy line run across the water, multiple light lines with hooks on the end were placed about three feet apart across the heavier line, and the hooks baited. Lines with weights were attached to pull the entire line to the bottom of the river.

He got a roll of the small cord from the shack, cut fifty lines about three feet long and then tied a hook to one end of each line. He found several old rusty gears in the shack he could use for weights and tied a length of cord to them. Lastly, he found a length of cheesecloth that could be used to make a seine to get minnows.

A stand of bamboo below the landing provided two cane poles to complete the seine. He cut another cane to use as a fishing pole. He went up the branch to the deep waterholes he'd seen earlier, seined and in a few minutes had a good supply of Chub and red tail minnows in his bucket.

Before the sun went down and the sky darkened, Rep had finished running the trotline from the landing to the small island. Afterward he used the cane pole to catch brim to use as bait on ten limb hooks in the slough below the landing. When he crawled into the bunk in the shed that night, he was dog-tired.

The sun was just rising in the eastern sky when he pushed the bateau away from the landing and began fishing the trotline. He was nervous, not having any idea what to expect but hoping not to completely strike out on his first day. When he picked up the line and felt a fish pulling and got the first channel cat in the boat, he immediately felt better. After checking the trotline, he had ten fish in the boat, including two large blue cats.

He paddled down the slough to check the limb hooks. He'd baited with live brim in the hope he'd catch a flathead, but it didn't happen. The water here was too shallow, and he'd have to find deeper holes as he'd used on the Flint. He felt sure he'd find them somewhere on down the slough when he had time to look.

He hurried back to the landing and dressed the fish, filleting the large blue cats. He felt good about the morning's catch. He went up the trail toward the farm with the bucket full of meat and went to the kitchen.

When he knocked on the door a black woman he'd never seen pushed open the screen. When she saw the bucket of fish, she screamed, "Oh lordy, chile, what be that you got? That's mo' catfish than we done seed in a month." She carried the bucket inside and when she brought the empty bucket back, she handed Rep a plate filled with scrambled eggs, sliced ham, two buttered biscuits and a cup of scalding coffee. Rep sat on the steps and ate the best breakfast he'd had in years, then went back to the river. This would be his schedule for the next several days. Breakfast was waiting every morning.

~

R ed Hogan was at his desk in the barn when Mose walked in. "That white boy sho can catch fish," he said. Everybody be talkin' about them fish he caught, and he brangs in a big mess 'bout ever day."

Red looked up. "Have you talked to him today?"

"Naw, suh. He come in early ever mornin' and heads right back to the river. Sleeps down there in that shed and don't talk to nobody when he come. Hattie Mae in the kitchen done bout dopted him, says he be the sweetest boy she bout ever did see. She say he be 'bout like a ghost, all of a sudden he be there and then he be gone."

Red nodded. "He damn well seems like a ghost. I've had people checking all over the country about him and they can't find a soul who knows who he is or has ever heard of him. I wonder where the hell he came from."

"Well," replied Mose, "maybe what he say bout runnin' away from home and bein' on the road all them years be true. Maybe he ain't been in one place long enough for nobody to know 'im."

Red nodded. "That may be, but I'm sure he's not with the law or anything like that. I've had that checked out all the way to Atlanta. Maybe he is telling the truth, but you keep an eye on him."

"I'll do dat," replied Mose as he headed for the door.

9

Rep had been on the river three weeks. Fishing had been good, and he had everything set up as he wanted. He hadn't caught a flathead, but he was certain they were in the river, he hadn't found the right place yet. The next day he found a deep hole about a mile below the landing in a bend on the Georgia side where the water was swirling or eddying. This seemed to be a perfect place and he put set hooks along the bank above and below the eddy.

He was there at daylight the next morning and one limb was in the water. When he pulled the limb up, the flathead boiled to the surface, then headed for the bottom. After a short battle he had it in the boat. He estimated it weighed between fifteen and twenty pounds. It wasn't the biggest he'd ever seen but it would serve the purpose. This was what he'd been waiting for.

He carried a bucket of dressed fish and the live flathead to the kitchen later that morning. Hettie Mae got so excited when she saw the big fish that she told everybody he'd caught a whale. He put the fish in a horse trough across the road from the kitchen so everybody could see what he'd caught. He felt the flathead might offset some of the hard feelings still harbored by some and show everyone he knew what he was doing. By that afternoon everybody on the farm knew about the fish and most had been to the trough to see the whale. Nobody had seen such a fish before and were impressed by what he'd done. Later that evening he went to the horse trough, got the fish out and returned it to the river. He had made his point.

He had intentionally stayed away from the farm since he'd arrived, talking to no one except Mose, to avoid any confrontation with Joe or anyone else. Mose didn't think Joe had forgotten and had warned him to be careful.

He had explored the area around the landing and down south into Back Slough. Not far down the slough he'd discovered a small island, about an acre in size, nestled against the larger Big Island. A small slough cut through behind the island, water was about ten feet across, separating the island from its larger neighbor. There was a higher flat ridge in the center of the island that was about the right size for a house or cabin. There was a stand of water oaks on the lower end and dogwoods were in bloom all over. Just over the narrow slough he could see a hillside covered with hickory trees and he knew squirrels would be plentiful.

Straight across Back Slough on the Georgia side was a spring-fed branch so he'd have a good supply of drinking water. He immediately decided that sometime in the future he would build a log cabin on the island and that would be his permanent homeplace. He wasn't concerned that he didn't own the island or know who did. It was unoccupied and available so he would use it until somebody objected. Later he discussed the possibility with Mose who agreed it would be a good idea for him to have a place away from the farm. The shack at the landing was too close to the farm. Mose told him to let him know when he was ready to start building and he would get people to help.

The island was called Sallie White, but nobody knew why. Nobody knew anyone named Sallie White or had never heard of such a person, but everyone agreed that was the name of the island. The history made no difference to Rep. He planned to homestead there. It was a perfect place and he wouldn't have to worry about somebody easily sneaking up on him at night. They'd have to go across water to get to him.

~

That evening when Rep got to the landing, he heard music coming from the direction of the farm. Mose had told him earlier that once a month Red held a big shindig or party at the barn. This was his big night and he enjoyed being the center of attraction. According to Mose, there were usually over a hundred people attending. Special customers, local dignitaries and even some law enforcement officials from the surrounding area were invited. Sometimes even some Alabama customers showed up, although they were never invited.

A band with fiddles and guitars was brought in, bars were set up inside and outside the barn with plenty of liquor and beer. Food was plentiful, barbequed pig being the specialty. Mose suggested it would be best if he stayed away, at least for this first time. He was concerned about him getting in trouble since some people, like Joe and Brit, still had hard feelings and both would be drinking.

Rep had agreed with Mose when he suggested he stay away. He didn't know any of the other farm people, so he planned to clean the fish from that day's catch and remain at the landing. But as he was cleaning the catch, the music got louder, and the crowd noise reminded him of how long it'd been since he'd been around people. On farms where he'd been, there were parties but not with a crowd this large. Finally, the temptation was too strong, so he decided to leave the fish in the live basket till the next morning and do something for himself. He'd been alone long enough, and he was ready to be around people.

He went to the shack, got a bar of soap, shucked off his clothes, jumped naked into the river and washed off for the first time in several days. He put on his one good shirt and clean jeans, brushed his teeth and started up the trail toward the farm. He figured he'd been out of sight long enough. If there were still hard feelings from people this long after the fight, it was time to face them.

When he topped the hill at the kitchen the entire barn area was lit up. It reminded him of the county fair he'd seen in one town in Georgia. Strings of lights were strung in the trees surrounding the area. He was surprised by what he saw. A bandstand was set up outside, the music was loud, and a large crowd was milling around in and out of the barn. He realized this would certainly be the largest crowd he'd ever been around.

He moved into the shadows under a large oak in the edge of the woods on a slope and watched. He was out of the lights but could see everything around the barn. He'd decided staying out of sight and watching was best for the time being. He could see what was going on and later, if he wanted to, he could walk down and try out the barbeque.

Red Hogan was standing outside the barn and seemed to be the main attraction, with a large group of men and women gathered around him. He wore a white Stetson and had a large cigar in his hand. He seemed to be enjoying the moment. Based on what Rep had seen of Red, the way he was acting was expected.

Rep let his eyes drift over the crowd. He'd only met three people by name since he arrived other than Mose - Red Hogan, Brit and Joe Hyde – so he knew none of the other people. He spotted Joe standing on the far side of the barn talking to some other men and Brit was at one of the bars with a blond wrapped around him. She was hanging on like she was afraid he would run away.

He'd been there for about ten minutes when he sensed someone standing behind him. He looked over his shoulder. Mose was in the shadows shaking his head, obviously displeased to see him there.

"How come you be here? You know this ain't smart."

"I got tired of talkin' to the possums."

Mose shook his head. "You gonna thank talkin' to possums. They be people here what ain't never liked you and now you done caught that big fish and everbody be talkin' 'bout you. Joe sho been talkin' bout you and what he gonna do to you. Brit runnin' his mouth too.

They gonna get too much liquor in 'em and if they see you, they gonna come at you. That's when the fight gonna start. They gonna' all be piling on you, it ain't gonna be just one."

Rep shrugged his shoulders. "I'm just watchin' here in the dark," he replied. He didn't intend to leave. "I ain't gonna leave this tree and start nothin', but I be stayin'. Ain't nobody runnin' me away."

Mose was unmoved. "It be best you be back to the river."

"I'm stayin' right here."

"Best you stay that way," he said, as he faded into the darkness.

Rep stared at the darkness for a moment after Mose disappeared. When he turned around and his eyes refocused toward the crowd, he was eye-to-eye with a woman not twenty feet away. She was standing in the light and was staring directly at him. She was strikingly beautiful, tall and statuesque with dark hair. He couldn't tell if the hair was brown or black, but it didn't matter. She was stunning. She had a drink in her hand and started walking straight toward him with her unwavering eyes focused on his face. He stared in wonder as she walked up the slight rise toward him.

"Why are you hiding here in the dark?" she asked as she stepped beside him in the edge of the shadows. Her voice was soft and smooth, self-assured, she knew she oversaw all around her. The scent of her perfume enveloped him. The aroma and her presence made him unsteady. "I've looked all over for you and thought you weren't even here. I was about to be disappointed. You were hard to find."

Her question and comment surprised him. Why would she be looking for him? "I wasn't hidin'," he replied, "just watchin' the party." Her face was just inches away from him and it bothered him. Who was she?

"I'm Lila," she said as she offered her hand.

"Rep," he said, as he took her hand.

"I know who you are, couldn't help but know, you're right famous," she said. "Everybody on the farm has been talking about you since you beat the hell out of Joe Hyde," she said, still holding his hand, "and then you catch the biggest fish anybody here has ever seen. You're somewhat of a folk hero." She squeezed his hand playfully. "And you've only been here three or four weeks."

Rep wasn't sure what a folk hero was, but the main question was who the devil is this woman? Why was she talking to him? Why would she be looking for him? He was aware of her soft and warm hand holding his and her perfume filling the air and the aura surrounding her. Her standing so close bothered him greatly.

She gently pulled him out of the shadows into the light. Still holding his hand, she stepped back and looked him over from head to foot, sizing him up. "They said you looked like a mountain man and they were right. My God, you are one handsome creature." She stepped back against him. "Are you as tough as everybody says you are?" she said playfully.

Rep stood without moving, speechless.

She leaned against him, put her hand on his bicep and squeezed his arm. "You don't look so tough, but you must be because everybody said Joe was tough and you whipped him." She looked up and smiled. "Course, I'm glad you brought him down a notch. I've always thought he was an ass and never liked him."

He knew this beautiful woman was teasing him and all he could think of was Red's warning about messing with any of the women. Right now, he had no choice but to go along with her, she had him by the hand and seemed to be in control. Regardless of the warning, he was enjoying being with her, although he had no idea why this was happening.

"Come and get a drink with me. I'm not going to bite you," she said as she linked her arm inside his and led him to the bar. She didn't ask what he wanted but ordered a beer and handed it to him. She moved close against him. He could feel her warmth and softness against his side. He was aware of every place she was touching him. It was obvious she was accustomed to having her way with men without an argument. He had no intention of arguing with her and messing up whatever was going on.

He took the beer, wanting to tell her he didn't drink but afraid if he did, he'd wake up and find his being with this beautiful woman was a dream. "I don't believe I've seen you around here before," he said lamely. He could think of nothing else to say. He felt like a complete idiot in her presence.

She laughed. "You haven't seen me before. I've been at school and just got home today."

"Oh," he said weakly, "but you know all about me. You know about Joe Hyde and the flathead and that I only been here a short time. I don't understand how you know all that and I don't know you."

"My daddy told me all about you," she said, her face only inches away. She knew her presence was bothering him, and she was enjoying his discomfort. "My daddy's been worried about you cause he can't figure you out and it bothers him. So, I said I must meet this young man who everybody is talking about. I wanted to see if you were real. So here I am, and you are most certainly real. I never expected anybody like you, even though everybody was talking about you so. Now that I've seen you, I'm acting like a schoolgirl and I never act like that. I don't know what to do with you." She took his other hand, and while facing him, pulled both his hands behind her back and her body against his, her breasts against his chest. His hands were around her as if he was holding her, but she had his hands. "What do you think I should do with you?"

He could feel her breath on his face. Her closeness was stirring his blood and he didn't want to move away. However, he was enjoying the feeling of her body plastered against him, but her comments about her daddy concerned him.

"You haven't answered my question. What should I do with you?"

He stood there with this beautiful girl holding both his hands, her body pressed tightly against him. She laughed at the questioning look on his face. "Have I confused you? You know my daddy. Everybody knows him." She turned and pointed at Red Hogan. "He's the guy wearing the white hat and smoking the big cigar."

Rep was stunned, as if somebody had poured a bucket of cold water on his head. Mose's words, "It be best you stayed away," ran through his mind, but it was too late. His body stiffened. He didn't know what to say but he knew he should get away from this woman or he could get into a lot of trouble, and he didn't need any trouble. He was trying to think of what to do when there was a commotion on the far side of the bar and he heard loud voices, screaming and cursing.

The crowd's attention turned toward the uproar and then the people around them began to move and shift towards the noise. Rep had a view over the crowd and could see two men fighting on the far side of the barn. They were in the shadows and he couldn't see them clearly. Then they moved into the light and he saw the red hair and knew one was Brit. He'd never seen the other man before.

The crowd surged around them as people moved toward the fight. Lila was standing beside him; she lost the grip on one hand and was pushed away. She tried to hold onto his other hand, but the pressure was too strong, and her hand slipped from his and she was shoved back. She tried to push back towards him, but the crowd pressure was too great. He watched as her eyes swept back and forth over the crowd, searching for him. Several men and women had stepped between them and blocked her view.

He could have moved toward her and probably could have reached her, but he didn't. He moved away toward the trees, quickly melted into the crowd and into the shadows. He looked back and saw her amid the crowd being pushed away. He moved into the trees and didn't stop until he was at the boat landing.

He was sorry their meeting had ended so badly, but he planned to stay far away from the farm until she was gone.

Despite his common sense telling him he was right, the memory of her holding his hand and the warmth of her body pressed against him didn't fade away. For a few short minutes that beautiful woman had touched him in a way he'd never dreamed about before. If she was of this world, she was from a part where he'd never been. The farm girls he'd known were like him. He understood them and how they thought, but this Lila had left his mind in turmoil.

He went to the shack, got in bed and sometimes in the wee hours went to sleep.

H e came out of the shack the next morning at daylight and Mose was waiting on the bench. He stood up and shook his head as he looked at him. "I told you last night to stay here."

Rep shook his head. "I know what you said, but I didn't go down cept to watch. That Lila come in the dark and got me fo' I knowed what happened."

Mose nodded and laughed. "I seed it. That Miss Lila done latched on you like a leech."

Rep nodded. "I didn't know who she was. Then she told me Red's her daddy and that scared the hell out of me."

"That be the truth, she be his oldest girl. She have two more sisters, but she be the pick of the litter. The other two look like they mama, sorta hefty."

Rep smiled. "I looked up and there she was comin' toward me. I ain't never seen a woman like her. She grabbed me and pulled me out of the dark. I didn't have a chance to git away till that fight started. I saw Brit was fightin' some man. What was that about?"

"He fightin' some man from cross the river. I ain't never seen 'im before. Brit say he say somethin' to that girl he be with and he beat him bad. If they hadn't stopped him, I believe he woulda sho' kilt 'im. Brit don't like Alabama people no way, but I doubt that man meant no harm. I done told you Brit be meaner than a snake. He don't like you no how and you know that. Best you stay away from 'im."

Rep shook his head. "I plan to stay away from 'im, and I'm gonna stay away from that Lila too."

Mose laughed and shook his head. "She be used to havin' her way, so she gonna come back at you. Best you stay down here outa her way."

"I aim to," Rep muttered as Mose went up the hill.

Rep went down the slough, fished the trotlines and set hooks after Mose left and came back to the landing about noon with a bucket of fish. As he came in sight of the landing, he spied Lila standing on the bank, hands on her hips, her eyes on him. The look on her face said she wasn't happy. The worry he'd had the night before about her being Red's daughter was staring him in the face and waiting in person for him. There was no way he could avoid her.

He beached the boat, tied the rope to a tree, stepped out and faced her. He had no other choice. A thousand thoughts raced through his mind as he looked at her. She was wearing jeans and a blouse instead of the dress she'd had on last night, but the perfume was the same. He noticed her hair was brown with a hint of red. He thought she was the most beautiful woman he'd ever seen, and she scared the hell out of him.

"You ran away from me and left me alone by myself in that crowd last night," she said, accusingly. "That wasn't nice, I could have been trampled."

"I didn't run away, just sorta walked slow."

She shook her head. "That's a smartass answer. You can do better than that."

Rep shrugged his shoulders. "I didn't know what I was supposed to do. I sho' didn't know I was supposed to look after you. I'd just met you. You'd told me Red was yo' daddy and right then I knew that you could be trouble for me. I didn't mean or try to get separated, it just happened. But that did seem like a good time for me to leave."

She didn't seem to understand. "Why would you being with me be trouble for you because Red is my daddy? What difference would that make to you?"

He didn't believe she would be so naïve. "Damn it, girl," he said, shaking his head, "you seemed to know all about me. You know why it be a problem. I'm hired help. I work for yo' daddy for a livin'. Me and you be from different worlds."

"I know you work for daddy. That had nothing to do with me talking to you. I told you I'd heard about you and wanted to meet you. That was all there was to it."

He looked at her, remembering her holding his hand and her body pressed against him. "Well, it does make a difference to me. I work for yo' daddy. What would he thank 'bout you bein' seen with me?"

She shook her head. "Why would he care?"

"Cause you're his daughter and you know what I am."

"So what?"

Rep could tell he wasn't getting anyplace with her. "Tell me, what do you do for a livin'?"

She was puzzled by the question. "I don't work, I go to school in Atlanta."

He shook his head and laughed. "And yo' daddy pays for it."

"Yes, Daddy pays for my schooling."

"And you come home sometimes and mess with the hired help." As soon as Rep spoke, he knew he had said the wrong thing.

Her demeanor changed immediately. Her face turned red and for a moment he thought she would hit him. "I don't mess around with anybody, anywhere." She spat the words out, then stepped back and took a deep breath. "You certainly think a lot of yourself. All I did was speak to you for a minute, that's all. What did you think I was doing, flirting with you? I thought you'd be interesting to talk to and I thought your story was interesting, that was all."

Rep wanted to turn and run, but he had to stand and take it.

"Let me tell you this, smartass, if I wanted to mess around with anybody, I have a covey of guys at school running around after me like Boar hogs in heat. I have plenty of opportunities to mess around up there." Her breath was coming in gasps she was so mad. "I don't need to come down here and mess with the hired help, especially not with you."

Rep realized he'd gone too far, and he wanted to stop this conversation now. "You're right. I was out of line. I was wrong. I be sorry." He picked up the bucket of fish and started away, wanting to avoid any further conversation, because he could see it wasn't going to get any better. "I got fish to clean." He walked toward the shack. He got half-way when she called him.

"Do you have an extra knife?" Her words stopped him cold.

He turned and stared at her. She was serious; her eyes cut into him. "I got extra knives." He walked on to the cleaning table with her right behind him. He dumped the fish out on the table, picked up a knife and handed it to her, unsure what was about to happen.

She took the knife, staring at him. Abruptly she grabbed a channel catfish off the table, swiftly cut off the head, slit it down the stomach and pulled the guts out. She threw the dressed carcass in the water bucket, rinsed it off, set it aside and grabbed another one.

Rep didn't say another word, nor did Lila as they dressed fish. He knew and understood she was sending him a message about who she was. She was showing him she was more than just a pretty face.

When the last fish was cleaned, she set the knife aside on the bench and stepped back. He watched as she stood there, her bloody hands shaking she was still so mad. Then she turned to him. "I intended to talk with you, that was all. I thought you were interesting, all the things you'd done were interesting. Never did I intend to mess around with you, regardless of what you thought. Now you listen to me, if I ever do decide I want to mess around with you, one night I will just come to the shack and crawl in your bed. Unlike today, there won't be any doubt that I want to mess with you. But I'll tell you this, if I do crawl in your bed with you, it'll be a night you won't ever forget. Until I decide to do that, smartass, you can go to hell." She wheeled around and went up the hill without looking back.

Rep watched her go with mixed emotions.

The next day Mose told him she'd gone back to Atlanta. The encounter with Lila was on his mind for the next several days. He never came to a clear-cut decision as how he felt about what had gone on, but he knew he wished he'd handled it differently. But she didn't leave his mind for some time. With Tish he'd not had anything to do with the split, this time with Lila it was all his fault. He felt he'd missed something special and it was going to haunt him.

10

River Bluff, Alabama, a small town on the banks of the Chattahoochee River, was located across the river from Shoal County, Georgia. The natives pronounced the name as Riv' Bluff. The town, established in eighteen sixty-five, sits atop a hogback ridge in a long bend of the river. With water on three sides and one road leading into town, it was somewhat like living on an island with a single bridge leading to the outside world. The local joke was, "Nobody came through River Bluff heading someplace else, so if a stranger showed up, they had to be lost."

River Bluff is a company town, in every sense of the word. The only employer in town, the Bluff Creek Cotton Mill, owns the mill supplying the only jobs in town. They also own all the land in and around the town, plus all the houses and all other buildings in town. Bluff Creek Cotton Mill built the town and it was theirs to run as they please. To get a house in town, you had to work in the mill. If you lost your job, you lost your house, which was incentive to do your job well.

Local planters built the mill and established the company the year the Civil War ended. The planters had the foresight to hide cotton bales in swamps on the river to keep them away from Yankee forces, then shipped the contraband cotton to England and sold it at a huge profit. They used the money from the sale of the cotton to purchase land on the river and build a cotton mill. The location on the river allowed water wheels to power the mill equipment via a channel of the river diverted to flow under the mill.

With the mill under construction, thoughts turned to workers who would operate the machinery. The area was sparsely populated; there was no town nearby. The South's economy was devastated by the war, people were poor and needed jobs. But if workers came, they wouldn't have a place to live and couldn't afford to build houses. Worker's houses would need to be near the mill, so the workers could walk to work. To solve the problem, the mill company built houses and rented them to the workers at a reasonable price, thus the town of River Bluff was born.

The promise of employment drew people from all over, primarily farm people. Families, tired of trying to eke out a living on their worn out, red-dirt farms, put their few possessions and children in a wagon and moved to River Bluff. One young man said the first time he saw his future wife, she was riding into town sitting in the back of wagon with her eight siblings with a milk cow tied behind. They came with nothing, hoping for a better future.

With the town established, the company constructed stores, churches, a high school, a gymnasium and a post office in the following years. Although the town was technically a "Company Town", usually a negative term, River Bluff was a good place to live and grow up. Someone once said, "Nobody in town had anything, but they didn't know any better, so everybody was happy."

Rolley Hill was born and grew up in River Bluff. Those families that came to work when the mill was built were prone to sire large families and his family was no exception. His father worked in the mill as a loom fixer, his mother was a spinner in another part of the mill. Six of his uncles and seven aunts also worked in the mill. Various other cousins were scattered throughout various departments. A high percentage of the total employees throughout the mill were Hills or their cousins.

When he was born, his family lived in one side of a mill house and another family lived in the other side. His father worked in the weave room and earned ten cents per hour. For a forty-hour week he made four dollars. When he was seven his father was promoted to loom fixer and his pay increased to twenty cents per hour and his family moved into their own house.

Rolley started to work in the mill on weekends at age sixteen as part of the clean-up crew. This was the normal route for the young people to get into the workforce. During the summer he worked every day when needed, regardless of shift. Now, as a senior in high school, he continued to work after school.

Cotton mill work wasn't easy, as he quickly found out. The mill was hot and dusty, and the work was hard. Cotton lint was in the air constantly and everyone was rubbing their eyes and scratching their nose to get relief. Many people ate their lunches in the bathroom to get out of the lint. Everyone leaving the mill after their shift was covered with cotton.

Rolley's father was an avid hunter and fisherman, as were most of the men in town. The Chattahoochee offered ample opportunity to do both. Rolley began hunting with his father at a young age and killed his first duck at eleven. By age seventeen he had his own wooden boat chained to a willow tree at the boat landing and he was free to roam the river when he pleased. He and other of his young friends were on the river most every day, either hunting or fishing or camping on one of the many islands in the river. On one of the smaller islands downriver, Squirrel Island, one group had built a cabin that they all shared.

One summer he and several of his friends worked on the second shift, from three in the afternoon till eleven at night. When they got off work they would go straight to the cabin on the river and spend the night. Some nights they would gig frogs on the way. The next morning, they would fish or do other things until time to go back to work. Some weeks they would follow this schedule for days at a time. Rolley's parents always insisted he leave the river on Sunday and attend church.

There was only one limitation to the freedom Rolley was given to roam the river. He was warned to stay away from the Georgia side around Shoal Creek. The reason for this warning was because the people up Shoal Creek made illegal whiskey and were very protective of their territory. Parents were afraid the young people might wander into places they shouldn't be and get hurt.

River Bluff was in a dry county, which meant all alcoholic beverages were illegal. To circumvent this law, local men would paddle across the river, walk up the creek and buy whiskey at Shoal Creek. Sometimes there was trouble. This didn't happen often, but it didn't take much to alarm the local community and brand the people across the river as bad and dangerous people. The general attitude in town was anti-alcohol.

Parents weren't the only ones who warned against the danger on the other side of the river. The Hill family attended the Baptist Church and throughout his young life, Rolley had heard sermons with the topic, "Those Godless heathens across the river." He knew about heathens from lessons in Sunday School. Heathens were ungodly people like the Philistines who the Israelites fought wars against in the Old Testament of the Bible. Goliath was a giant of a man and a famous Philistine. As a young boy, Rolley wasn't sure how these heathens had arrived in Georgia, but it was preached from the pulpit that they were there, so he believed it. Later, when older, he learned about local men paddling from River Bluff across the river, walking up to the Hogan farm and drinking and buying shine liquor. This made him wonder who the real heathens were? He never mentioned these thoughts to anyone, certainly not to his father.

Later, because of the stories he'd heard about how bad the people across the river were, he motored to the mouth of Shoal Creek and saw some people sitting on the bank fishing. He thought they looked just about like the people on the Alabama side, but he wasn't certain, he'd never talked to them. Later that same day he saw a boat come out of Hogan Landing. The driver, a tall young man with shoulder-length brown hair, stared at him as he passed, then turned down Back Slough and disappeared. The man didn't look dangerous.

Rolley vowed that if he saw the young man again, he would try to speak to him.

That night he talked to his daddy about the young man he'd seen in the boat. His father listened to his thoughts, then ordered him to stay away from Shoal Creek in the future and never speak to anyone from the Georgia side, regardless of how honest or harmless they looked.

11

It had been a week since the encounter with Lila. Regardless of how hard Rep tried to forget what had happened, it had been in his mind constantly. He had replayed each step, each word, what she said, what he said, over and over throughout each day. He was frustrated and confused.

He had taken a bucket of fish to the kitchen and was sitting on the bench by the road eating breakfast when Mose came up. "Red be wantin' you at the barn."

"What far?"

"He don't say. Just say come git you."

Rep took a sip of coffee and looked up at him. "I been wantin' to thank you, Mose. You've been good to me since I've been here, and I wanted you to know I preciate it." Mose didn't move, just looked at him. "I just wondered why you done it?"

"You be like a lost puppy when you showed up that day. There be bad folks here and I thought you'd be eat up, so I be wantin' to help you. I ain't got no use for some of them what be here." He laughed. "You done fooled me and everbody else. You be done good."

Rep finished eating and fell in beside Mose as they walked toward the barn. He wondered what Red wanted.

Red was sitting behind the desk when they entered. Mose went to his regular place against the wall and stood with his arms crossed. Rep looked around the room. Nobody else was present. He'd half expected Brit to be there. Red motioned for him to sit in the chair in front of the desk. He was surprised, since he'd never been asked to sit before. He eased into the chair, waiting for Red to tell him whatever was on his mind.

"You've surprised me, boy," Red began, his eyes on Rep. "I still don't know who you are and where you come from, but you've done alright here."

Rep sat very still, waiting for whatever came next. He had no idea what this was about, but he was certain Red didn't bring him here to brag on him.

"You've stayed out of trouble, which is good." He looked at Mose. "You were right, the boy can fish." He turned to Rep. "How did you know about that flathead?"

"Farmer on the Flint told me 'bout the flathead and showed me how to fish for 'em."

Red opened a desk drawer, took out paper and a can of Prince Albert and very deliberately rolled a cigarette. He lit it, took a puff then looked at Rep. "I didn't see you there, but I understand you were at the party the other night."

Rep didn't move, unsure what was coming next, but he thought he knew.

"Understand you talked to my girl, Lila, at the party. Is that right?"

"Yes, suh, I talked to her."

"Somebody told me she went down to the landing the next day after the party. I asked her about that, and she said she did go to the landing and talked to you." He leaned forward on the desk, staring at Rep. "Why would she come down to the landing to see you? Hell, she didn't even know you before that night. What reason would she have to come down there unless you asked her?"

Rep shook his head. "She come to the landin', but I didn't ask her to come. You have to ask her why she come."

"I did ask her, but she wouldn't say nothing except she went to the landing, talked to you and helped you clean some fish. That didn't make no sense to me."

"She did help me clean fish. I didn't ask her to, but she did."

Red leaned on the desk. "I told her I didn't want her going to the river alone again to see you or clean fish or for any other reason. And I damn well don't want you to ask her to come. You don't ever ask her to come down there. Is that clear?"

"Yes, suh, it be clear."

"It better be. Lila is young and I don't know what you said to her at the party to get this started, but that's the end of anything getting started between you and her, if that's what you had in mind. Do you understand?"

"Yes, suh, I understand."

Suddenly Mose spoke up. "You bein' hard on the boy, Red. I be there and saw and heard everythang at the party. He was standin' in the trees watchin' and Lila saw him, and she come and got him. She was just talkin' about him whippin' Joe Hyde. You know she ain't never liked Joe."

Rep watched Red's face, expecting him to explode at any moment. He didn't know why Mose had gotten himself into this discussion, although he appreciated the help, but he didn't think Red would like it.

Red stared at Mose for a moment and puffed on the cigarette. Then, very calmly he said, "Maybe so Mose, but I don't want Lila at the river again by herself, not ever for any reason." He looked back at Rep. "You know what I'm saying to you?"

Rep nodded. "Yes, suh. I know what you're sayin'.

Red motioned toward the door. "You get the hell out of here.

Rep almost raced to the door; he was so relieved to get away. He started up the road and Mose came alongside. "I 'preciate what you said and helpin' me out, but I expected Red to cuss you out for buttin' in like that."

Moses smiled. "Naw, suh, he wasn't gonna say nothin' to me."

Rep stopped. "I know he depends on you about thangs but why

weren't he gonna to say nothin' to you? I thought he would jump all over you cause you took up for me."

Mose stared across the corn field for several moments in deep thought and then looked at Rep. "I gonna' tell you som'em tween you and me." He paused and took a long breath. "Red don't say nothin' to me 'bout what I said cause he be my brother." When he saw Rep's shocked and confused look, he hurried on. "Well, he ain't my whole brother, we just got the same daddy."

Rep was so shocked he couldn't comment.

"My daddy, Mr. John, as everbody call him, run the farm after his daddy died. He weren't married and lived by his self. My mama, a fine-lookin' woman, she was a maid in the big house, and she got pregnant with me. Mr. John never said he was my daddy at that time, but he never said he weren't neither. Everbody on the farm knowed he be my daddy."

Rep finally found his voice. "Does everbody know that now?"

"The older folk do, but they don't talk about it. Red's chilluns don't know."

"So, then what happened?"

"Mr. John met Miss Gertrude later and that's when he built my mama the house where I live now. Mama moved in that house and never did have to work again. Mr. John and Miss Gertrude got married and Red was born."

"How did Red find out you be his brother?"

"Mr. John told him. One day he called me to the barn, Red was there, and he told Red I was his brother. Red was bout ten and I be older, bout twenty. He told me to look after Red while he growed up and told Red to treat me as his brother. He made him promise. Mr. John died some years back. Red took over the farm and that's where we be now."

Rep shook his head, amazed at what he'd just been told. "Red has treated you right?"

Mose nodded. "Most of the time. Now he ain't perfect by no means, he has some good in 'im, but he has a bad temper and a mean streak if riled. I don't like all this liquor stuff and he knows I don't. Mr.

John started that liquor business, but Red kept it goin'. Liquor causes troubles like at that party other night. Somebody gonna get hurt bad fo' long. I done told Red it was bad but he don't pay me no mind." He changed the subject. "You heard what Red said about Lila. I don't know Red loves nobody else, but he loves that girl and he meant what he say. It be best you stay away from her."

Rep laughed. "Don't worry about that. He didn't have to tell me all that. I was already gonna stay away. When she had that knife cleanin' fish, I thought she be gonna cut my throat. She has a temper and I ain't gonna cross her again." He continued to digest all he'd heard as they walked up the road.

As they neared the bunkhouse, Brit and Joe Hyde came out the front door, they both stepped off the porch and stood side-by-side in the center of the road. It was obvious they were looking for a confrontation.

"Brit, you better git on down the road now and don't start no trouble," said Mose.

"You go to hell, Mose," replied Brit as he stared at Rep, "you ain't got nothin' to do with this." He moved towards Rep. "This is the son of a bitch I'm lookin' for." He put his hand on Rep's chest and pushed hard.

Rep stumbled back but quickly regained his balance. He stepped to the side of the road and held his hands out toward Brit. "I don't want to fight you," he said and started to walk around him.

Brit grabbed him by the shoulder, jerked him around, and swung. His right hand hit a glancing blow on Rep's temple, sending him staggering back. He then swung his left which Rep blocked but a right to his shoulder knocked him backward.

Rep quickly regained his balance and reacted. He set his feet and hit Brit in the jaw with his right hand and followed with a left to the mouth. The two blows sent him staggering back across the road. His butt hit first, then the back of his head hit the concrete-hard dirt. He lay stretched out on his back and didn't move.

Joe made a step toward Rep, then stopped and put his hands up. He wanted no part of this.

Mose grabbed his arm. "You git into this, Joe and I'll put you down," he said quietly. Joe glanced at him, then ran and knelt by Brit.

"You done it now," yelled Mose, "you git on down to the river. You don't need to be round here for a while."

Rep nodded. "I'm goin' to Sallie White and finish my cabin. Be gone about a week and then I'll check with you. Do you have two good men what can help me?"

"I send three. I already got some stuff ready and you'll need boards and tin for the roof. You go on down and they be comin' tomorrow. They bring everthang you need."

Rep started up the road toward the landing.

"Don't worry about this here," Mose said as Rep disappeared, "I'll talk to Red and tell him what Brit done."

Rep hurried to the landing, entered the shack and grabbed his pack which he always had ready in case he had to leave suddenly. He threw everything in the boat and headed down Back Slough. He didn't second-guess hitting Brit, it was bound to come sooner or later. It wouldn't do any good to worry about it anyway.

Rep had the cabin on Sallie White almost completed. He'd known he couldn't continue to live in the shack at the landing. Sooner or later Brit or Joe would get drunk and come after him. Neither one would dare face him during the day again, they'd come in the middle of the night, so he knew he had to leave. That was why he'd discussed the idea of the cabin with Mose some time back. Sallie White was isolated and therefore much safer.

During the past weeks he'd worked alone preparing the site. He'd figured he'd need more than sixty logs to build the cabin. He knew he couldn't handle this work alone, felling the trees and preparing them was too heavy for one man. Mose allowed two men to join him at times and they started cutting trees. There weren't enough suitable trees on Sallie White, so they built a temporary bridge across the narrow inlet to Big Island where there were more than enough pines and oaks. They cut the trees, debarked them and painted the ends with a mixture to hold moisture in to avoid the log drying out and cracking. The foundation was prepared, and the walls constructed, one log at a time. The walls and gable were finally up and if Mose sent tin sheets, they would take off the covering and finish the roof.

The three men arrived the next morning as promised and immediately started to work. The tin for the roof and other items needed to complete the work inside came with them. At the end of the week the cabin was livable. There was still much to do but Rep could do that as time permitted. Now his next concern was what was going on at the farm and what was Red's attitude toward him. His question was answered that afternoon when one of the men arrived and told him Mose said to come to see Red the next morning.

12

Mose was waiting at the landing when Rep stepped out of the boat. One look at his face let Rep know he was concerned. "You look troubled," he said.

Mose shook his head. "Red be raisin' hell since you left. He wanted to know where you be, so I told 'im the truth, told 'im you was at Sallie White. Then I told 'im you comin' back in a week and he settled down."

"What else?"

"He all over Brit about startin' trouble. He say he gonna send 'im away if he don't straighten out. I don't reckon he cares if Brit fights with you but he's afraid the law will come in here and hurt the liquor business."

"So, what do we do now?"

"Red be waitin' at the barn."

Both Rep and Moose were quiet on the long walk to the barn, each absorbed with their own thoughts as to what was about to happen.

When they entered the barn Mose went to his regular spot against the wall. Red was sitting behind the desk smoking a cigarette. Rep was surprised to see Brit seated in a chair at the far end of the desk. Red looked at Rep and pointed at the chair at the near end of the desk. He eased into the seat. He glanced at Brit, noting the right eye was still black and he had a cut on his mouth.

Red leaned back in the chair and puffed on the cigarette, seemingly paying no attention to those in the room. The three other occupants sat quietly. Finally, he leaned forward and stared at Rep. "You've been a pain in my ass ever since you got here. I still don't know who you are or where you came from, but I do know you are trouble. I had to tell Lila to stay away from you and now she's arguing with me about that. Said she's gonna see you if she wants to. She's 'bout crazy as hell."

"Then you beat the hell out of Brit." He paused and looked at Brit. "I know he started the fight, that's the only reason you're still here." He looked back at Rep. "I think the best thing to do is put your ass on the road if this happens again, regardless who starts it." He looked across the room at Mose. "I understand he's built a cabin on Sallie White."

Mose nodded. "He stay there 'cept when he comes to the kitchen to brang fish."

Red looked at Rep. "That right?"

"Yes, suh. I ain't got no other reason to come to the farm, unless you tell me to."

Red shook his head. "I damn well don't want you up here. I don't want you to come past the kitchen. Is that clear?"

Rep nodded.

"It damn well better be clear." Red turned to Brit. "You stay the hell away from him on the river and Sallie White or anywhere else. If you can't do that, we'll settle it right now. I'll put you both outside in the road right now and let him beat the hell out of you again, unless you think you can beat him. Do you want to try him again, right now?"

Brit stared at Rep, hatred in his eyes. He shook his head. "No, sir."

"Good, I better not hear another word about all this." He turned to Rep. "You get the hell out of here and keep your ass on the river."

Rep went out the door and trotted up the road toward the kitchen, trying to get as far away from the barn as he could before Red changed his mind. Mose followed him up the hill.

"You stay low, I be watchin' out for thangs here," Mose said.

"I intend to stay far away," replied Rep. He continued up the hill and Mose turned off toward his house.

~

W hen he rounded the corner by the kitchen, Lila was sitting on the bench beside the road looking at him. He stared at her as if he was seeing a ghost, or the devil, unsure what he should do, but his first thought was to turn and run. He stood like a statue, staring at her.

She got up and walked slowly towards him. She had a small bag slung over her shoulder. As she came closer, he could smell her perfume and memories rushed through his mind, not all were good. She put her hands on his shoulders, reached up and kissed him on the cheek. "It's good to see you again, Rep," she whispered.

Rep realized that was the first time she'd said his name. He stepped back and held up his hands as if to ward her off. "What are you doin'? Red told me to stay away from you and he said he told you the same thang."

She smiled. "He did tell me that the other day, but today I told him I was a grown woman and I didn't give a damn what he said. He wasn't going to tell me who I could see or not see."

"Then what did he say?"

"Well, he hemmed and hawed a bit with some cursing sprinkled in, but then he gave up and here I am."

Rep was confused. "What does all this mean?"

"I heard you have a cabin on Sallie White."

Rep nodded. "Yes, I do. What does that have to do with anythin'?"

"I would like to see it."

Rep was so startled he could hardly speak. "You want to see the cabin?"

"Yes. I would like to go see it today."

Rep was about to tell her she was out of her mind when he heard a door slam behind him. He turned just as Brit and Joe came out of the kitchen. They both stopped and stared at them. Brit said something to Joe and stepped off the porch, but Joe grabbed his arm and pulled him back.

Lila put her hand on Rep's arm. "Let's go to the landing. Don't worry about them." She pulled him away toward the path to the landing.

Brit stood on the kitchen porch watching until they were out of sight.

Rep followed Lilla down the path to the landing, wondering all the way what was happening. It seemed he was going to the cabin with this woman who he had been told specifically to stay away from. Earlier, she had told him he could go to hell and now she wanted to be with him. He was totally confused.

He helped her get in the boat and pushed away from the pier. He cranked the motor and headed down Back Slough, glancing back up the path to see if they were followed but didn't see anyone. There was one thought in his mind, "What is this beautiful girl, with everything in the world, doing here with me?" He went about a hundred yards down the slough, shut off the motor and let the boat drift with the current. He looked at her. "You tell me what's goin' on here."

"I want to see your cabin. That's very simple."

He shook his head. "It's not simple. That's bullshit and you know it. Nothin' you do is simple. I remember the last thin' you said to me was about me going to hell."

"You're right, I wasn't totally honest the way I came on to you last time. I can see why you reacted as you did. When I came home, everybody was talking about the new guy on the farm, who whipped Joe and caught a giant fish. I asked daddy about you and he told me the story you'd told him, about running away from home and being on the road for four years. Of course, at that time he thought you were a spy sent here to cause trouble. I thought your story was interesting and I wanted to meet you and that's why I went to the trouble to find you. The problem was you turned out to be more interesting than I had planned on and I was attracted to you."

Rep sat without moving.

"Then we were separated, and I acted foolishly and chased after you the next day. I assure you I've never chased after a man like that. But then when I came to the landing, you accused me of messing with you, which was what I was really doing, and it pissed me off that you saw through me."

"You got me in trouble when you came to the landin'."

"Got myself in trouble too."

"So where are we now?"

"I've had time to think about everything and I want to spend time with you, so I plan to see your cabin."

He glanced at the bag and then at her.

"That's my clothes. I plan to stay the next two nights."

Rep leaned back and stared wide-eyed at her. "Are you serious? I've seen you two times in my life and neither time ended good. And now you're gonna spend the night with me?" He shook his head. "Lila, I don't understand this. You're from another world, so different from mine. You can't be serious."

"Yes, I'm serious. I've told you what I want to do."

Rep shook his head. "Red has threatened to kill me if I even speak to you and you plan to stay two nights with me. None of this makes any sense."

"I told you I have cleared that up with him. You don't have to worry."

Rep shook his head. "That may be easy for you to say, but I have to live here."

She smiled. "Let's talk about something else. Is the story you told Daddy about how you got here true?"

"Yes, it's true."

"You left home and were on the road for over four years alone?"

"Afraid so."

"That's amazing. Did you go to school before you left home?"

"Not much, my folks didn't think much of school."

"That is so sad, but you've done well."

Rep laughed. "Done well? I doubt that. Years ago, I was on the road, dead broke, and a fellow found me wanderin' around and told me I didn't have a pot to pee in. That's still true. I still don't have a pot."

"I disagree. I think you have a lot to offer. You underestimate yourself."

Rep could see he wasn't getting anywhere. "Let's start over. Why are you here? I still don't understand that."

"I want to spend time with you and get to know you better. I haven't been able to stop thinking about you for a month. I wanted to be with you, and I thought this was a good time to do it." She looked at him. "Tell me you haven't thought about me."

He shook his head. "I can't say that. I've thought about you."

She smiled. "Then we go on. I remember you accused me of messing with you and I told you if I ever came back, I would crawl in your bed. Do you remember that?"

"Yes, I remember that."

"I intend doing that tonight as I promised, however, there is one condition."

Rep was even more dumbfounded. He couldn't believe she'd just said she was gonna get in the bed with him. He'd never thought she'd meant she'd really crawl in his bed. He couldn't think of a reply.

"I will stay in the cabin and sleep in the bed with you on the condition you just hold me. Just hold me all night. Nothing more than that, just hold me."

Rep sat shaking his head. "Damn, girl, that be crazy. You even sayin' that is crazy. I never thought you sayin' you'd get in my bed was a promise. Remember, you were so mad I thought you said that because the idea was so crazy. How could I ever sleep a wink with you in the bed with me like that?"

Lila smiled. "Neither will I, but that is the condition. If you don't agree as I've asked, you can take me back to the landing now." She watched his face.

Rep sat staring at her for what seemed several minutes. "You really want to do this? As crazy as this is, you really mean to do this?"

She nodded. "I really do."

He turned around, started the motor and headed toward the cabin. His mind was racing full speed during the ride down the slough. He wanted to be with this girl, he had since the first time he saw her, but all this was too much and too fast to digest. As he'd said, they'd only met twice and now she had decided to not only stay with him but get in the bed with him. He had no choice in the matter. She was in control.

They landed at the pier. Their welcoming committee was two small pigs and a flock of mixed- breed chickens that came running thinking it was feeding time. He helped her out of the boat and carried her bag to the cabin. Lila's reaction was as expected of a woman. She walked in, looked at one bed, a cast iron stove and a homemade table with two chairs. There were no rugs on the floor and no pictures or anything on the walls. She turned to Rep and said, "Seems a little bare." He didn't understand her concern. It worked for him.

That afternoon Rep caught brim and went downriver to bait the set hooks -- Lila stayed at the cabin. When he returned, she had a mason jar on the table filled with yellow flowers from the yard, had washed the pile of dirty dishes and swept some of the dirt off the floor. She had hung a blanket across a wire in one corner of the room to make her a small private place.

He looked around at the changes. He liked what she'd done.

"How do you take a bath?" she asked. "It's been a long day and I want to bathe."

He laughed. "Don't bathe very often but when I do, I get a bar of soap and jump in the river."

She didn't comment, found a towel hanging on a nail in the wall, grabbed a bar of soap and headed for the pier. He watched as she shucked off her clothes and jumped naked into the water. She came up and yelled at him, "I'm not sleeping with you if you're not clean."

"What the hell," he muttered as he ran to the pier, took off his clothes and jumped in. "Throw me the soap," he said. He swam around but stayed away from her.

She finally swam to the pier, climbed up the ladder and picked up her clothes. He watched her all the way. She saw him watching her, so she turned, smiled and stood facing him for a full minute as he watched. Then, laughing, she ran into the cabin.

Late that evening he started a fire outside, then walked to the back side of the island and gigged four frogs. He dressed them and cooked the legs in the small skillet the farmer's wife gave him so long ago. They sat around the fire and ate. "This is the way I ate all those years I was alone on the road," he said.

Lila realized with this statement Rep opened a small crack into his very private inner self. "You grew up rough?"

"Wasn't very good."

"Do you wonder about your family?"

"Haven't thought much about them but I had two younger brothers and two sisters. I worry about them without me bein' there."

"Do you think you'll ever see them again?"

He shook his head. "Doubt it."

"That's sad," she said. "You worked at farms on the way up the road from time to time?"

He nodded. "I worked on farms."

"You meet any girls on the farms?"

He cut his eyes at her and smiled. "I met some."

She reached over and punched him. "I bet you left them crying all over Georgia."

He didn't answer but reached up and pulled her to him and kissed her. He turned her loose. "You ask too many questions."

She didn't ask any more, afraid she would pry too much into his past and shut his talking down. She pulled him to her and kissed him back.

Later they went inside. He had no idea how this was supposed to work. She went behind the curtain, he undressed, crawled into bed and waited, unsure how he would handle what was coming. She came out in a nightgown and eased into bed. She squirmed around until her back was against him. She was soft and warm. The effect on him was immediate. He was aroused, and he knew she felt it too. She stopped squirming and was silent.

The tension was interrupted by a loud whistling noise from outside the cabin. The sound startled her, and he felt her jump. "What is that?" she whispered.

"It's a whip-poor-will' calling his mate," he said, as the loud call came again. "It's a bird, just outside the window. He's lonesome." The loud call came again. He put his arm around her and pulled her close.

"Sounds like he's under the bed," she said. "It's so loud he must be six feet tall. How long does he keep this up? How can we sleep with that going all night?"

"He'll stop in a bit," he said as he moved his hand and cupped her breast, "but while we're awake there are other things we could do."

She didn't move. "You promised," she said.

He moved his hand and pulled her close. "Good night," she whispered. He squeezed her tightly. Sometime later they both went to sleep.

They were both up early. After eating a breakfast of eggs and bacon she cooked, they went swimming where he found she could outswim him. He was treading water near the pier when she swam toward him, smiling mischievously she put her hands on his shoulders and pressed her breasts against his chest. He automatically reacted as if a hot poker had touched him, pushing her away and paddling back. She laughed, playfully splashed water in his face and swam to the pier. As she climbed up the ladder, he watched her all the way.

He didn't fish this day, just stayed with her. It struck him that he didn't know where all this was headed but he felt the time they had together was precious. Even though they seemed to be equal at this moment in time at this place, he knew that in the light of day that wasn't true. She was indeed from another world, and try as they might, it would always be that way.

Later they lay in the sun on the pier and talked. He'd never had such a long conversation with a woman. She eased into the conversation a few more questions about his trek north and he opened up and talked freely about his experiences. As the time passed, she was more and more impressed with what he had accomplished.

The afternoon passed quickly, the sun disappeared behind the trees to the west and the sky darkened. They sat at the table drinking coffee and talked until late. She went behind the curtain and prepared for bed. He, as the night before, climbed into bed and waited, wondering how he could survive another night with her so close. She came out in her nightgown, eased under the covers and pushed back against him. She was warm against his body. Her warmth aroused him as it had the night before. He put his arm over her and held her. She lay silent.

"It's been a good day," she whispered.

"Yes, it has," he replied, pulling her closer.

"You were a good sport last night, you showed respect for me and I appreciate how you acted."

He chuckled. "It wasn't easy, I didn't sleep much."

"Wasn't easy for me either." She lay close to him for a minute, then moved a little away. He thought she was getting out of bed. Suddenly she turned over and faced him. "I've only done this one other time," she said, her eyes staring straight at him. "That happened after I'd been with him a long time. I loved him." She ran her hand over his face. "I have no idea what I'm doing here with you, but I wanted to be with you, so here I am."

He started to speak but she put her hand over his mouth.

"There are no conditions tonight," she whispered as she ran her hand over his chest and down his stomach. I'm all yours." She kissed him and pulled him close. Then she pressed her body against him, threw her leg over his legs and held him tight. Already aroused, he reacted to her advances.

They stayed in bed until mid-morning, touching and loving, passion running high. Both knew she was leaving but neither wanted to begin the process so they held each other for as long as they could.

There were no promises made and no talk of the future. A light rain was falling, Rep heard thunder in the distance and knew they had to move quickly to avoid being caught in a downpour.

Finally, she sat up, looked down at him for a moment and then leaned over, kissed him on his forehead and jumped out of bed. He watched her walk across the floor and disappear behind the curtain. He didn't move, just lay there with his mind trying to figure out what had happened during the last forty-eight hours. He still had no idea how all this had come about or what it all meant.

After a minute he gave up trying to understand, got up and dressed. He grabbed her bag, wrapped his heavy coat around her and hurried to the boat. They said little on the trip to the landing. Sadness seemed to have invaded them both.

He helped her out of the boat. The pier was wet and slippery. He carried her bag and held her hand as they walked up the path toward the kitchen. They stood on the porch under the cover for several minutes holding each other, nothing was said, then she kissed him and walked toward the big house. She never looked back. Rep stood in the rain and watched her all the way to the house, then went to the landing.

The trip to the cabin seemed to have the proper setting, dark and wet and somber. When he walked in the cabin and smelled her perfume and saw the yellow flowers in the mason jar he felt as if someone close to him had died. He undressed and stretched out on the bed where she had slept, surrounded by her warmth and the smell of her. Finally, sometime during the night, he went into a restless sleep.

~

The next morning Rep was on his regular routine. Up early, fished the trotline and limb hooks, dressed the fish and headed for the landing. Mose was waiting on the pier when he landed. He didn't greet him as usual and waited until Rep stepped out of the boat to hand him an envelope.

Rep didn't make a move to take the envelope. He looked at Mose's somber face and then at the envelope, as if hesitation would change the outcome. Finally, he took the envelope without speaking and walked slowly to the shed. He sat with it in his hand for several minutes before tearing it open.

`Dear Rep,

I have not been completely honest with you and I ask for your forgiveness. A long time ago I decided this farm and river life was not for me. I had never doubted this decision until I met you, but you made me question what I had never questioned before. How this could happen in such a short time puzzles me and I have no answer. This weekend was wonderful, all I could ever hope for and I thank you for it. I will never forget the conversations and the private feelings you shared with me. But you are a wild creature, like the animals that live around the cabin, and you must be free to lead this life. You have no other choice. We are from different worlds, I realize that now, so I will leave you free. I think that is best for both of us. I am moving away as I had always planned to do and will be gone while you are reading this. Lila

He read the note several times. It was always the same message - - she was gone. He sat slumped over on the bench with the note clutched in his hand, a thousand thoughts running through his mind. Lila had flitted into his life, stayed for a short time and then flitted away. It made no sense.

Mose sat on the pier and watched. Finally, he got up and walked over to where Rep sat. "I don't know what ya'll be doin', but here you sit all tore up and Miss Lila, when she give me that note was cryin' and all tore up." He walked away shaking his head. "Ya'll white folks be mighty strange."

Rep went back to the cabin with his mind in a fog. He walked inside, picked up the mason jar, walked to the door and threw the yellow flowers out into the yard. He took down the blanket she'd used as a curtain in the corner and opened the doors and windows to clear the air of any perfume still drifting about. He took the sheets off the bed, went out in the yard and put them in the black wash pot and poured a bucket of water over them, planning to wash them later. Lastly, he took the bar of soap she'd used, walked down to the pier and threw it across the slough into Georgia. He stood on the pier and let out a long mournful cry that sent the chickens in the yard running for their lives. When he walked back to the cabin, he didn't feel one bit better.

For the next week he threw himself into work, from daylight until dark and after, thinking this would help ease the emptiness he felt. He stayed away from the farm. He knew Brit had seen him leave with Lila and if he met him and Brit said one word about it, he was afraid he'd kill him. Thankfully, he never saw him on his trips to the kitchen, nor did he see Red Hogan.

After several days the pain subsided to a degree, although he still felt an emptiness inside, but he was more able to function and think about Lila without getting depressed. If he had done something that drove her away, he could at least blame himself for being so uncaring or a complete idiot. But that hadn't happened. He thought their time together had been perfect. Her note said she felt the same way.

That evening when he walked into the cabin and looked at what he had that was his, the words she'd said about being from different worlds hit him. But he already knew that, he knew it before she ever left. He was happy with this life, living in a log cabin on land he didn't own without a pot to pee in, but her other statement that it was best for both of them for her to go, brought him back to his senses. Right now, he was hurt and disappointed, but if they had gone further, she would have broken his heart. He realized this was probably best, but it didn't make him feel a bit better and his whole being was wound up tight. He was not happy with the world.

∼

When he got to the kitchen the next morning Mose was waiting. "Red want to see you."

"I spect I know what he wants," Rep muttered. "When does he want to see me?"

"He say right now."

"Any idea what he wants?"

"He ain't said."

Rep started towards the barn with Mose alongside, as they came around the corner of the kitchen, he saw Brit and two other men coming up the road toward them. He didn't know the two men but since they were with Brit, their presence didn't bode well. All three stopped in the middle of the road and waited.

Mose spoke to Brit as they approached the trio. "You betta not start no trouble here, Brit."

"You go to hell, Mose, this ain't got nothing to do with you." He pointed toward Rep who was coming toward him. "This son-of-a-bitch is gonna answer for what......"

Brit never finished his sentence. Rep didn't slow down but walked right through him and with all his force slapped him on the side of the face with an open palm. He put all the hurt he felt about Lila into the blow and if he'd hit him with his fist, he'd surely have broken his jaw or neck. The force of the blow staggered Brit, he stumbled awkwardly to the side of the road and fell to his knees, then slowly slumped over on his back and lay still. Rep stepped over the prone body without pausing and continued walking toward the barn.

Rep's action stunned Mose. He'd seen violence in his time, but nothing like he'd just witnessed. The other two men didn't move. All three looked down at Brit lying unconscious on the ground and then at the retreating Rep.

Mose quickly gathered his composure and trotted after him. Red Hogan was standing at the barn watching what happened. He threw down his cigarette, slowly turned and went inside.

They continued to the barn without speaking. Mose opened the door and they went in. Red was sitting behind the desk, drinking from a mason jar. He didn't look at them as he lit another cigarette. Finally, he looked up at Rep. "I saw what happened. Brit ain't got any damn sense and he's bad outclassed fighting you, and he oughta know better, but he don't. But if you ever hurt him bad, I'll have to kill you. You know that, but I'm telling you plain out."

Rep stood in front of the desk with his arms crossed. "Then tell him to stay the hell away from me or he's gonna get hurt."

"I've done told him that. I told Lila to stay away from you too, but that didn't do no good either." He looked up. "You know she's gone?"

"I know."

"I don't know what the hell happened with you two, but I told her she was acting like a bitch dog in heat, running around after you with her tail up looking for somebody to scratch her itch." He puffed on the cigarette. "She flat out told me it wasn't my business and then she went off with you. I reckon you bedded her. That seemed to be what she wanted. But she's gone now and that settles that."

Rep stood without moving, trying not to think of Lila.

Red took another drink from the mason jar and looked back at Mose. "What the hell do we do with this, Mose? Ever time I turn around I'm dealing with a family problem because of this son of a bitch."

"Brit ain't got no sense about this boy," replied Mose. "This boy ain't looked for no trouble but Brit set on comin' at 'im. You gotta stop this foolishness from Brit." He paused. "Now Miss Lila, she come at this boy at that party that night, then she come to the river that next day and now she done gone to the cabin on her own. Miss Lila a grown woman and she sho know her mind. She done all that herself but now she be gone. This boy be done what you say he do on the river and he ain't causin' no trouble."

Red puffed on the cigarette and stared at Rep. "Mose is right that I need you on the river or else I'd run your ass off, cause you ain't been nothing but trouble since you showed up here. You listen to me careful cause this is the last time I say this. You stay on the river and away from my family or I'm gonna sic my dogs on you. I'm gonna come after you myself." He leaned forward, put his elbows on the desk. "Do you understand what I'm telling you, boy?"

Rep nodded. He saw no need to push this further.

Red leaned back in the chair and changed the subject, as if nothing had happened with Lila and Brit. "We got other things to do besides talking about this. Cold weather's coming, and I want you to keep bringing fish, but we want squirrels and ducks, so get them too."

Rep didn't see any need to prolong the discussion, so he stood silent.

"You ever hunt quail?" Red asked.

Rep shook his head.

Red turned to Mose. "You need to teach him. We're gonna have a big bird supper in another week or so and I want lots of birds because we got a lot of people coming. Ya'll need to get busy hunting now. There's several coveys down by the cornfields so it ought not be a problem." He looked back at Rep. "Have you been downriver to Walnut Creek?"

"I've been to the creek but not up it."

"Lick Shell lives up the creek a piece on the right bank. He's a crazy bastard, but he trains good bird dogs. He says he's got a good pointer bitch he wants to sell. Go down there tomorrow and get the dog. We'll try her out and see if she's worth a damn." He looked back at Mose. "When he gets back ya'll see what the pointer's got. You understand?"

"I heared what you say," replied Mose, as he started for the door.

"You stay the hell away from Brit," said Red, looking at Rep, "I meant what I said."

Rep got up and walked out without replying.

"You know Red ain't foolin' about what he said," Mose said as they walked up the road toward the kitchen.

"Neither am I," Rep replied. At this time, he hated everybody in the world.

13

Rep left the cabin at daylight the next morning and headed downriver. He was glad to have something new to do on his mind. Lila was gone and he could do nothing to change that. He flushed several flocks of mallards and wood ducks as he went down the slough and turned into the main river. The sun was well up when he got to Walnut Creek and he found the house and barn on the right bank a short piece up the creek as Red had said.

He was not impressed with what he saw. The barn was badly in need of repair and the house, while larger, in some respects reminded him of the house where he'd grown up. A well was in the side yard, a two-hole outhouse in the back and chickens of various colors running everywhere.

He beached the boat and walked up the bank. He was about ten steps toward the house when a man holding a rifle stepped on the front porch and yelled, "Better tell me who you are right quick before I start shootin'."

Rep held up both arms. "Red Hogan sent me to get a bird dog," he yelled back.

"Why the hell didn't you say that to start with," the man said as he walked down the steps. He stood in the yard, the rifle in the crook of his left arm as he waited for Rep. "You work for Red? I ain't never seen you before."

"I ain't been there long. I do the fishin' for the farm."

"Hey, I heard about you. You be the one what caught that big fish?"

Rep nodded. "I caught the flathead. My name's Rep Doe."

"I heard 'bout that big fish but ain't never heard of no flathead. You come to get the dog? You a bird hunter?"

Rep shook his head. "I just come to get the dog."

Lick turned back toward the house and yelled, "Bess!"

Rep looked up as a tall young girl with long black hair walked out on the porch. Her hair looked badly in need of a brushing but beneath the unruly mop he saw a pretty face. The dress she wore was decorated with a pattern of small yellow flowers and it immediately caught his attention. Long ago he'd seen the same pattern on dresses his little sisters wore and forgotten memories flooded his mind. Her sudden appearance, the dress pattern and the memories caught him off guard and he stood there gaping at the girl in the flour sack dress. These are my kind of people, he thought. This is what I come from, folks just like these. It was the first time he'd had these thoughts in years.

"What the hell you be lookin' at!" she yelled, leaning over the porch railing and staring straight at him.

Her accusing voice brought him back to his senses. "I'm sorry," he stammered, "you surprised me."

"Ain't you got no good sense?" She stood with hands on her hips and glared at him. "You be standin' there lookin' like a idjit."

Rep just stood there. He didn't know what to say to this wild-haired girl in the flour sack dress who made him think of his sisters.

Lick interrupted. "Hush yo' prattlin', gal, and take him to the pen and get that bitch pointer. Put her on a leash so she don't run away."

She came down the steps, brushed by Rep and walked toward the barn. He fell in behind her, noting she was older than he'd first thought and how attractive she was, despite the unruly hair and the flour sack dress.

"You work up at that Shoal Creek place?" She didn't look around, just kept walking.

"Yes."

She stopped and turned to face him. Her tone was accusing. "You make liquor? Lick say that's what they do up there."

Rep laughed. "Not me, I don't make no liquor. I fish."

She turned up her nose. "Lick gets mean when he dranks. He used to hit my mama. I don't like liquor and I don't like them what make it."

"My daddy was a drunk and he was mean. That's why I left home," Rep replied. As soon as he uttered these words, he wondered why he'd told this stranger anything about his life. Why would he open up like that to a girl he'd never seen before?

She nodded. "I done thought about runnin' away too."

Rep shook his head. "You better stay with yo' folks. Bein' by yo'self ain't easy."

"Ain't nobody here 'cept Lick and my three sisters."

"Where's yo' mama?"

"She left some time back. Lick be drunk and hit her, so she whopped him in the head with a skillet, knocked him out cold. Then she run out the door and we ain't heared from her since."

They got to the pen, she opened the door, got the leash off the post and secured the dog quickly. Rep was impressed with the way she handled the dog and the dog's reaction to her. "You handle the dog good," he said.

A tight-lipped Bess turned and faced him. "Don't start that sweet stuff with me," she said, stepping right in his face, "My mama done told me about men like you. Mama said you'll come here sweet talkin' me like you care and then after you do what you want, you be gone. Don't you start that crap with me." She turned and walked toward the house, the dog trailing behind. She handed the leash to Lick, went up the steps, into the house and slammed the door.

Rep watched her walk away, wondering what he'd said that stirred her up so? Shaking his head, he followed her to the house, remembering prior lessons that women are strange creatures. Lick stood by the steps holding the dog and staring at him.

"What the hell you do to Bess?" he asked.

"I don't know," Rep replied, shaking his head. "We was just talkin' and yonder she went."

"She's just like her mama, crazy as hell," said Lick. "Their mama run off and the damn bitch like to kilt me before she left. She hit me in the head with a fryin' pan and left me with them four girls and they be drivin' me crazy. I can't do nothin' with 'em." He stood with his head bowed, totally frustrated. "I don't know what the hell I gonna' do.

He started to walk up the steps and suddenly he wheeled about and stepped back toward Rep. "By damn it," he said as a smile crossed his face and he looked at Rep. "You be a young man. You got a woman?"

Rep stepped away and shook his head. "No, I ain't married."

"Boy, you ain't got no woman, then you sho-nuff need a woman. By God, I'll give you one. I got four, so you can have airy one of the four I got. You pick the one you want." He stopped and looked back toward the house, his brow furrowed in thought, then looked back to Rep. "It be best you take Bess, cause she be the oldest, about sixteen I thank, and she can cook. Hell, you wait, I git her back out here."

Rep held up his hands. "I don't want nobody, specially no woman. I come for the dog, just give me the dog and I'll go."

He reached for the leash, but Lick jerked it away and yelled at the house, "Bess, get yo' ass out here, right now."

Rep looked up as the door opened. Bess slowly walked out on the porch and stood at the railing. The look on her face showed she wasn't happy.

Lick motioned to her. "Come on down here, gal. This man be needin' a live-in woman and I told 'im you be goin' with 'im. He'll look after you and God knows you shore need lookin' after. Go git yo' thangs right now and go with 'im."

Bess walked to the edge of the porch, leaned over the railing and stared at Lick, her face livid. Then she turned her eyes on Rep. "I ain't goin' nowhere with no man!" she screamed, and pointed her finger at Rep, "and I damn well ain't goin' nowhere with that son o'bitch!" She wheeled about, went in the house and slammed the door again.

Rep stared at the closed door, his mind trying to grasp all that had just happened. Finally, he walked over, took the leash from Lick and slowly started leading the dog toward the boat. He thought he had seen a lot in the past four years, but this beat it all.

Lick was behind him yelling. "Don't you be worryin' about her, boy, I'll get her straightened out. You just come on back and she be ready."

The ride upriver was filled with memories and confusion -- memories of the life he'd once had and confusion concerning this family he'd just met. He'd rarely thought of his family during the past four years and now he was overwhelmed with thoughts he'd stuck far back in the recesses of his mind. He'd never intended to ever bring them to light again and it was all due to a wild-haired girl in a flour sack dress.

He decided the matter of that crazy Lick offering his daughter to him as a live-in woman would be forgotten. He couldn't see any good to come from discussing any part of his trip with anyone. The best thing for him would be to stay far away from Walnut Creek and them crazy folks.

Mose was waiting at the landing. "See you got the dog." he said. He chuckled. "That Lick be one crazy white man."

Rep thought that Mose didn't know it, but he'd never uttered a more truthful statement in his life. "No problem," he replied, as he tied the boat up and handed the leash to him.

For the next two weeks Rep and Mose hunted quail in the mornings and shot doves in the afternoon. He'd never hunted quail with a dog before and it took him some days to get the hang of it. The first time he walked across a sedge-brush field with the dog standing motionless on point, he had no idea what to expect. Mose told him to be ready and walked forward, so Rep followed. As they walked past the dog, the covey exploded into the air all around his feet and he was so startled he almost dropped his gun. When he recovered and fired both barrels, he hit nothing. Mose laughed at him, he'd seen the same thing happen before. But after a few days Rep learned to anticipate the covey rise and shot well and could nearly match Mose. Lick's dog pointed and retrieved better than any of the other dogs and Mose was well pleased.

Dove hunting was easier. He stood at one place on the edge of the field and could see the birds coming in time to shoot. By the end of two weeks they had enough birds to feed half the county.

~

The next morning Rep was outside the kitchen eating breakfast when Mose came up and handed him an envelope. "I told Red the dog be good. He say for you to go to Lick's place and pay him."

Rep stared at the envelope, not wanting to touch it. He'd been worried about this possibility for days. He had no idea how he would handle Lick and his crowd again. "What if Lick wants me to take that wild-haired girl to the cabin with me?" he thought. "When do he want me to go?"

"He say you go today. That be a problem?"

Rep shook his head. "No, not a problem." He sat on the bench until Mose was out of sight, thinking about what he should do. He got up, went to the kitchen and talked to Hattie Mae. She gave him a bucket of dressed fish, a package of ten quail and a cured ham. He put them in a croker sack and headed for the boat.

As he went downriver, he grappled with his feelings as to exactly what he was doing and why he was doing it. He tried to tell himself it was his job to go, Red had told him to, plus he felt sorry for this poor family that reminded him of his own. But the image of Bess, the wild haired girl, for some reason kept getting in the way of and muddying his thoughts. He couldn't get her out of his mind. He grappled with these confusing feelings as he went downriver.

He turned off the river into Walnut Creek and landed. He picked up the box of food and started toward the house. He didn't see anyone on the porch or in the yard, so he yelled out, "Anybody home?"

The front door cracked open and he could see a small face looking at him. "What you want?"

"Looking for Lick. Want to pay him for the dog."

The door opened and a young girl walked out on the porch. He figured she must be one of the sisters. "He ain't here. You be that fellow from Shoal Creek? You come to git Bess?"

"I'm from Shoal creek but I didn't come to git Bess. I come to pay for the dog. Where is Lick?"

"I don't know, he left this morning to go see a man up the road."

"You be here all by yo'self?"

"No. My sisters be here, and Bess be at the barn."

Rep walked up on the porch carrying the box of food. "Let me put this in the house and then I'll go talk to Bess." The young girl stepped back and opened the door. He walked into the kitchen and it was like going back in time to the house where he grew up. He sat the box on the table and fled from the memories.

He walked to the barn but didn't see anyone. He heard cackling around back. He went around the corner and Bess was in the chicken yard throwing corn on the ground, chickens feeding around her feet. She was wearing overalls much too large for her and her hair was as wild as it'd been when he last saw her. He stood and watched, fascinated.

Finally, feeling his presence, she turned and looked at him. She didn't move for what seemed to be a minute. "What you be doin' here?" she asked. Her tone wasn't combative, which an improvement over the last time.

"I got Lick the money for the dog."

"He ain't here." She unfastened the gate to the pen and walked toward him.

"I know, your sister told me. I brought some fish and birds and ham for ya'll too."

"What you do that fir?"

"Thought it might help you out."

She stared at him for a minute. "You really run away from home?"

"I did, like I told you last time."

"Where you stay now?" Her tone seemed friendlier.

"I have a cabin on Sallie White Island."

She walked around the side of the barn and on toward the house. Rep fell in beside her.

She stopped and looked in his face. "I don't care what you thank. Lick ain't never gonna give me to nobody I don't wanta' go with. I wouldn't never go, no matter what he say."

"I never thought you would."

"Mama said a girl what go off with a man and ain't married ain't nothing but a whore."

Rep had no idea how to reply to this statement, so he kept walking.

When they reached the house, he handed her the envelope. "Give this money to Lick for the dog."

Bess took the envelope, started up the steps, paused and turned around. She stared at him. "Lick say you ain't got no woman."

He nodded. "I don't have a wife. I'm not married."

She looked at him for several seconds as if studying over his answer, then walked up the steps to the porch, stopped again at the railing and looked back at him. "Lick told me to go with you and be yo' woman," she said accusingly. "Did you tell Lick to tell me to go with you?"

Rep shook his head. "No. I would never ask Lick about nothin' like that without talkin' to you first. I wouldn't never do that."

One side of her mouth turned up in the beginning of a smile. "That be good." She turned and went into the house without another word.

Rep stood there for a bit then went to the boat. He dwelt on their conversation all the way to the cabin. When he got out on the pier he was still as confused as he'd been earlier.

14

Jack and Ruby Hobb lived in River Bluff and both worked in the mill. Years before they had come to the town by wading across the river from the Georgia side of the river with all they owned in a brown paper sack. They were hungry, hopeless and destitute. Mill management felt sorry for their pitiful situation and they were hired for menial jobs at the mill. Management would regret this decision in the future.

Jack was a sweeper on the night shift and Ruby cleaned bathrooms. To date neither had risen above that initial hiring. Uneducated and ignorant in many ways, they had both quit school at an early age and aspired for no more learning.

Nobody knew anything about their upbringing in Georgia but based on their actions in River Bluff, they had no idea how normal people should act. They claimed to be married but nobody had seen any paper to prove it. Local citizens looked at how they conducted themselves and decided they were living in sin. Drinking and fighting seemed to be their normal daily routine. The town constable made regular trips to their house to settle various domestic disputes.

They were given the least desirable house in the least desirable location and managed to make it even less desirable. They contributed nothing positive to the community in any way. They never darkened the door of any church, never helped in any community activity and were an embarrassment to the community by their actions.

Over several years they birthed four children, two boys and two girls. The town's women saw her constant pregnancy and said, "Ruby Hobb is pregnant as an alley cat again." They gave the children no positive moral guidance as they grew up because they practiced none themselves. The children's home environment was challenging. They were never subjected to discipline, never held accountable, regardless of their actions. The oldest three quit school early, following the example of their parents. The Hobb family was considered by most of the local citizens to be at the bottom of the town's social strata. No family wanted their son or daughter to marry or have anything to do with one of the Hobb children.

Boot was the oldest son. He was tall, well-built and a capable hunter and fisherman. He worked in the mill and could have been a good worker but lacked any desire to excel. Now twenty-five years old, he had a reputation for drinking and fighting, most of the time in beer joints in the next county. He had been warned repeatedly that his actions would cost him his job or even jail time if he continued down this path. These warnings had little if any effect. He was prone to violence and the men in town tried to avoid him.

Star was the oldest daughter. A pretty girl, she matured physically at an early age and caught the eye of the town's young men. As a result of her lack of any thought of right or wrong, she was promiscuous at fifteen. Her parents were proud she was so popular with many of the town's young men. They did wonder why none of her dates picked her up before dark. She ran away from home and was found in Texas three days later. When Jack was told she'd been found, his only comment was, "She made damn good time, didn't she?" Soon after, she decided River Bluff was too small for her talents and she discovered soldiers at Fort Benning and left town. The women in town were glad she was gone; it lessened their concern she might be carrying their grandchild. Many of the town's young men weren't so thrilled. Her parents said she'd married an officer and was in Germany, but nobody believed that was true. She was gone though, and no one had seen her for several years.

Harold, the youngest son, was twenty years old. He had been promoted from one grade to the other because the teachers wanted to get rid of him. He didn't make it to the sixth grade. He worked in the mill more than once, but each time ended up being fired for absenteeism and poor work performance. He was living with his parents and doing nothing to improve his situation. His fifth-grade teacher, Miss Sands, had told him repeatedly, "Harold, if you don't change your ways, you're going to end up sorrier than gulley-dirt," which she considered worthless. The other fifth-grade students heard that comment and it ended up being Harold's epithet. His parents never encouraged him or the other children to strive for excellence in school or in any other effort. He wasn't stupid, he just chose the path of least resistance in every aspect of life and his parents never guided nor disciplined his actions. At an age when most young men were well on their way to a meaningful life, he lived with his parents, ate at their table and showed not one iota of ambition.

Some of the boys his age remembered an incident some years before when he was with a group on Big Island roaming around as boys do. Harold discovered a mama racoon with young ones in a hollow tree. Shirtless, he climbed up the dead tree, made a loop with his belt and dropped it like a lasso over the mama coon's head. Disregarding warnings from the other boys of the danger, he tightened the loop and dragged the coon out of the tree. While he had the mama coon under control initially, that quickly changed. For the next several minutes he was fighting to get loose from the enraged mama, who was doing her best to tear off his head. Needless to say, the results to his head and back were similar to a person being dragged through a briar patch.

The only potential exception to the Hobb family's sorry record with their children was their youngest daughter, May. She was fifteen, in the tenth grande and was an outstanding student. Therehad never been a hint of any of any questionable moral issues on her part, though she'd been watched closely because of her sister Star's past reputation. However, she was still a Hobb and therefore she wore the mantle of the name, no matter how undeserved and unfair it might be. The attitude of the community and the actions of her classmates made this clear and she realized it.

Jack and Ruby kept liquor in the house which they drank daily for years and all the children joined them at an early age. Jack paddled across the river and walked up Shoal Creek to replenish their supply at least once each week. Both boys would accompany their father at times and knew the territory well. The Shoal Creek people also knew the Hobb family and had no use for them. When they were on the farm, they were closely watched because of their record of stealing and causing trouble. Jack knew, as all Alabama people knew, that Red Hogan wanted them to buy liquor and head back across the river. If you tarried too long and especially if caught in off-limit areas, the consequences could be dire. The most serious offense concerned the Flat Shoals women. They were completely taboo, and the penalty was a severe beating or worse. This usually happened when someone drank too much, their judgement was impaired, and hormones took over.

The Shoal Creek women weren't lily-pure by any means. They lived far away from town, worked on the farm throughout the week and were not above looking for excitement. Lonely women and alcohol made a dangerous mixture, which was especially true for the younger unmarried women. It was the dream of some that one of these outside young men would take them away from their present life, so they made themselves available. It didn't bother them if a man wanted to try out the merchandise before buying it.

~

Harold Hobb knew the rules too, but as usual, didn't choose to follow them. He'd never followed rules, but he wasn't the only one to ignore the rules. Two young girls whose parents lived and worked at Shoal Creek were also guilty. They slipped out of the house one night and ended up at the barn where they ran into Harold. The meeting wasn't planned, he'd never seen them before, but he was certainly willing to join in any mischief they planned. They found an empty room and began to get acquainted.

Later that night the parents discovered the girls weren't in their room and sent their brother to find them. The brother ran into Brit Hogan while he was searching, and Brit was glad to help in the hunt. After an hour they discovered Harold and the girls in a shed behind the barn. The girls were partially clothed as was Harold. Brit took control of the situation. He told the brother to take the girls home and he would handle Harold.

Harold was no match for Brit, who was bigger, a more experienced fighter and loved to hurt people. Harold tried to get to the door, but Brit was too quick and trapped him in the corner and began to pound him unmercifully. Very quickly Harold was a bloody mess and Brit showed no signs of letting up. The blood lust was on him and he had no control over his actions once he started. The girl's brother hadn't left the room as Brit had ordered him to do but told the girls to go home and he stayed at the door to watch the fight. As the beating continued, he became concerned, rushed forward and grabbed Brit and held his arms. "You gotta stop, Brit. You gonna kill him," he said, pulling him back.

Finally, Brit's breathing settled down and he got under control. "Let me go," he finally said. He walked to where Harold lay huddled against the wall and pulled him up. He dragged him to the back door and pushed him outside. "If I ever catch you over here again, I'll kill you." He shoved the stumbling half-blind Harold toward the woods and went back inside."

Harold staggered into the woods, falling over debris as he went down the hill toward the creek. He finally got to the well-worn path leading to the river and knew where he was. His eyes were almost swollen shut and blood was still dripping from his nose as he made his way toward his boat. He was on his knees crawling when he reached the river, pulled himself into the boat and finally pushed away from shore. Then he collapsed in the bottom. The current took the boat and it drifted aimlessly down Back Slough.

~

R ep was up early, checked the trotline and set hooks and had started toward the landing when he saw the boat drifting toward him. He wondered what was going on as he approached the seemingly empty craft. He came alongside, grabbed the gunnel and then saw the young man lying in in the bottom in a pool of blood. He saw that the man was breathing so he reached over, grabbed his shoulder and shook him. "Hey," he said. There was no response, so he shook him again. "Hey," he yelled.

The man moved his head a bit and partially opened one eye. He was trying to focus on Rep's face. His mouth moved but nothing came out. He tried again. "Red-headed man hit me," he said weakly.

Rep's first thought was, "Brit did this". He wasn't sure why he thought that. "Where you live?"

"Across the river."

"You live in River Bluff?"

The man nodded.

"You stay where you are. I'll take you home." Rep didn't know how bad the man was hurt but he looked a mess so the best thing to do was get him to his folks and let them take care of him. He moved to the front of the boat, grabbed the rope, cranked the motor and started up the river, pulling the boat behind. As he started up the slough, he thought about what Red had said about staying out of Alabama. But he couldn't see he had a choice.

R olley Hill went to the boat landing early, planning to go to the shoals and fish for bass. He was about to crank up when he saw a boat come out of Back Slough with another boat tied behind. He always watched boats coming from that direction. It was coming across the river in the direction of the landing. This immediately got his attention because nobody from Shoal Creek ever came to the landing. He got out of his boat and walked down to an empty landing spot and waited. He saw the driver was the young man with long brown hair.

The stranger beached in front of him and pulled the other boat alongside. "Got a hurt man here," he said to Rolley.

Rolley walked over and looked in the boat.

"Do you know him?"

Rolley wasn't sure to start with because the man's face was bloody and swollen, but then he realized who it was. "That's Harold Hobb."

"He live here?"

Rolley nodded, "He lives on Pot Licker Lane."

"He's hurt bad, better get him some help."

As they were talking, other people were walking down the bank toward the boat. The arrival of a boat from Shoal Creek had gotten people's attention. Several men gathered around the boat.

"What happened to him?" one of the men asked. "Somebody beat the hell out of him," another said, "look at his face." Three of the men got in the boat and lifted him out. They started up the bank with him. "Put him in my truck," a man said, "we'll take him to Miss Neal, the mill nurse."

"I don't know what happened to 'im," replied Rep. "I found the boat driftin' with him in it."

"Never seen you afore," said one of the men. "Who the hell are you?"

"I live on Back Slough." Rep could see it was time for him to leave before these men asked too many questions.

"You work for Shoal Creek?"

"I fish for 'em."

"Sorry ass crowd over there," said one of the men as they carried Harold to the truck. "People oughta have enough sense to stay out from over there."

Rep pushed away from the bank and moved back to the rear of the boat.

Rolley walked toward the front of the boat. "Some of the men said

Harold had been up Shoal Creek," he said. "He said a red-headed man beat him up."

Rep looked at him. "I don't know bout nothin', I just found 'im."

"Harold's daddy and brother are crazy and mean folks," Rolley said. "They ain't gonna like him getting beat up like this. I spect they'll be looking for whoever did it."

"That's up to them," replied Rep. He cranked the motor and headed upriver.

~

The men got Harold to Miss Neal's office at the mill and she was tending to him when his daddy and Boot got there. They were quickly brought up to date on his condition, what he'd said about the red-headed man beating him and the man from Shoal Creek bringing him to the landing. Both men reacted as the crowd expected; questions followed by threats and then curses. Miss Neal finally had enough and told everybody to get out of her office or she wouldn't do another thing for Harold.

Once outside, Jack wanted to get up a posse to invade Shoal Creek and get the red-headed man who beat up his son. The men had been glad to help Harold, they would have done the same for a hurt dog, but they didn't want a part in anything Jack and Boot was planning.

The Hobb family had always been troublemakers, an embarrassment for the community and they wanted to stay away from them. They didn't know what had happened to get Harold such a beating but based on his past, they figured that he probably deserved it.

Failing to get any support from the group, Jack cursed them all and walked away. By the time he and Boot got to the house, they had decided they'd slip into Georgia and kill the red-headed man themselves. They began discussing how to do it and Boot quickly took over the planning. He knew his daddy didn't know his ass from a hole in the ground about planning and would screw up everything.

"There's two red-headed men over there," said Boot. "We don't know which one did it."

"Don't make a damn," replied Jack, "just kill 'em both.

$\sim$

Rep rode upriver with mixed emotions. Red had told him to stay away from Alabama people and now he'd not only rescued one, but he'd taken him to the Alabama shore and talked to the people. Making the situation worse, it seemed Brit had been involved in whatever led to the person being injured. Based on what the young man said, the family of the injured man were mean people. If they were intent on retribution and were able to do it, there could be a problem. He had no choice but to tell Red Hogan what he'd done and what he knew.

Mose was waiting at the landing and he didn't look happy. "We got trouble," he said as Rep got out. "Brit had a fight last night with some Alabama man and they say he hurt 'im bad. The man went to the woods but he ain't been found."

"Damn," muttered Rep. "I can tell you what happened to 'im." He told Mose about finding the boat with the man and then taking him to Alabama. He also told him what had been said at the landing.

Mose shook his head. "Red sho' ain't gonna like nary bit of this. He sho gonna be mad."

Rep shrugged. "He'll just have to be mad then. Let's go tell 'im."

They were right that Red would be mad. After Rep related what had happened, he pitched a fit. "You took the son of a bitch back to Alabama!" he screamed. "Why didn't you just let the bastard die?"

"I didn't know what happened to 'im," replied Rep. "He was hurt, and I didn't know who he be."

Red threw his arms up. "Now we gonna have ever bastard in Alabama raising hell about us. What did you say his name was?"

"Harold Hobb."

"Oh hell," yelled Red. "I know that crazy ass family. The old man is stupid, and Harold is like his daddy but that other son, Boot, is one mean bastard. We've had problems with that bunch ever time they've been over here." He walked around the room shaking his head. "You said he told them a red-headed man beat him?"

Rep nodded. "He told me and the men at the landin' that be what happened."

"Damn Brit," he said as he looked at Mose. "I'll have to send him to Atlanta till this all blows over. He don't need to be around here. I ain't worried about them telling the law here, I can handle that. But that crazy-ass Boot might come over here looking for him."

Mose nodded. "That be best to do."

Red looked at Rep. "You said the boy was beat up bad but he won't die, so this might settle down."

"They might let it go, but you said they're mean and crazy people" replied Rep. "Course I don't know 'em but the boy at the landin' said they wouldn't let it go."

Red agreed. "Anyway, we can't ignore it. Mose, send two men to the mouth of the creek. Tell them to watch across the river. If they see any of the Hobb people coming this way, tell them to shoot the bastards."

15

The next week was quiet and by Saturday the farm was about back to normal. Each day Rep would leave the landing, ride into the main river and pass on the far side past the River Bluff landing to see if there was any unusual activity going on. He watched closely but never saw anything that caught his attention. The situation at the landing seemed normal with fishing boats coming and going.

On Saturday he passed the landing and instead of turning back toward Shoal Creek as he had intended, he continued downriver. He did this without any prior planning. He continued past the mouth of Back Slough and in a short while was at Walnut Creek. He had no idea how he was going to explain what he was doing there when he beached the boat at Lick's house. However, in his mind he knew why he was there. He'd come to see Bess. He left the boat and walked toward the house. A dog asleep under the front steps was aroused and his barking awoke the house.

The front door opened and two of the younger sisters walked out on the porch. They both wore flour sack dresses as they stared down at him. "What you want?" they asked.

"Lick here?" He wasn't really interested in Lick, but he had to say something.

"He ain't here. You be comin' to git Bess?"

Rep laughed. "I don't know. She be ready to go?"

The girls giggled, looked at each other and ran back in the house.

Rep was watching the door when Bess came out. Her appearance surprised him. Her hair was brushed, and she wore a dress he'd never seen. He was struck by how attractive she was.

She walked to the railing and looked down at him. "He ain't here."

"They told me." He was in a quandary as to what excuse to use as a reason for being here. "Do you know where he be?"

"He at that widow woman's house up the hill. He goes up there and helps her out a lot." She walked halfway down the steps and cut her eyes at him. "She must have a lot she needs help with, cause sometimes he has to spend the whole night with her to git ever thang done."

Rep looked at her, trying to see if she was serious or making fun of him.

She stared back, her face a mask. "Why you want 'im?" He could see in her eyes she was deviling with him.

"Well, the last time I was here he said since I didn't have a woman, he'd give me one of the four he had. I've been thankin' on that and tryin' to decide what one I oughta pick."

She stared at him for a moment, then turned and walked toward the barn. "While you be thankin', I got to git the eggs."

He followed behind her, aware she wasn't a little girl anymore, but a filled-out woman. "I ain't never talked much to yo' sisters, so I don't know them much. One of them might be good but I ain't sure."

She didn't turn around, kept walking with her back to him. "They be too young. They cain't go."

He walked faster and caught up with her. "Then if they cain't go, you be the only one for me to thank about?"

She walked into the barn and turned around. "You can thank all you want to. It don't matter what you say or who you pick, or what you say to Lick. I done told you before, it be up to me, not Lick, bout what I do."

"I know that. So, what do you think?"

She turned up her nose and looked at him. "I don't know you much neither, not nough to be thanking bout goin' off with you. I ain't hardly ever seen you till now."

Rep nodded. "That be true. Maybe I'll come down more often and we'll get to know each other better. Maybe you can go up and see the cabin. That be where I live."

She shook her head. "I ain't stayin' at no cabin with you cept we be married. You know what mama say."

Rep smiled. "Yeah, I know what yo' mama say but I ain't said nothin' bout stayin' with me. I said you could look at the cabin."

She stared at him for a moment, then walked in the chicken yard and went in the henhouse. He stood and waited. She came out with a basket of eggs, walked past him into the barn and looked back at him. "When you be comin' back down here, if you do thank you be coming back?"

"I'm comin' back, be back in three or four days. I have some thangs I have to do before then."

"Why you be comin' back?

"I want to get to know you better."

She walked over to him and looked up in his face, with serious eyes. "I want you to know, any man thank he can hit me or beat me, one night he be asleep, I cut his throat. I wouldn't put up with that. I sayin' that be true sure as I be livin'."

Rep looked down at the little wild girl and smiled. "I don't doubt that for a minute, Bess. I would never hit you though." He stepped back. "I'll see you in a few days."

She laughed. "I be thankin' about who I pick."

He thought about what she'd said all the way to the cabin. Lila had messed his mind up, briefly appearing and then leaving. He knew she was alien to everything he knew, and she wasn't going to change. Her note had outlined her feelings plainly, she didn't like the farm or the river and had no intention of staying. There was no way she'd ever live in a log cabin on Sallie white. She was gone and he had to deal with it.

Bess was different. He was happy in the cabin on land he didn't own and fishing for a living. He felt she would also be happy in the cabin. She had grown up as he had, having nothing. Although he'd only had a few conversations with her, he thought the attraction was mutual. He decided he would continue seeing her and if things progressed as he expected, he would move quickly. Cold weather was coming, and he wanted to be settled before it came.

$\sim$

Rep went to the landing earlier than usual the next morning, then to the kitchen and bunkhouse looking for Mose. He found him at the barn. "Mose I need to talk to you."

Mose seemed surprised at the tone of urgency. "What be wrong?"

"Nothin' be wrong, but I need help. It's gettin' cold weather and I need a bathtub in the cabin. And too, I'm tired of going off the island across the slough to the spring on the Georgia bank to get water. I need to get a well dug on Big Island."

Mose was puzzled by both requests. "This be sorta quick."

Rep nodded. "I know but I want to do this before freeze comes. I was hopin' you could help me."

Mose shrugged. "Ain't no trouble. I'll get a tub and some men down to dig a well. Just you ain't said nothin' bout this before. You ain't got no problems, have you?"

Rep shook his head. "Just tryin' to get the cabin in better shape."

Mose felt something was going on but had no idea what.

16

Boot and Jack were at the boat landing well before daylight. They didn't see anyone as they loaded the boat, pushed away and headed downriver. They knew there would be guards watching at Shoal Creek, so they'd decided the best plan was to come up Back Slough and come at the farm from the south side. They continued down the main river and turned up into the mouth of Back Slough. As they neared the farm, they slowed the motor down and crept up the bank. They pulled into the mouth of a branch on the Georgia side and Boot pulled the boat into some bushes. They had agreed that Jack would stay with the boat and Boot would go to the farm. He would wait in hiding near Red Hogan's house until he got a shot at him and then hightail it to the boat. When Jack heard shooting, he was to have the motor running and be ready to leave. Boot didn't believe anybody could outrun him to the boat and they'd get away safely and head to Alabama. Nobody had seen them leave the landing that morning so nobody would ever know they'd been in Georgia.

～

Rep was up before daylight to go duck hunting. He walked over the log bridge across the slough to Big Island and started walking down toward the lower end. He planned to be at the lagoon and set up in his blind before the ducks started coming in. He loved this time of day, when all the creatures in the woods were waking up. He was almost to the lagoon when he heard a motor coming up the slough. That surprised him. He'd not seen another boat in the slough in all the time he'd been there, certainly not this early. Someone coming up the Georgia bank before daylight really made him suspicious. He slipped to the bank and waited. The motor was idling as the boat, making little wake, came slowly into view to his right. It was obvious the occupants in the boat were trying to move as quietly as possible. As they passed by, he could see two men in the dim light, one in the front and the other in the rear driving. The boat continued up the slough at the same slow pace.

He got up and followed, easily keeping up with them as he walked. About one hundred yards up the slough the boat pulled into a small inlet on the Georgia bank, a light came on and he could see the two men. He'd never seen them before. The man in the front was big and the driver was smaller and seemed older by his posture. The bigger man was holding a rifle. He could hear them talking but couldn't make out the words. The man with the rifle got out on the bank and dragged the boat up into the inlet until it was hidden by overhanging bushes. He said something to the other man and disappeared in the trees. The other man settled in the boat.

Rep felt sure he'd just seen the two Hobb men they were concerned about. He thought they were smart by coming up Back Slough and approaching the farm from the south. They probably thought there would be guards posted at Shoal Creek and this way they could avoid them. Now, if his suspicions were correct, Boot Hobb was headed toward the farm armed with a rifle. He had no doubt about his purpose. Boot would be after the red-headed man that beat his brother up. The other man settled down in the boat. Rep got up and started in a trot toward the cabin.

At the cabin he dropped off his shotgun and got his rifle. He wasn't sure what he could do with it, but he felt safer having it. He ran to the pier, got in the boat and paddled quietly to the Georgia bank. The man in the boat on the Georgia side was only a short distance down the slough and he didn't want to stir him up, so he didn't start the motor. He knew the man with the rifle, who he now considered to be Boot, had such a head start he'd never catch him. His only chance was to head straight to the farm as fast as he could and cut him off.

R ed Hogan came out of the house as the sun was lighting up the eastern sky. He saw Mose and two of the men who had been guarding the creek standing at the barn. About halfway down the hill he stopped, took out paper and tobacco and had begun rolling a cigarette when the bullet hit him in the left shoulder, knocking him down and scattering tobacco everywhere. Two more rounds were fired harmlessly in the dirt near him.

The two men with Mose saw the smoke from the shooter's rifle at the top of the hill and quickly returned fire. They both emptied their weapons toward the top of the hill. They ran to where Red lay on the ground, the two men reloading as they ran. Mose knelt by Red, saw that the wound wasn't life-threatening, took one of the rifles and told the men to see after Red. He ran up the hill toward the house. As he topped the crest, he saw a man disappear into the woods far below. He figured the man would head to Back Slough eventually, so he cut across to the right toward the slough.

J ack was half asleep in the boat when the first shot was fired. He roused up as the next two followed. He was halfway up the bank to untie the boat when the volley shook the ground and echoed through the trees. "Damn", he muttered as he ran back to the boat, jumped in and pushed out of the bushes into the slough. Hurriedly he started the motor, turned the boat around and started at full speed downstream. He came out of the mouth of Back Slough into the main river and turned toward the River Bluff landing. He felt he was justified in leaving and not waiting for Boot as they'd planned. They'd agreed that if Boot couldn't get back to the boat, he'd hide in the woods and make his way home later. Jack felt he could do that easily.

~

Rep was almost to the hill behind the Hogan house when he heard the first three shots and then the thunderous volley that followed. He stopped and dropped to his knees. The shooting was directly in front of him and he figured that Boot, if he had survived, would come off the hill and head for the boat. He ran through the trees, branches slapping him in the face, to the edge of a sedge brush field where he had an open view.

Suddenly Boot broke out of the trees on the far side about a hundred yards away and came running straight across the field toward him. Rep watched him approach, undecided what to do, never having been in this position before. Boot had probably killed or tried to kill somebody with all the shooting he'd heard. But he didn't know for certain about what had happened and killing a man was serious business. However, regardless of his concerns, he felt he had to stop him somehow. Boot was now about twenty-five yards away when Rep stepped away from the tree, yelled loudly and fired a shot over Boot's head.

The yell and shot startled Boot. He had no idea anyone would be in this area and had no idea where the shot came from. He'd expected any pursuit to be from his rear, so this was surprising. He stopped, squatted halfway down while looking around. It took him several seconds to locate Rep in the trees. When he saw him, he quickly turned and fired. The bullet ricocheted off the tree beside Rep's head, sending slivers of bark against his face.

Rep instinctively jerked to the right as Boot fired again. He was trying to get behind the tree when another shot rang out. Out of the corner of his eye he saw Boot stagger forward in the brush, fall to his knees and pitch forward on his face. He didn't understand what had happened. Then he saw Mose standing in the tree line on the other side of the field holding a rifle. Then the shakes hit him. It was at least a full minute before he got control of his functions. Still shaking, he walked toward Boot's body.

Mose came across the field and met him there. He stared at Rep, not understanding how he was there. "A damn fool thang you did there, boy," he said. "Man bout kilt ya with the yellin' and shootin' in the air. Where the hell you come from no way? Why come you be over here?"

It took Rep a minute before he could speak. "I saw 'em come up the slough and figured it was them. I saw Boot start toward the farm, so I followed him. There's another man, probably his daddy, in a boat down the slough. He may still be there but with all the shootin' I spect he's gone."

Mose shook his head. "Let 'im go, this be enough." He looked at Rep. "We done kilt this boy and that be 'nuff."

Rep looked down at Boot's body. He'd never seen a dead man before, certainly not one he'd had a part in killing. "What do we do now? We gotta call the law."

Mose stared at him for a minute. "Now we two be all what know this boy be kilt." He shook his head. "Ain't nobody else know but us. Us killin' him gonna start a war with them folks cross the river if we haul him in daid. Then they know we kilt 'im, it won't never stop."

Rep nodded. He didn't doubt what Mose said was true. "So, what do we do? We ain't got no choice but to call the law."

Mose shook his head. "We ain't gonna call no law. We stop it now. We drag him to the river and throw 'im in. He just be gone away, and it be over. We be the only two what know what happened."

Rep shook his head. "Damn, Mose. You gonna do that? What if he comes up right away?"

"The water be runnin' sho'nuff fast, and he be way down that river by then and they don't know who he be. It gonna take a while noway."

"What will we tell everybody about us chasin' him?"

"Ain't no us, you ain't in this. Folks don't know you be over here. It just be me here." Mose chuckled. "I tell folks he done got clean away." He reached down and picked up Boot's arm. He nodded at Rep. "Git the other arm. It ain't far to the river."

Rep stood for a minute before he responded. He understood what Mose had said but something about it didn't feel right. Why didn't they just turn his body over to the law? He'd tried to murder Red. Then he gave in and did as Mose instructed him to do. It didn't take long to get Boot to the riverbank and throw him in. He floated down the slough for a bit and then sank.

Rep stood on the bank and watched until Boot's body went under. He didn't feel right about what they'd done.

～

Earlier that morning Rolley Hill was camping at Second Branch when the noise of a motor awakened him. He looked out the tent and saw a boat leave the landing and come downriver. He wondered who that could be on the river so early. As the boat passed by, he could see the forms of two men in the dim early morning light. The shape of the boat seemed to be like one owned by Boot Hobb. If that was Boot, he wondered where they would be going this time of the morning. They disappeared down the river and he crawled back in his quilts.

Later in the morning he was fishing at Big Eddy when he heard shots on the far side of Big Island, seemingly in Georgia. He was accustomed to hearing shooting in that area with people duck hunting, but these shots sounded like high-powered rifles. Then the volley opened up like thunder and he knew something different had happened, but he had no idea what it was. It wasn't long after all the shooting that he saw Jack Hobb came back up the river in the boat alone. He watched as Jack went to the landing, jumped out of the boat and ran up the road toward town. That seemed odd to him, Jack seeming to be in such a hurry. He wondered what happened to the other man.

~

M ose walked to the boat with Rep, then rode to the landing with him. He told Rep about Red getting hit in the shoulder, but it didn't seem to be very serious. They both were quiet afterward, each contemplating what they had just gone through. They hurried up the hill where they were told Red was in the barn and the doctor was on the way. When they walked in the barn, he was lying on a table with several women tending to him.

When Red saw Mose he motioned for him to come over and asked the women to move back. Mose knelt by the table, leaned over close to Red's ear and whispered for most of a minute. Red nodded several times as he talked, midway through the conversation he cut his eyes toward Rep and nodded. Mose finished talking and moved away. The women moved back around the table. In a few minutes the doctor arrived, and later Red was moved to his house.

Mose walked outside and Rep followed. "I told Red what happened. He said we done the right thang." He looked at Rep. "I told him what you done. He said you done good."

Rep shook his head. "I didn't do nothin' 'cept 'bout get my dumb ass shot. You saved me." They walked on up the hill. "Do you reckon this will settle down or keep on?"

"Them people cross the river done lost they shooter. I 'spect he be the only one to try, they won't come back. Red can handle the law here, so it be over."

Rep heard what Mose said but he wasn't sure he was right. Something about all this didn't feel right. He still thought they should have called the law and let them handle it.

The Shoal County Sheriff came to the farm after the doctor reported the shooting and talked to Red. Red told him everything was under control and that satisfied the sheriff. Red was satisfied so why should the sheriff be concerned? He didn't talk to anybody else. Brit's fight with the man from Alabama wasn't discussed. He was told they had no idea who the shooter may have been, had no idea why he shot Red and he'd gotten away. Two deputies went over the area where the shooter had been and picked up spent casings and then left. Since they had no idea or evidence as to who the shooter was, they didn't know who to look for, so they considered the case closed. Red told them that was the best thing to do and thanked them for coming. Since he seemed to be recovering well, everyone at the farm breathed a sigh of relief and things began settling back to normal.

17

Rolley sat on the front steps waiting for his daddy to come home from work. He needed to talk. The whistle blew at the mill to end the shift and a few minutes later he saw him coming. He ran to meet him in the street and began telling him about what happened that morning. He told him about the two men in the boat leaving the landing before daylight and it looked like Boot's boat. Then he told about them going on downriver in the dark. Later he was fishing, and all the shooting started. Then he saw Jack Hobb return alone in the boat and that was not long after all the shooting.

"Have you mentioned this to anyone else?"

"No, sir. Everybody is talking about all the shooting sounding like a war. I heard it and didn't have no idea what it was about."

"Are you sure it was Jack and Boot in the boat early?"

"It was dark, and I couldn't really see them in the dark, but it looked like Boot's boat. And then when I saw Jack come back, I knew it was them that went this morning."

His daddy nodded. "I 'spect you're right. They've been saying all week they were going to get even with the red-headed man for beating up Harold. With that shooting and them on the river, they might have tried." He looked at Rolley. "Since we don't know for sure what happened, we need to keep all this between us and not stir up more trouble. This has to do with the Hobb family, and it's best we don't get involved in their problems. We'll wait till we learn more about what happened."

Rolley nodded. "Yes, sir, I won't say nothin'."

"Son, you have to understand the Hobb family ain't like us. They're different from regular folks and I don't have any regard for them because of the way they live and act. They don't care about right and wrong, or any laws. They do whatever they want, especially the boys. I wouldn't put anything past Boot; he's a mean man. They came here with nothing and they still got nothing, and they don't want nothing, it seems. All this trouble came from Harold being over in Georgia where he had no business. Jack raised both boys to drink and fight, they're just like him. I don't know what happened across the river to get Harold beat up but if he hadn't been there, it wouldn't have happened. Now if they were involved in this shooting this morning, and they probably were, it could be dead serious, and I don't want you in it."

After talking with his daddy, Rolley decided to go to the landing to check on his boat. He had left in a hurry after all the day's excitement and wanted to make sure everything was in good shape. He was in the boat dipping out water with a tin can when he heard somebody walking on the bank behind him. He turned and saw a girl standing on the bank watching him. The evening sun was to her back so he couldn't tell who she was.

"Do you know where my brother's boat is parked?" she asked.

He shielded his eyes with his hand so he could see her clearly. The blood drained from his face when he recognized May Hobb, Boot's younger sister. "What did you say?" he stammered as his daddy's talk about avoiding the Hobb family replayed in his mind.

"My daddy left his coat in the boat this morning and he sent me to get it and I don't know where the boat is. Can you show me?" she replied.

Rolley stood in the boat staring up at this forbidden girl. If she had been a tiger, he couldn't have been more scared. He couldn't speak.

She was puzzled at his inaction, just standing there frozen. "I know who you are. You're Rolley Hill," she said.

Her statement awakened him from his stupor. "I know who you are, May." He stumbled over the paddle in the bottom of the boat and staggered forward, embarrassed. "I'll show you where the boat is," he said as he climbed up the bank. She followed as he walked through the trees.

He knew May Hobb but had never spoken to her, much less had a conversation with her. She was two grades behind him in school. She was the only one of the Hobb children who had stayed in school past the sixth grade. She was a pretty girl, tall with dark hair. He had noticed her in passing but her Hobb name made her off limits to most of the boys he knew, and she certainly was off limits for him. Some of the boys had tried to sneak around and talk to her, but she had rebuffed their advances. He'd never heard any bad talk about her, and he knew if there had been anything bad some of the boys would have bragged about it. As they walked up the bank toward Boot's boat, he found himself hoping nobody would see her with him.

"Do you have your own boat?" she asked.

The question and her interest surprised him. "Yes, I do."

"My daddy said he sees you on the river a lot."

"I like to fish and hunt." They walked on in silence. That she had talked about him with her daddy got his attention. She talked with better sense than most of the girls he knew. Too bad she's a Hobb, he thought, she might be interesting. "Here's Boot's boat," he said when they reached the tree where the boat was tied. He saw a coat on the back seat, so he got in the boat, picked up the coat and handed it to her as he got out on the bank.

"Thank you," she said. "Daddy and Boot left the house early this morning but Boot ain't come home yet. Daddy said he stayed on the river, but he didn't know why."

Rolley didn't comment. "I bet I know", he thought.

She turned and started walking away but stopped and looked back at him. "Thank you for being nice to me Rolley. Most folks ain't nice at all. I know why they act that way, it's cause of my family drinking and fighting and raising hell all the time. I don't like it and I try to do right but it's hard when you're alone and don't have no help." She turned and walked up the road toward town.

Rolley watched her go, his mind in disarray.

18

Two days after all the excitement the bathtub arrived at the cabin and men came to begin digging the well on Big Island. Rep was glad for the activity. Having this going on helped keep his mind off the happenings earlier in the week. He'd not been to the farm since he'd left the barn with Mose after seeing Red. The men working on the well said Red was doing well, had even been to the barn with his arm in a sling. Not one person had come from Alabama to buy liquor in the past three days. That business would probably be dead for a while anyway.

He thought about going to see Bess but wanted to get the well dug before bringing her to see the cabin, so he put visiting off for a few more days. Mid-afternoon he decided to go up and talk to Mose. He still had some misgivings about what they had done with Boot's body although he felt the reasoning had made sense.

When he pulled into the pier at the landing Mose was waiting for him. He wondered how he could be waiting when he'd not even known he was coming today.

"Thought it be time you come up." Mose said. "Red said you come see 'im at the barn when I see you.

"How's he doing?" Rep asked as they walked up the trail.

"He sho'nuff mad at Brit for startin' all this and bout gittin' him kilt.

Rep shook his head. "Bout got me too."

Mose stopped and looked at Rep. Rep knew by his serious face he was about to tell him something he didn't want to tell him. "Lila be here," he said, his eyes on Rep's face. "She come last night."

Rep stiffened all over as if a chill had hit him. He turned away, staring blankly at nothing as his mind took in and attempted to deal with this news. After a minute he looked back at Mose. "Where she be?"

"I spect she be at the barn with Red. She come see bout him."

They continued walking toward the barn. Rep walked and felt like a man on his way to the hangman, having no idea how he would deal with seeing Lila. One part wanted to grab her and kiss her and the other wanted to tell her to go where she had once told him to go. He hoped he wouldn't make a complete fool of himself.

When they walked inside Red was sitting behind the desk smoking a cigar and a half-filled fruit-jar was on the desk. Lila was standing at the far end of the desk. Mose spoke to her and walked to the wall.

Smiling, Lila walked around the desk to Rep, put her hands on his shoulders and kissed him on the cheek. Her perfume surrounded him as it always seemed to do. It was all he could do to keep his hands by his side. She turned, walked to the desk and sat down. Red motioned for him to sit.

Red puffed on the cigar and looked at Rep. "Damn boy, in all the time you been here, this is the first time I've talked to you and don't have to raise hell about something you done." He chuckled and puffed. "Mose told me what you done. That was good. How come you was over there anyway?"

"I was duck huntin' on the island and saw 'em come up before daylight. I figured it was them and when I saw Boot with the rifle, I knew it was. I paddled across and tried to cut 'im off, but he was too far ahead. Then the shootin' started, and I figured he'd head for the boat, so I waited and that was it."

"Mose said you stopped him, and he shot him."

Rep nodded.

"It was right to put him in the river. Maybe that will stop it." He looked at Lila and back at Rep. "You done good here. I was wrong about you." He took another puff. "I think you can do more here on the farm than fish, maybe come up and help Mose with the farming and all. Mose agrees it would be good. I realize this is a lot to think over but take your time. I don't want you to answer me now."

Rep was completely surprised by the offer. His first reaction was to say no. But he'd asked him to think it over so he would at least do that. "Thank you, that's a lot to think about." Right off, he couldn't see any way he would leave the cabin and fishing, but he'd wait.

"Good," said Red. "You go ahead, I need to talk to Mose."

Taking care not to look at Lila, in a few steps Rep was out the door and almost off the porch when he heard her call. He stopped and looked back.

She was walking toward him. "Aren't you even going to speak to me?"

"I don't know what to say. I thought you'd already said it."

"I never intended to return this quickly, so I was unprepared to meet you and talk to you. But it has happened so here we are. I imagine you are mad or hurt with me and I'm sorry."

"Were you just messin' with me and then you run away? Was that all there was to it?"

He saw her eyes tear up and begin to flow down her face. "My God, Rep. If you believe that, it kills me. Do you know how hard it was to leave you? How hard it was to write that note? I cried for three days. Surely, you can't believe it didn't mean anything. I'd never done anything like that with anybody before you."

Rep saw he'd hurt her. The phrase - messing with me – seemed to always set her off. "Anyway, regardless you was right," he replied. "I was mad and hurt but I thought about it and you did right. I didn't have nothin' to offer you. If you'd stayed and weren't happy and then left, you'd have broke my heart."

She wiped her eyes; make up ran down her cheeks. "Maybe so,

and I said that myself in my note, but I'm not sure I'm right." She shook her head. "I've never been torn up like this before." As she looked at him through the mist in her eyes, she knew if he asked her to go to the cabin, she would go.

I'm standing here talking gibberish, Rep thought, and all I want to do is pick her up and take her to the cabin and never let her leave. But all that'd do is start the pain over again.

Lila noted his silence and wondered what he was thinking. "Mose told me you're having a tub put in and a well dug. What's with that?"

"I got tired of haulin' water from the spring and the water is gonna get too cold to jump in the river."

"I thought you liked the cabin the way it was."

"I do, but times change. I'm thankin' about getting a fulltime live-in woman and she'd like it better."

Lila was stunned. He'd never joked about anything like this with her. She laughed but stopped when she saw his serious face. "You may have been kidding but did you say something about getting a live-in woman? Have you really thought about that?"

He nodded. "Yes, I have."

His comment almost made her speechless. "This surprises me, if you're serious. Do you have someone in mind?"

"I do."

This entire conversation was so out of character for him that she was completely flustered. "You got over me so quickly," she said, smiling, trying her best to not show her true feelings.

He didn't blink. "You can still come with me if you want to. I ain't done nothin' yet."

God don't ask me that she thought. "We've already been over that if you remember?" she said, wondering where this talk about another woman came from.

"Yes, we done gone over that. After I read yo' note I went to the cabin and threw yo' yellow flowers out in the yard and threw the soap you used across the slough into Georgia. I opened all the doors in the cabin to get the perfume out and then I washed the sheets that smelled like you. Yes, we done been over all that."

She watched his face and heard the pain and hurt in his voice. "I'm sorry Rep. It's my fault. I shouldn't have messed with you."

He reached out, grabbed her and pulled her against his chest and held her close. He looked straight in her eyes. "Don't you ever say that." Then he kissed her, whispered, "Thank you," then turned her loose and walked away.

She watched him walk up the road, her heart dying with every step he took. "Did I do this to him?" she thought. "Is he looking for someone else so quickly to get over me?" It was all she could do not to run after him. Finally, she turned and went back in the barn.

19

The news that Red Hogan had been shot went through River Bluff like wildfire. The excitement at the news was somewhat dampened by him being wounded and not killed. Most felt the person doing the shooting should have been a better shot. On Sunday all three pastors in the town's churches preached sermons titled, "Those who live by the sword die by the sword." In each sermon were references to the evils of drink.

Those citizens who had paddled to Shoal Creek at times in the past put any plans to go there again on hold. Their action had little to do with the sermons, but they'd rather do without liquor than risk the wrath of the Hogans. It was felt they would be looking for someone to blame for the shooting.

The other news making the rounds was the disappearance of Boot Hobb. He hadn't been seen in over a week. It had been learned, and not denied by Jack Hobb, that he and Boot had left the landing before daylight the day all the shooting was heard, and Jack had returned later in the day alone.

Rolley had heard this talk and he didn't know the source, but he knew it wasn't him. He hadn't talked to anyone about what he'd seen. He'd been on the river every day and watched for any movement at

Shoal Creek landing but there was none. He wondered about the young man with the long hair who'd brought Harold to the landing and then left. He still believed he was a good person and if he ever had an opportunity to talk to him, he would take it.

Then, after days had passed and Boot still hadn't showed up, the talk turned back to his whereabouts. Several people were heard to say, "Boot was a damn good shot, how come he just winged the son of a bitch?"

The sequence of the shots was then discussed. Many people had heard the shooting so there were many witnesses who gave their opinion. It was generally agreed that there had been a single shot, then quickly followed by two more shots. There was little debate about these facts. The volley that followed was a different story. Estimates of the number fired ranged from fifty to several hundred. One man said there had to be at least twenty people firing to have that many shots in such a short time.

Cooler heads soon prevailed, and the number was lowered to a reasonable figure, although everyone didn't agree. But the majority did agree that the volley fired by the Shoal Creek bastards had killed Boot, they had no doubt this was true. If Boot was alive, as good an outdoorsman as he was, he would have made his way back home by now.

Someone asked, "If he's dead, where's the body?" This question set off a bevy of theories about the disposal of Boot's remains. Most people believed he was buried somewhere on the farm. Other, more fanciful theories were put forward but were quickly dismissed. One man suggested they'd killed him and simply thrown his body in the river. "Hell, they wouldn't do that," said a doubter, "he'd come up and everybody'd know he was dead and he was killed on the farm. Right now, we can't prove he's dead." Everybody agreed this was a foolish suggestion.

When several men took their theories to the County Sheriff and demanded he do something about it, he pointed out they had no evidence to prove anything they claimed. Also, if a crime had been committed, it happened in Georgia and out of his jurisdiction. The sheriff didn't tell them but there was no way in hell he was gonna get involved in this mess. Those people across the river were dangerous and tolerated no interference in their business. He intended to stay on his side of the river.

~

J ack Hobb hadn't been seen or heard from in days, staying in his house where Harold was still recovering from his foray into Georgia. But he'd heard the talk and on one point he agreed with the conclusion--Boot was dead. When he'd heard the first shots and then the volley, he knew the odds were that Boot would never return. When one day passed with no sign of him, he knew he was dead. As the days passed, Jack, who had never finished any task he started and Harold, who had never started a task, sat and plotted how they would make the Shoal Creek bastards pay for killing Boot.

They had learned that Boot had shot the wrong red-headed man. Harold knew the man who beat him was a young man and Red Hogan was old. So, their target would be the younger Hogan, Brit. They'd both seen him on their visits to the farm and had little regard for him. The challenge would be to get close to him. At present they didn't have a single idea how they might do that.

~

R olley was walking to the next class with two friends when he saw May coming down the hall toward him. Her eyes were looking straight at him without wavering. As she neared, he smiled and said, "Hey, May," and kept walking.

One of the boys punched him on the shoulder and said, "Dang, Rolley, you trying to get some of that white-trash stuff?"

"Won't do you no good," said the other boy. "She don't fool around with nobody."

That afternoon Rolley was in his boat putting new line on a reel when he heard someone walking in the leaves on the bank. He looked around as May came out of the trees and stopped at the end of his boat.

"Thank you for speaking to me this morning," she said.

Rolley shrugged. "It wasn't nothing, May."

"It was to me. Your friends don't ever speak to me. I hear the words they say when I pass by."

"I'll always speak to you, May. I'll talk to you at school if we meet."

"I wouldn't ask you to do that. Your friends will make fun of you and I wouldn't want that. But I thank you anyway." Then she squatted down and motioned to him. "Will you come to the front of the boat. I want to tell you something, but I don't want anyone to hear."

Puzzled, he walked toward her.

"You know about all this talk about Boot."

He nodded.

"I wouldn't tell nobody else this, but I heard my daddy say Boot shot that man over cross the river and now he says Boot is dead. He says them people across the river killed him. Now he says him, and Harold are gonna go over there and kill a boy named Brit. That's what they talk about all the time."

"Why are you telling me this, May?"

"I had to talk to somebody and you're the only friend I got."

"What do you want me to do?

"I don't know."

Rolley shook his head. "Maybe they're just talking. Maybe they won't do anything."

"Daddy's full of hate and Harold don't know no better."

"I'm your friend, May. If there's trouble you come see me."

She smiled. "Thank you, Rolley. I won't ever forget this." She turned and walked back into the trees.

He stood without moving. "Why did she tell me this?" he thought. "What am I supposed to do?

20

The encounter with Lila had confused Rep even more about what he should do.

He'd thought the feelings he'd had for her had been put away for good because he knew it was best. As she'd said so in the note, it was best for both of them to let it go. That was true and he believed it, but when he saw her and touched her, all that logic went up in smoke. He had to do something to offset the effect she had on him. Then he thought of Bess, the wild young girl who intrigued him so and reminded him of his upbringing which he'd tried so hard to forget. Maybe if she was with him, that would keep his mind off Lila.

He was physically attracted to her, but there was something else there that drew him. They were birds of a feather because of their similar raising. He wasn't sure that was enough to build a commitment on. One thing he did know, cold weather wasn't far away, and he wanted to get settled before it hit. He wanted to get all this doubt out of his mind.

That afternoon, regardless of his questions and doubts, he got in the boat and headed to Walnut Creek. It was a warm sunny day as he went down the river. As he rode, he couldn't help but wonder where

Boot's body was in the river, maybe he'd just passed over it. He quickly pushed that thought aside. Nothing he could do about that anyway. He went up the creek, pulled his boat up on the bank and started toward the house. Lick was standing in the yard. When he saw Rep he yelled, "Hey, I hear Red got his ass shot. I thought somebody woulda shot the sona'bitch years ago, sorry bastard he is."

Rep had little use for Lick because he reminded him of his daddy. He considered them both ignorant, liquor drinking, overbearing bastards. In the past four years he'd met other fathers who led their families with dignity and neither of these two had even a smidgen of it. Even if a person was dealing with hard times, they could have dignity.

Lick watched Rep approach. "I heard somebody from Alabama shot Red. Y'all catch 'im?"

Rep shook his head. "He got away."

"That's too bad. If they'd caught 'im, old Red woulda hung the po' bastard for sure. Wouldn't have been the first neither, so I've heard." He cocked his head at Rep. "You come about Bess?"

"I come to talk to her."

"Talk? There ain't no need to talk. I done told her she be goin' with you. I'll tell her to git her thangs and she'll go tonight. Ain't no need of waiting. Hell, I'll call her." He started to turn around.

Rep grabbed him by the arm and stopped him. In a quiet voice he said, 'You tell her I want to talk to her." He still had the arm in his strong grip, his eyes on his face.

Lick stared at him for a moment, then turned and hollered back toward the house, "Bess, man wants to talk to you out here."

The front door opened, Bess walked out on the porch to the steps and looked down at Rep. "What you want?"

"I want to talk to you."

She walked down the steps, completely ignoring Lick, took Rep by the hand and said, "Let's go to the barn." Inside the barn she walked over to a bench, sat down and pulled him down beside her, still holding his hand. "You talk."

He looked at her, so young and trusting, her eyes searching his face. "Bess, we been talkin' about things for a time now. I want to see what you thank. I'm askin' you to go with me, live with me at the cabin and be my wife."

Her eyes never left his face. "If I go, I wouldn't 'cept the preacher say the words and I get the paper."

"I know that and that's what we 'll do."

"You know what else I say, you ain't never gonna hit me."

Rep nodded, smiling. "I never wanted to hit you and I ain't gonna hit you. Not never. I be good to you and you be good to me."

She shook her head. "You ain't gonna be like Lick hitting mama?"

"I won't be like Lick."

She reached up, tenderly touched his face and stared in his eyes. "I'll go with you and be yo' wife, if that be what you want, cause that be what I want."

"That's what I want," he said as he pulled her to him and kissed her for the first time. He held her close and kissed her again.

When he turned her loose, she looked up at him. "I know what wives do, mama done told me, but I ain't never been with no man.

"We'll work that out. That ain't gonna' be no problem."

"You been with a woman?"

"Yes, I have."

"Then you show me what to do."

"I'll show you what to do."

They got up and started toward the house. "I have to do somethin' back at the cabin. You get your clothes and I be back in a week. We'll go to the preacher and get the paper."

"I ain't got much to git."

"It's fixin' to get cold. Do you have warm clothes?"

"Nothin' 'cept some old stuff mama left. It ain't much."

He hugged her to him, for the first time feeling responsible for her. "Don't you worry, I take care of that for you. I get you some warm clothes."

They walked to the boat, he kissed her and then headed upriver.

He'd made the move with Bess and he felt good about it. He had no intention to let Lila bother him again. He had made a promise to Bess and he intended to keep it, regardless of the temptations Lila might put in his path.

~

B rit returned from his exile in Atlanta, but not as the conquering hero. Red was still irate that his actions had set into motion the events leading to him being shot. So, every menial and dirty task he could find was assigned to him. In addition, he wasn't allowed to use a car and none of his friends, either male or female, were allowed on the property. So instead of taking this punishment as a learning opportunity, he became more and more bitter every passing day.

He was kept in the dark as to any details about the day of the shooting. He wasn't considered trustworthy, so he knew nothing. He did learn that Rep, for some unknown reason, was now considered to be a candidate for promotion by his father. He took this to be a direct attack on his position as heir apparent to the family's domain. Unknown to him, his father had never considered him capable of manning any position in Shoal Creek but considered him to be a wastrel. As far as heir apparent, that position belonged to Lila.

Brit had learned one thing, direct physical combat with Rep was a good way to get your ass kicked and he didn't intend to try that again. He still intended to do harm to Rep, he would just be smarter in the future. He would bide his time and when the opportunity arose, he would move.

~

R olley was walking to the landing when he saw a boat coming downriver from the direction of Shoal Creek. Any boat from that direction always got his attention. He stood at the landing and waited as the boat continued straight toward him. As it got closer, he recognized the young man with long brown hair who'd brought Harold back when he got hurt.

The boat landed, the man got out and tied up to a tree. He walked up the bank to Rolley. "That man I brought back here get alright?" he asked.

Rolley was still trying to figure out why this man from Shoal Creek was here at the landing and the question surprised him. "I don't know. He's at home but he's getting better, I heard."

He offered his hand. "I'm Rep."

Rolley was surprised at the offer and it took him a second to respond. "I'm Rolley," he said as they shook hands. As he did, he saw two men up the bank and he knew it wouldn't be long before the arrival of this alien from Shoal Creek would be known all over town."

"You got a store here what sells women's clothes?"

This gets stranger every minute, thought Rolley. "In town we do."

"I ain't never been here before. Can you tell me how to git to that store?"

Without thinking of the possible consequences, Rolley said, "I'll show you, if you want me to."

It was Rep's turn to be surprised. "That would be good."

Rolley started walking away from the landing and Rep followed. "It's up the hill in town," he said. "We can walk up the road." His mind was filled with questions he wanted to ask about Shoal Creek. "You do the fishing over there?"

Rep nodded. "I fish down Back Slough and do some huntin'."

"I heard a lot of shootin' over that way last week."

"I heard it too."

Rolley waited, hoping for more information but Rep was silent.

They came to the edge of town, the street lined on both sides with houses that looked alike and all were painted white. "All the houses be the same," said Rep as they walked.

"The mill owns all the houses and they built them. They just use white paint, no other color."

"You live in one of these houses?"

"Yes. My daddy works in the mill. You have to work in the mill to live here."

"I ain't never lived in no town."

"You always lived at Shoal Creek?"

"Naw. I just been there a little while. I lived on a farm down south."

As the conversation progressed, Rolley felt more at ease talking to Rep. He decided to venture out. "Lots of people here don't like the people at Shoal Creek."

"Cause they make whiskey?"

"That's part of it but mostly they don't like what they did to Harold and some other people too. They think the Hogans are bad people."

Rep walked several steps before he answered. "That fellow, Harold you say, got caught messin' with a young girl and got beat up. He be lucky he didn't get killed. If her daddy'd got holt of him, he would have kilt him."

"Harold is always in trouble, so everybody thought he probably got in some trouble over there. But Harold's daddy blamed Shoal Creek and they said they were gonna get even. Harold's brother went down the river the day we heard all the shootin' and he ain't been seen since. Folks say he went to Shoal Creek and some say he shot that red-headed man."

Rep stopped. "Whoever shot him got away." He turned and walked up the hill.

Rolley felt he had pushed about far enough. Nothing else was said until they got to the store in the center of town. Rep looked around at the buildings. They were standing in front of the largest store, which he figured was the general store. Across the street was a drugstore and a barber shop. Down the hill was a theatre and next door was the gymnasium. It seemed the town had even more than he'd seen in most of the towns in Georgia. He didn't like towns, but he could see advantages in living here.

"This is the store that sells women's stuff," Rolley said as he walked up on the porch, opened the door and went in. Rep followed.

Rep looked around. The store looked like the store he'd seen the day he got to Shoal County where the owner told him about Shoal Creek. There was the marble top counter lined with candies and the shelves of canned goods. This wasn't a farming town, so all the feed and chicks weren't in back like other farming stores.

An older lady walked out from behind the counter. "Hey Rolley," she said. "What are you doing?"

"Hey, Miss Williams, this is Rep. He wants to buy some women's clothes."

"Well, we will certainly help him," she said as she turned to Rep. "Exactly what do you need, honey?"

For the next thirty minutes Rolley watched as she and Rep walked through the store looking at various items. They looked at dresses and coats plus other smaller items. Rolley wondered why this young man was interested in women's clothes. They left the store with several sacks and headed back down the hill toward the landing.

When they reached the boat and loaded the sacks, Rep turned to Rolley and shook his hand. "Thank you for helpin' me out. I never woulda found it by myself." He turned to get in the boat.

"I want to tell you somethin'," said Rolley, "but you can't tell nobody I told you."

Rep turned back around. "I ain't gonna say nothin'."

"Boot Hobb shot that man at Shoal Creek. Harold and his daddy say they're sure Boot got killed at Shoal Creek after he shot that man. They say if he was alive, he would of come home by now. They say they gonna go over there and kill some red-headed man named Brit for beatin' Harold up. I'm telling you this because I don't want nobody else to get killed."

Rep looked at Rolley's face and knew he was telling the truth. "Does everbody know this?"

Rolley shook his head. "I'm the only one, but it's the truth. I can't tell you how I know."

Rep nodded. "I believe you. Do you thank they'll really try?"

"I don't know. They're mean people but they ain't real smart. Boot was the only one I thought might do somethin' and he's gone. Maybe they're just talkin'."

Rep nodded. "I thank you for tellin' me this. Sometimes when you're on Back Slough, come see me." He climbed in the boat, cranked the motor and went upriver. Maybe Mose was wrong, he thought, as he went toward Shoal Creek. These people may not quit.

Rep went directly to the Shoal Creek landing and found Mose. He told him about his trip to Alabama and they decided to go to the barn and tell Red what he'd learned there. They knew Red wouldn't be happy but there wasn't a choice.

Mose stood against the wall and watched, a slight smile on his face. He was enjoying the show.

"You went back to Alabama? What the hell you do that for?" Red was fuming.

"I went to buy some clothes."

"Clothes? Why go over there to buy clothes? You know what I told you about that."

Mose interrupted. "He has a woman and she be needing winter clothes."

Rep cut his eyes at Mose and frowned. He hadn't wanted him to tell anybody about Bess.

Red looked at Mose and then back at Rep. "What the hell is going on here?"

Rep answered quickly, trying to get the conversation back on the right track. "That ain't got nothin' to do with it, but I found out somethin' you need to know." He went on to tell Red what the young man had told him.

"Do you think he knew what he was talking about?"

Rep nodded. "I don't know how he knowed it, and he told me he couldn't say. I thank he be tellin' the truth."

"He mentioned Brit by name?"

Rep nodded.

Red rubbed his sore shoulder and looked at Mose. "What do we do now?"

Mose shrugged. "When folks over here be botherin' us, we send folks to beat hell out of 'em but we can't do that over there. They ain't got no use for us no way."

Red nodded his agreement. "Damn, we didn't need this." He thought for a minute, then looked at Rep. "What's this about a woman?"

Rep sat with his head down looking at the floor. He wanted to choke Mose for mentioning Bess.

Mose wasn't about to let it drop. He was enjoying Rep's discomfort. "He be seein' Lick's gal, Bess, down on the creek."

Red furrowed his brow as he looked at Mose. "Bess?" he said. "Ain't she the one that beat the hell out of Joe's boy when we sent him down there to git one of Lick's puppies? If I'm right, he jumped her in the barn and she kicked him in the balls and damn near made a steer outa him. He hobbled around here for a month."

Mose laughed. "That be her."

Red smiled and looked at Rep. "Is that right?"

Rep cut his eyes at Mose. "I figure that's my business."

"Shore it is," replied Red. "Ain't nothing wrong with getting some young thing to use for a while. Cold weather's coming and she could warm your bed till spring. Better be careful with that one though, they say she is mean."

Rep stared at Red. "I gonna marry her," he said. His tone was matter of fact. His face emotionless.

It was Red's turn to be surprised. "Marry her? Damn boy, shacking up for the winter is one thing but marriage is another. You saw Lick's place. Didn't you see what she come from?

Rep didn't blink. "She come from the same place what I come from. We be the same kind of people."

Red looked at Mose and then back at Rep. "You're serious?"

Rep nodded.

"What did Lick say?"

"Lick don't have no say bout nothin'. It be up to me and Bess."

Red smiled at that remark. He looked back at Rep. "When are you gonna do this?"

"Right away."

"Ya'll gonna live in the cabin on Sallie White?"

Rep nodded.

"Have you thought about coming to the farm and working with Mose?"

"I have but maybe in the spring. I want us to spend the winter on Sallie White."

Red shrugged. "That's up to you." He looked at Mose. "So, what do we do about them folks in Alabama? All this trouble already dried up the business from over there. I don't want to sit here and wait for another bastard to take a shot at me."

Mose shook his head. "Ain't much to do 'cept watch that way. We done got guards watchin' the landin'."

"Guards didn't do no good last time," said Red. "We gotta stop this somehow."

Rep and Mose left the barn and started up the hill. Halfway up Rep stopped and grabbed Mose's arm. "I gotta ask you this, Mose. Does it bother you, killin' that man? Killing Boot?"

"Bother me?" replied Mose. He shook his head. "He come over here and shot Red, tried to kill 'im and bout killed you too. Why it bother me? It be like killin' a snake. Dead snake won't never hurt nobody no more." He turned and walked on up the hill. He didn't intend to discuss it anymore.

Rep followed him up the hill. Sometimes logic makes sense.

Brit didn't appreciate being kept in the dark about Red's wounding, so he asked around, talking with different people until he knew most of the story. He didn't know what happened to the shooter but didn't believe Mose's story that he escaped. Most of the people on the farm believed the shooter was dead and buried somewhere on Back Slough, but that was just conjecture. Brit believed it to be true. He learned that Rep was somehow involved in the shooting. There were no details as to his involvement but his father's sudden high regard for him indicated his part was significant.

All this fueled his hatred more than anything. However, even with the hate he felt, it wasn't enough to make him forget the beatings he'd encountered when he faced Rep. He wanted to get even but it wouldn't happen face to face. He had to come up with a plan that would leave him blameless, otherwise he would face his father's ire.

21

The town of River Bluff wasn't incorporated as a city; therefore, the town had no elected officials. Since the Bluff Creek Cotton Mill supplied all jobs in the town, owned all the houses and buildings and decided who lived where, the de facto mayor was John Gill, the Mill Manager. Mr. Gill, as he was called by everyone, answered to no one. His decisions were final.

He was born in River Bluff and went to work in the mill at sixteen. At age thirty he was a department overseer and Manager at forty. He was fair, demanding and didn't suffer fools. Now, at age sixty, he was revered by the mill workers.

Jack Hobb worked as a sweeper on the night or graveyard shift in the opening room where the bales of cotton entered the mill. This had been his job since the first night he went to work years before. He neither wanted nor deserved anything better.

He'd never talked to John Gill and had rarely seen him. That morning he was ten minutes from finishing the shift when he saw Mr. Gill walk in the room and come toward him. He stopped sweeping, propped on the broom and waited, unsure why Mr. Gill would be coming up to him.

"Jack, do you know who I am?"

Jack took off his hat and nodded. "Yes, suh, Capt'n."

"I understand your son Harold went over in Georgia and got beat up. Is that true?"

"Yes, suh." Jack didn't have a good feeling about the direction of this conversation."

"I also understand your son Boot hasn't been at work in several days. Some people are saying he went to Georgia and shot Red Hogan and hasn't come back. Is that correct?"

Jack held his hat against his chest, nervously twisting it in his hands. "Boot ain't been home. I don't know nothin' 'bout no shootin'.""

Mr. Gill nodded and looked straight in Jack's face. "Now I'm told Harold is going around telling people ya'll are planning to go to Georgia and kill Brit Hogan."

"Nah suh, that ain't true. Harold, he ain't right sometimes and say too much. We ain't doing nothin' bout shootin' nobody."

"Jack, we hired you and your wife years ago because we felt sorry for you. That was a mistake. We should have sent you back across the river from where you came. Now both you and your children are nothing but trouble and an embarrassment to the town. That's been true for years. As of today, you are on notice that if there is any more trouble or even any more talk about your family causing trouble, I will fire you and your wife and evict you from your house. Evict means I will put you and your family in the street. Do you understand what I said?"

Jack nodded. "Yes, suh Capt'n, I sho do."

"Now, you tell me what I said."

"We ain't gonna cause no more trouble or look like we gonna cause trouble, or my ass be in the street."

"Well put, Jack," replied Mr. Gill as he turned and walked away.

That afternoon Jack called Ruby and Harold into the kitchen and told them what Mr. Gill said. He pointed out he didn't appreciate being talked to like that after all the years they'd worked for the company. However, that aside, he warned Harold to keep his mouth shut about anything about Georgia to anybody and to stay away from the river. He had decided they would lay low until spring and then do something to make that redheaded man pay for killing Boot. Regardless of what might happen, they couldn't let it pass. It was a matter of family honor although he didn't use these exact words. But now wasn't the time to do anything. May was standing in the doorway listening.

Harold sat and listened to what his daddy said but he didn't agree. Regardless of what Mr. Gill or Jack said, he wasn't waiting till spring. It was easy for them to say sit and wait but he was the one who got beat up and suffered. He didn't have a job to lose and he damn well didn't care about this house. He would do something by himself and he wouldn't wait long.

~

R olley found himself looking for May at school, taking every opportunity to talk to her. Most afternoons after school he would go to the river and she would show up. Her parents didn't know or care where she was so she could come and go as she chose. He liked being with her, but he also felt sad for her. She knew how the town felt about her family and regardless of what she did in school or anywhere else, she felt she was still regarded as a white-trash Hobb. All the recent talk and gossip about Harold and Boot hadn't helped.

He had dated other girls, taking them to the movie or the local café, but he was still hesitant to be seen with May in public. His reluctance made him feel bad, but he hadn't overcome it. He hadn't even let his own family know about his friendship with May. He knew what their reaction would be.

May, like her sister Star, was mature physically for her age. Rolley was aware of this but it wasn't the main reason he was attracted to her. He liked being around her and talking to her. One afternoon as they were walking up the riverbank she tripped and started falling. He instinctively grabbed her arm and pulled her toward him. She reacted by wrapping her arms around his neck and pressing her body against him. They stood face to face for a moment and then, embarrassed, both jumped away. This was the first time their bodies had touched, even for an instant but from that point on they were aware of each other in a different way.

The next afternoon when Rolley got home from school, his daddy was waiting for him on the front porch. He wasted no time getting to the point. "Rolley, Mr. Bill White told me he's seen you at the landing with that Hobb girl, May. He's seen you several times in the last week with her. Seems like ya'll are there together bout every day. You want to tell me what's going on?"

"She came to the landing and I just been talking to her some."

"Do you remember what I told you about the Hobb family?"

"Yes sir, but May ain't like the others."

"She has the same blood and has been raised up with them. They're not like us. Not one good thing has ever come from that family. They have no redeeming values. I don't want you around her anymore. Do you understand me?"

He looked at his daddy for several seconds, but he knew he had no choice. "Yes, sir."

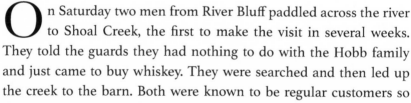

On Saturday two men from River Bluff paddled across the river to Shoal Creek, the first to make the visit in several weeks. They told the guards they had nothing to do with the Hobb family and just came to buy whiskey. They were searched and then led up the creek to the barn. Both were known to be regular customers so there wasn't a problem getting served.

They told Mose about the gossip in River Bluff about Boot, that most people thought he was the one who shot Red Hogan since he hadn't been seen since. The general feeling in town was that Boot was dead and that feeling was shared by his daddy and brother. The trouble had started when Harold was beat up, but most people had no sympathy for him, they figured he deserved whatever he got. If Boot then tried to get even by shooting Red Hogan, he also deserved what he got.

Lastly, they told about the warning to the Hobbs that if they stirred up any more trouble they would be run out of town. The people in River Bluff had no love for the Hobbs and hoped they would leave. Mose passed this information on to Red. It seemed this chapter in Shoal Creek's story was over. Everybody breathed a sigh of relief.

~

Rep left the cabin and headed down Back Slough toward Walnut Creek. He has several sacks in the boat containing the winter clothes he'd bought for Bess. His mind was in turmoil. The recent visit and conversation with Lila had undone all the logical conclusions he'd thought made sense. Her standing in front of him with tears streaming down her face and saying how hard it was to leave the cabin had torn him up. Saying how hard it was to write the note did the same. Now, uninvited, she was in his mind and fouling up everything.

He was headed to see Bess. He'd asked her to marry him and she'd agreed. For all he knew, she was expecting him to come today, go see the preacher and get married. None of this was her fault. Like a hound running a fox, he'd run Bess to ground. She was so young, so inexperienced and so honest and, as he was four years ago, she was looking for a way out of her home situation. Maybe he was that way out for her, as going on the road had been the way out for him. He'd only seen Bess three times, not exactly time enough for either of them to decide to be together the rest of their lives. As he turned up Walnut Creek, he was still confused about what he should do.

He beached the boat, gathered up the sacks and started toward the house. He'd noticed that Lick's boat wasn't at the landing. He reached the steps with still no sign of life from the house, not even a dog barking. He walked up and knocked on the door. It cracked opened and one of the sisters stood looking up at him. "Where's Bess?" he asked.

"She ain't here. She be gone up to the bridge with Lick to see Preacher Snow. Are you gonna marry Bess?"

"Yes, I am."

"Are you gonna take liberties with her?"

"Do what?"

"Take liberties. Mama said we have to be careful cause men try to take liberties with young girls."

"Do you know what that means?"

"No. But I think it has som'um to do with having babies."

Rep laughed. "Who are you?"

"I'm Sassafras, Bess' sister. They call me Sassy."

Rep laughed again. "I don't doubt it. How old are you?"

"I be twelve next June."

"I have these sacks for Bess. I want to put them in the house." Sassy opened the door and stepped back. He went in and put the sacks by the table. The other two sisters were sitting on a pallet on the floor watching him. As it had before when he came in this house, memories flooded his mind. He turned, walked out on the porch and took several deep breaths, trying to get his mind straight. He walked to the railing and saw Bess and Lick coming from the landing. He walked down the steps and waited.

"You come to get Bess?" yelled Lick as they walked toward him. Rep ignored him. His eyes were on Bess, as her eyes were on him.

"You come back," she said as she wrapped her arms around his waist.

"Told you I was." He pushed her back so he could see her face. "I have you presents in the house."

She looked up, questioning. "Ain't nobody never give me no presents."

"Well, you have some now." He took her hand and led her up the steps into the house.

She ran over to the sacks and pulled out two new dresses, night gowns and a warm winter coat plus several smaller items. Her sisters stood and watched, completely mesmerized. She looked at Rep, tears streaming down her face. "You done this for me?"

He nodded. "They're all for you."

She rushed over and hugged him. He wrapped his arms around her and led her out to the porch. "Bess, before we go any more, I want you to be sure about everthing. The cabin I live in ain't much, just one big room. It be mighty rough for a woman. It's on a little island with a cooking stove, a table and chairs and one bed in it. I want you to know that."

"I ain't never had much myself," she said, still holding on tightly.

"I know you said you wouldn't never go to the cabin till we be married but maybe you oughta go and look at it. Sassy could go with us if you wanted."

She looked up at him. "You gonna be with me at the cabin, ain't you?

"Yes, I'll be with you 'cept when I'm fishin'."

She reached up, pulled his head down and kissed him. "That's all I want."

All his doubts about what he should do disappeared. "If that's what you want to do, I'll be back in a week. You have everything ready with the preacher, we'll be married and then go to the cabin. Does that suit you?"

She nodded. "I be wearin' my new dress." She took his hand and walked down the steps. "Let's go to the barn. I want to be with you by myself."

They went in the barn and lay on feed sacks and held each other and talked. It was the first time they'd been alone for more than a few minutes at a time.

Later she stood at the landing as he left in the boat. For the first time he felt sad about leaving her. As he rode up Back Slough, he thought of what he needed to do to get the cabin ready. He thought of what Lila had done when she was there, especially setting up a small private place. He would get Mose to send a carpenter down and build a small room in the corner. Also have a place to put the tub with privacy. Otherwise the cabin was what it was and not much else could be done. Maybe in the future they could add a room. But like Bess had said, she'd never been used to having much.

22

There's an old saying, "Even a blind hog finds an acorn." Harold Hobb had never heard this saying and wouldn't have understood it if he had heard it, but it meant everybody has some good fortune sometimes. Harold would have argued that the saying hadn't been true for him to this point in his life.

He was fixated on getting even with Brit Hogan for the beating he'd suffered. The fact that he was guilty of molesting two underage girls never figured into his thinking about the episode. As far as he was concerned, they had been willing participants. That he had done anything wrong never entered his mind. The beating he took made him the victim.

He'd never been focused on any single thing in his life for more than ten seconds, but he was completely focused now. He said nothing to his daddy about his thoughts, keeping them to himself. Jack would be no help anyway; he was too worried about losing the house.

Harold wasn't very intelligent, but he wasn't completely stupid. It seemed during this period of fixation on revenge, he could understand and see situations clearer than ever before. It seemed parts of his brain mostly unused in the past had come to life. He was aware of the tremendous obstacles he would face in getting even with Brit and the Hogans. But in his present state of mind he was prepared to face any hardship, even willing to risk his life to accomplish this goal. The thought of working hard and suffering hardships to accomplish anything had never crossed his mind in his entire life.

He knew the men who had recently gone to Shoal Creek to buy whiskey had told everybody about being searched by guards and how tight security was on Back Slough and up the creek. The men also told everybody that the Shoal Creek people were especially looking for anyone named Hobb. Harold took these facts into consideration, thought up plan after plan and then discarded them all. He was about to give up when something he had nothing to do with happened.

Harold Hobb found an acorn; the rain came.

R ep woke up during the night and heard hard rain pounding on the cabin's tin roof. He normally liked the sound of rain on the tin, it was restful, but this was different. The noise was louder and sounded threatening. Rain had never disturbed his sleep before, and it concerned him. He got up and looked out the window. He could barely see the slough. Then the thunder and lightning came, like a fireworks show. At times the outside was lit up for minutes on end. Streaks of lightning creased the sky, sometimes two or three bolts racing each other across the heavens. Occasionally a bolt would come to ground and strike a tree, causing a boom like a bomb dropped from the sky. The storm continued with the same intensity throughout the morning into the afternoon. The wind blew so hard it turned solid sheets of rain sideways and hurled them against the cabin wall.

Rep had never seen such a display of nature's power. Initially he was in awe of the storm, but as the rain and lightning continued throughout the day, he became worried about the tremendous damage the storm might bring. He knew if this deluge kept up and softened the ground, trees along the riverbank would fall into the river.

He watched but there was nothing he could do. There was no sense in going outside, he would be helpless to do anything and would only get wet and cold. So, he hunkered down inside the cabin and waited for the storm to blow over as they normally did. He checked the ceilings and walls for leaks, he'd never seen such rain since he'd been in the cabin. He hoped his chickens and pigs would survive.

The storm continued through the night and into the next morning. The storm's intensity hadn't decreased at all. He grew concerned about his boat tied to the pier. He had no idea how much rain had fallen, but he knew it was a lot, several inches at least. The amount of rain falling through the last day plus that falling now would soon fill up the boat and unless bailed out, the boat would sink. That would be a disaster. Without the boat he would be marooned on the island. He had to act before long.

Later that afternoon he felt he had no choice but to do something. He braved the lightning, dashed to the pier and bailed water out of the boat as fast as he could, all the while expecting to be struck by lightning at any minute. Soaking wet, he ran back in the cabin, dried off and put on dry clothes. Then he sat and watched the storm. There was nothing else he could do.

R olley was also worried about his boat. He hadn't been to the landing since the storm began and knew it was filling up with water. If he didn't get there soon to bail it out, it would sink. That afternoon he asked his daddy if he could go to the river and look after his boat. At that time water was running down the streets in town like rivers. The rain was falling so hard he couldn't see the river out his back window or even the trees in the back yard. Lightning lit up the sky and thunder rumbled constantly. Although his daddy knew what Rolley said was true, the boat would indeed sink, his answer was a definite no. There was no more discussion. He knew going outside in this weather was too dangerous. Rolley sat and worried, helpless under the conditions.

~

Harold didn't care at all about the rain or how much it rained; it made no difference to him. He was unaffected and was going to stay in the house regardless. He had no reason to go out, he didn't have a boat. He didn't care if all the boats at the boat landing sunk. The owners didn't like him anyway.

~

The storm continued into the third day with no sign of letting up. Upriver to the north all the creeks and branches were full and muddy and pouring their excess into the river. Rep knew if this storm continued much longer, the river would be out of its banks, the water level was already near covering the pier. The cabin was sitting on the highest point of Sallie White but if it continued much longer, it might be flooded. On the morning of the fourth day, the water was out of the banks and moving toward the cabin. He was forced to move the boat from the pier and tie it to a tree nearby. There was little dry land remaining on the island. The chickens were safe in the trees and it seemed all the pigs had gone to Big Island to higher ground.

He wondered about Bess and her family, but there was nothing he could do. They'd have to fend for themselves, he couldn't go to Walnut Creek. He had little faith in Lick to look after them. The river was rolling at flood stage. Huge trees were being washed from the banks and it was no time to be on the river. Limbs and logs captured against the banks formed rafts, then were swept away and floated downriver like small islands.

~

Riiver Bluff was located on a ridge much higher than the river, so there was no danger of the town flooding. Harold could see the river from his house. As he stood at the window looking down, he saw the high water had covered the road leading down to the landing. No one could get to their boats so many were already sunk. He not only didn't care, the situation pleased him. He had no sympathy for these River Bluff people that had made his life so miserable.

He had never been a thinker, in fact was a shallow person, only responding to what was happening now. As he looked at the raging river, it struck him that nobody in their right mind would be on the water in a boat. That thought morphed into the idea that nobody would be out in this weather anywhere, for any reason.

Suddenly, the thought dawned in him, if that was true, it would include the guards at Shoal Creek. They, like everybody else, would be somewhere out of the rain instead of standing guard. Why should they be concerned if nobody would dare cross the river in this storm? Harold's blending of several separate thoughts into a logical conclusion was a first for him.

These thoughts birthed a plan. What if he crossed the river to Flat Shoals amid this storm? Such a daring move would be unexpected and if he was successful, he could go where he pleased without anyone interfering. The more he thought about the idea, the more convinced he was he could do it.

He knew he wasn't an experienced outdoorsman; Boot had taught him what little he knew. But he'd been on the river many times, he could navigate a boat and he had fired a rifle. For his plan to be successful, he would have to do all three and do them well.

But regardless of the odds against him, he moved from thinking about the possibility of going across the river to preparing to go across the river. He made a list of the equipment he would need. Boot had left several rifles in the house plus ammunition and warm clothing. He found a raincoat to keep him dry; that would be most important. Quietly he gathered what he needed, taking care to avoid being seen by others in the house. He filled a backpack with clothing, canteens of water and food for several days. He especially liked sardines and potted meat with crackers. He wrapped a small tarp around a blanket and tied it to the top of the pack.

His plan was to cross the river, sneak into a position at Shoal Creek near the barn and remain there throughout the storm. When the storm moved through, and it couldn't last forever, he would wait for an opportunity to kill a Hogan. He had decided Brit was the main target. He had a score to settle with him, but Red Hogan would do.

He was so involved in the preparation he gave no thought to failure. He was focused on the thought of revenge and he wasn't worried about the risk.

Boot had kept a wooden bateau hidden upriver that he used when he fished in the shoals. Harold had been fishing with him several times and knew where it was hidden, and he knew how to operate the motor. The boat was never left in the water but covered with bushes on higher ground to keep anyone from stealing it. There was a five-horsepower motor with the boat, and it would ferry him across the river. A larger motor would have been better, but that was all he had.

Getting across the river was the main challenge. Once he pushed into the river's strong current, the boat would be sent straight downstream and making headway across the raging river would be hard to do. He couldn't try to go straight across from the present location, he'd have to go further upriver to begin. He wasn't sure how far upriver he'd have to go but the strong current would push him past Shoal Creek if he didn't go far enough.

Boot had shown him what to do when the river flooded. He would stay in the flooded trees away from the main river where the current was not as swift. Although traveling through the trees in the wind and rain wouldn't be easy, that was the only choice.

He left the house the next morning while his parents were asleep. When he walked outside and the wind and rain hit him for the first time, he got a taste of the upcoming difficulty. Carrying his pack and rifle he made his way to the boat, dumped the rainwater out and loaded his gear. He pulled the boat to the water, then started paddling and poling upriver through the trees. He didn't use the motor for fear he would break a pin or propeller in the limbs and debris. The storm hadn't let up and was still ferocious. He went upriver all day. It was tough making headway in the rain and wind, plus fallen trees blocked his path causing delays. He was cold and wet despite the rainwear. There was no use changing clothes, he couldn't stay dry.

He was exhausted. He'd done very little exercise since he'd been hurt, and he was sore all over. He slept that night in the boat covered with the tarp, after eating a supper of sardines and crackers. The rain and wind pounded on him throughout the night.

The next day he continued upriver and spent another night in the boat. Late the next afternoon he felt he'd gotten far enough upriver to reach the Georgia bank before he was washed past Shoal Creek. He hoped his calculations were correct, but it was all a guess. He attached the motor and cranked it to make sure it was running well.

He paddled to the edge of the trees along the river and sat for several minutes looking out across the main river run. Trees and other debris rushed past, any of which could overturn his flimsy boat in a second. If that happened, he wouldn't stand a chance to survive. He didn't have a life jacket and if he'd had, it wouldn't make any difference. The rain and lightning continued as he sat in the edge of the trees and looked across toward the Georgia shore. He knew that the river was about one hundred and fifty yards across, but the sheets of rain blocked his view, except when flashes of lightning showed glimpses of tree on the far bank. He was going to head in the direction of the Georgia shore and hope for the best. He said no prayers; he never had.

He revved the motor and without hesitation shot into the current, trying to keep the boat at a forty-five-degree angle as he made headway across the river. The current pushed him downstream. He could barely see the far bank, the rain was beating down so hard in his face, but he was making progress, although slowly. He leaned forward, fighting against the wind and rain. It seemed he was being swept downstream faster than he was going across and he was concerned. His calculations were all based on guesswork.

He hit something in the water and the boat shuddered but kept going. A large tree rushed by so close he could have reached out and touched it. Blindly he forged ahead, having no idea where he was in relation to the Georgia bank. He was so caught up in the moment that he felt no concern for his safety. He was focused on holding the motor at the right angle against the strong current as he knew he had to do to have any hope of success. It seemed he'd been on the water for hours.

Suddenly, he was out of the swift river current and tree limbs on the Georgia side slapped him in the face. He'd made it! He continued through the trees away from the river until he saw a spot of higher ground. He cut the motor and paddled forward and tied up to a tree on dry land.

He put the tarp over him against the beating rain and sat for a few minutes to allow his nerves to settle down. He decided to remain there for the night. He was totally exhausted. After a supper of potted meat and crackers and a cup of milk, he sat in the pouring rain and savored his achievement. Nobody would have believed him capable of such a feat. He doubted Boot would have tried it. But he knew this was just the first step.

The next morning, he untied the boat and started downriver through the trees, letting the current push him. The storm hadn't let up at all. Lightning was still flashing all around and the wind made it difficult to keep the boat steady. He stayed in the flooded trees until he reached the edge of Shoal Creek. He sat and watched but saw no sign of guards on the far bank, which he could barely see.

He started the motor and headed up the creek to a point he figured was well above the barn. He landed on a spot of high ground and unloaded his gear. He walked to the edge of the trees and made sure he was in the right position above the barn which he saw to his right. He walked back to the boat, gathered up his gear and stood staring at the boat. It was the only evidence showing he'd come to Shoal Creek. He thought for a moment, then took his foot and pushed the boat away from the bank and into the creek where the current caught it and sent it down toward the river. His main objective was to kill Brit Hogan. He couldn't risk compromising that by the boat being found. This decision to push the boat away eliminated any chance that he might escape later.

There was a big spreading magnolia tree about twenty yards from the edge of the trees with the lower limbs touching the ground. He'd have a good view of the barn about fifty yards away to his right. He dashed across the open space, the rain still beating against him and crawled under the thick limbs. The broad leaves offered some protection from the rain and provided a good hiding place. He spread the tarp on the ground and pulled part of it over him the best he could. He was tired and wet and cold. He turned on his small flashlight and with its dim light he opened a can of sardines and ate them with crackers. Then he settled down for a wet and cold miserable night. Sometime later he went to sleep.

Rep woke up the next morning and something seemed strange, then he realized it was the quietness that caught his attention. The rain wasn't beating on the tin roof as it had the last several days. He walked to the door and looked outside. The water was at the same level it'd been the day before and although the rain hadn't completely stopped, it was just a sprinkle.

By late afternoon it had completely stopped, and some patches of blue sky broke through the clouds to the east. The river was still rolling but without further rain it would quickly begin to recede and get back in its banks. He walked outside and looked at the damage to the island. Several trees were down, and limbs were scattered about. The receding water had left a layer of mud all around the cabin and the bridge to Big Island had lost several boards. He felt the damage was less than expected for all the high water and the intensity of the storm.

As he stood outside, he saw several of the pigs make their way back across the slough from Big Island.

～

H arold had spent two nights of misery under the magnolia tree, but the rain had stopped. He was well hidden and in a perfect spot to see the comings and goings at the barn. He didn't think anyone would suspect he was here so they wouldn't be looking for him. He wasn't as good a shot with a rifle as Boot but at this distance he felt he could hit whatever he shot at around the barn. He settled down and waited.

～

R ep was restless. The week was almost gone, and he'd not been able to do one thing to the cabin he'd planned on in preparation to Bess coming. The river was going down, and he'd moved his boat to the pier, but he was still afraid to travel to Walnut Creek. Maybe he could go the next day or two and see about her.

He knew it would be a while before he could fish again. The river was still rolling mud and would be for days. His trotline and set hooks would all have to be replaced. He started getting prepared for that.

～

R olley had avoided May at school since his daddy had talked to him. He wanted to talk to her and felt bad about avoiding her, but he didn't want to get in trouble. He was walking down the hall and saw her coming toward him. There was no way he could avoid passing her, so he kept going trying to avoid eye contact. She didn't let that happen but walked directly in front of him and stopped in his path. He stopped and looked at her.

"I know you've been staying away from me Rolley, but I have to talk to you."

"About what?"

"Harold's been gone three days."

He didn't understand why she was telling him this. "So what?"

"He took Boot's rifle and clothes and his boat is gone. Daddy says he's gone to Georgia to kill that man called Brit."

"What can I do?"

"I don't know. Maybe you could tell somebody."

"Who could I tell?"

"Maybe tell your daddy, he'd know what to do."

Rolley nodded. "I'll tell him when I get home from school."

"Thank you Rolley. You're the only friend I have," she said as she walked away.

That afternoon Rolley waited for his daddy to get home from work and told him what May had said.

"Why did she tell you this, son?"

"She don't want nobody to get hurt. She told me Boot shot that other man over there."

His daddy nodded his head. "I'll tell Hawke. Maybe he can call the people across the river and warn them." He got up and walked out the door.

Constable Jim Hawke was sitting in his regular spot at the gym when he saw Owen Hill coming up the street. Owen related to him what Rolley had told him about Harold Hobb being gone from home, where it was believed he'd gone and his mission. Jim thanked him and said he would call the sheriff in Shoal County.

23

With the sun shining and the weather warming, everything at Shoal Creek settled back to normal. Harold lay under the magnolia tree and watched people come and go at the barn. He saw Red Hogan and the black man who followed him around all the time come to the barn. He'd lost interest in Red Hogan; he was waiting for Brit to show up. He'd seen him several times in the past in his visits, even before Brit beat him up. He was certain he'd recognize him when he saw him again.

People continued in and out all day. Two men were on the road in front of the barn fixing a fence, others would stop and talk and then go up the road. Harold was concerned he was getting low on water and he had no idea how he could get a refill. The sun was leaning toward the west when he saw two men top the hill on the far side of the barn. He watched as they walked down the road towards the barn. Brit Hogan was on the left. Harold didn't know the other man. They were talking and laughing, seemingly without a care in the world. This was what he'd been waiting for. He took a deep breath to settle his nerves.

He rested his rifle on a log and watched them approach. He hands were sweating; he'd never shot at a man before. He waited until they were twenty yards from the barn, his sight centered on Brit's chest. He put his finger on the trigger and slowly began to squeeze. As Harold squeezed the trigger, Brit said something to Joe, good-naturedly turned to the left and shoved him in the shoulder. The bullet hit Brit in the back of his shoulder and knocked him to the side. Joe reacted, grabbing Brit to steady him. He was blocking the view as Harold fired again. This round hit Joe in the center of his back and knocked him flat on his face. Harold fired again as Brit dove for the corner of the barn but missed.

The two men at the fence hit the ground on the first shot but they spotted Harrold's position with the second. They were yelling and pointing toward the magnolia tree as two men with rifles came running out of the barn, saw the men at the fence pointing and opened fire toward the magnolia. Suddenly the limbs and leaves above Harold's head were shredded by a hail of bullets. He crawled to the other side of the tree. As he started to get up and run toward the woods his legs were knocked out from under him. He fell to the ground and his rifle went flying as he pitched forward. He quickly scrambled to his feet and staggered into the woods.

Red Hogan was at his desk when he heard the first shot. He was getting out of the chair when the second and third sounded. Several men with rifles were near him and they ran out the door. He knew something bad was happening and his first thought was, "Where's Brit?" Then he heard several more shots as he ran out the door. He saw Joe on the ground and Brit lying at the corner of the barn. "Call the doctor," he yelled to one of the men. He knelt by Brit and was relieved to see it was a flesh wound. He looked at Joe lying motionless in a pool of blood and knew he was dead. He motioned to one of the men, "Get him inside and cover him up." To another man he said, "Get Brit inside and get some of the women down here."

One of the guards came running up. "The shooter run in the woods, but we hit 'im. He ain't gonna' get far."

Red grabbed him by the arm. "Don't kill him. Catch him and hold him till I get there. Let me know when you got him."

The guard turned and ran toward the woods.

Harold was in intense pain. The bullet had gone through his left leg and he couldn't run any further. He heard men coming through the woods behind him and the creek was in front. He was trapped. He fell to his knees, slumped over and waited. Several men with rifles quickly surrounded him. "I'll go get Mr. Red," one of the men said as he started toward the barn.

Mose was in a heated conversation with Red at the barn. "You gotta call the law, Red. Joe is kilt and he have family, a wife and chillun. You gotta git the law out here."

Red reluctantly nodded. He turned to one of the men. "Call the sheriff. Tell him what happened."

As he finished talking the guard came running up. "We got 'im, Mr. Red. He ain't dead. He down by the creek."

Red turned to Mose. "Get a rope and come to the creek." He pointed to the guard. "Take me down there."

Harold was on the ground propped up against a tree when Red came through the woods. Mose soon followed. Red walked over and knelt beside him. "You shot my son, you son'bitch. Who was with you?"

Harold shook his head. "Just me," he stammered through the pain. "Weren't nobody else."

Red looked back at Mose. "Who the hell is he?"

"He that boy what Brit beat up. He that Boot boy brother."

Red nodded and motioned to Mose. "Throw that rope over that big limb."

Harold suddenly realized what was about to happen as two of the men pulled him to his feet. "You can't do this," he screamed. "You can't hang me."

"You oughta kept your ass on the other side of the river," Red said as he nodded to one of the men. "Tie his hands."

With his hands tied one of the men made a loop in the rope and dropped it over Harold's head. They turned and looked at Red.

"Hang the bastard," he said.

The three men grabbed the loose end of the rope and pulled, lifting Harold's feet off the ground. They held him in the air as he kicked and struggled, as he defecated and wet his pants. A stench filled the air. When he was no longer moving, they dropped him to the ground in a heap.

Red walked over and looked down at the body. "Cut the bastard loose and throw him in the creek."

One of the men cut the rope, leaving the loop around his neck. They carried him to the creek and threw him in. The body floated down the creek a ways and slowly sank.

Red looked at Mose and the three guards. "The bastard got away and jumped in the creek. We didn't see him no more, so we figure he drowned." He stared at the guards. "You understand that?" All three nodded. "We the only people here so if word about this gets out, I'll be looking for you." They all nodded again. "Alright, let's get back to the barn."

∾

Rep was at the landing when he heard the first shot. Two more shots followed and in a few seconds a volley. His mind went back to his experience with Boot. He knew something bad was happening with that much shooting. He started running up the hill and when he passed the kitchen he saw a crowd at the barn. He had started down the road when he met a man running up the hill. "What happened?" he asked.

"Somebody shot Brit and Joe Hyde," the man yelled as he ran past.

Rep stopped where he was, completely shocked. "Damn," he thought. "When will it ever stop?" Gathering his feelings, he ran on down the road. When he entered the barn, he didn't see Red or Mose. Brit was on one table with several women gathered around him. A covered body was on the other table. He figured that was Joe. He was about to ask about Red and Mose when both came in the door. Rep walked over and pulled Mose to the side. "What the hell happened?" he asked.

"That Hobb boy shot 'em, the one what Brit beat up."

"How did he get up here so close?"

Mose shook his head. "He musta come over in the storm. He be hid under that magnolia tree for days. Been eating sardines and potted meat. He sho did hate Brit to do all that."

Rep shook his head. "How could he come across the river in that weather? I woulda never tried it."

"Don't know but he sho done it."

"Where is he now? Somebody said he was wounded."

Mose smiled. "He done jump in da creek and musta drowned,"

Rep, with a questioning look on his face slowly shook his head. "You know I don't believe that."

Mose glanced over his shoulder and then the other way. "Don't you say nothin'." He leaned closer and whispered. "Red done hung 'im and throwed 'im in the creek. Nobody there but three guards, all what know."

Rep stepped back and took a deep breath. "You kiddin'?"

Mose shook his head. "He sho done it."

They were interrupted by the sound of sirens outside. The door opened and the sheriff walked in with two deputies. He went immediately to Red and they walked over to the corner and began talking.

Two men in white carrying a stretcher came in, loaded Brit and went out the door. They heard a car leaving and then the piercing sound of a siren.

Their attention turned back to the conversation between Red and the sheriff, which had gotten quite animated. The sheriff was red-faced while Red was yelling and waving his arms. This went on for several minutes with everybody in the room watching.

Another siren broke the silence and two other men with a stretcher entered, loaded Joe's body and left. Red followed them out with the sheriff and deputies. Soon they heard a car start, and they heard it pull away.

Red came back in, obviously upset, spotted Mose and walked toward him. Rep didn't know what to say to him, so he stood quietly. Red took Mose by the arm and started toward the other side of the room, then he looked at Rep and motioned for him to follow. They gathered against the far wall. Red was red-faced and obviously mad. "That damn sheriff said he was gonna shut us down if all this shooting and killing kept up. He said he's already getting pressure from Atlanta and this shooting will get more hell raised. I told him I paid him enough to keep them off my ass and I'd get somebody else if he wouldn't do it. He said he didn't give a damn about that. I wasn't paying enough for him to go to jail."

"What he say bout the shooter drownin'?"

"He said he didn't believe that bullshit, but he didn't really care what happened to him. Anyway, he didn't have a body to worry about."

Suddenly Red turned and faced Rep. "The bastard you saved in the river and took to Alabama has come over here and shot Brit. It's lucky he didn't kill him. It's all your fault for saving him. I told you back then you oughta let the bastard die. All you done is cause me trouble ever since you got here. First it was you and Brit having trouble and then Lila acted like a bitch and run off with you."

Mose started to say something but Red turned on him. "Don't you say a damn word. You been covering for him since he got here." He looked back at Rep. "I think it's best you pack up and go but I got too much on my mind right now to deal with it." He walked to the door. "You come see me Monday and we'll get it settled." Then his shoulders slumped, and he stood staring at the floor. "I've got to go to the house." He turned without another word and went out the door.

Mose watched him go. "Lordy, Lordy," he said, "Miss Sara ain't gonna be happy. Her boy done got shot and she gonna blame Red."

Rep almost felt sorry for him.

Mose's forecast was correct. Miss Sara was hysterical, and the two younger girls were packing their suitcases. She told Red as he walked in the door that she was going to the hospital to see about Brit and then she was going back to Atlanta, where civilized people lived. She didn't care what he thought about it; that was the way it was going to be. She wasn't coming back here, and neither were the girls. She'd had enough.

Red tried to interrupt but she stopped him.

"Don't you say another word to me. You ruined that boy, spoiling him and excusing every bad thing he did. You were proud of his fighting and meanness, encouraging him in it. You think I don't know what's been going on lately? Brit beat that boy up and now he came back and tried to kill him. Ya'll killed his brother too and bragged about it. The Bible says, "You live by the sword; you die by the sword."

She pointed at Red. "You need to go back and see about Joe Hyde's family. Have you even asked about them? If there's one decent bone left in you, you need to do something right." She walked over and opened the door. "You're a mean man, Red. You've lost all decency, if you ever had any. I don't know why I ever left my home to come here with you, but it's finished. The girls and I are going to Atlanta and we won't be back." She pointed to the door. "Now get out. I have to go see about my son. I want him to come to Atlanta when he gets out of the hospital and get far away from here."

Red bowed his head and walked out.

Mose and Rep left the barn and walked up the road toward the kitchen. They were both trying to come to grips with all that had happened.

Rep spoke first. "He blames me for Brit getting' shot and wants me gone. That don't make no sense. I don't understand it."

Mose shook his head. "I done told you Red sho' got a mean streak. He be upset right now. He gonna git better, Brit gonna be alright."

"I'm supposed to go get Bess in a few days. She'd gonna have the preacher ready. I can't bring her up here if I ain't got no place to live."

"I gonna talk to 'im. Just git her to wait," Mose said.

"I might can but I don't know. I go down tomorrow and see.

24

The newspapers the next day in Atlanta and Columbus had all the lurid details of the shooting at Shoal Creek. The Hogan family was well known in both cities and the shooting of Brit Hogan and the killing of Joe Hyde was big news. The attitude toward the Hogan's wasn't positive in all areas. There were many detractors. No reporter had actually been at Shoal Creek to see what happened, but they interviewed the sheriff and the deputies and the doctor who responded to the call. These men were professionals who knew what to say and what not to say.

Most of the details of the shootings and the wounding of Brit Hogan were supplied by the hospital attendants and the mortuary service driver. They not only reported details of the victims' wounds, but they included what they saw around the barn, who they saw in the barn and comments by onlookers outside the barn. These last comments had nothing to do with facts but were used as filler where facts were unknown.

The facts known about the assailant was his name, Harold Hobb. He was a resident of River Bluff, Alabama. Somehow, he had managed to get on the Shoals Creek farm without being seen and hid under a magnolia tree for several days before shooting the victims.

According to the sheriff, Hobb had managed to escape into the woods, where it seemed he attempted to swim the flooded creek and was never seen again. It was assumed he'd drowned. There was no mention of Hobb's motives for the attack. His involvement with underage girls which led to his being beaten by Brit Hogan was never mentioned.

In none of the articles were there any mention of any illegal activities at Shoal Creek.

Harold accomplished several things on his mission of vengeance - he killed Joe Hyde, wounded Brit Hogan and put River Bluff on the map. People who had no idea the town even existed were suddenly rushing to be there. Harold Hobb was big news and the reporters from the big cities were anxious to hear all about him. The fact he'd crossed the river in the storm had developed into the main talking point. Undoubtedly, he'd been a cross between Daniel Boone and Chief Crazy Horse to accomplish such a feat. They were looking for details as to how he did it and his reason for attempting such a crazy stunt.

Jack and Ruby Hobb talked to no one. They were locked in the house and dared not venture out. They'd heard the news about Harold, and they were waiting for Mr. Gill to kick them out of the house, which they expected to happen. They had no idea what they'd do then. They believed Harold had drowned, since that's what they'd been told. They were as amazed as everyone that Harold had crossed the river in the storm and killed and wounded those men. When the neighbor came over and told them about the newspaper story, Jack's comment was, "Harold musta made a damn good shot to hit both of 'em".

Jack, in his younger days had been a hell raiser, fighting with Ruby in his home, fighting in the streets of the town with other people and fighting in beer joints in the next county. The deaths of Boot and Harold had broken him. In the past he would have responded to their deaths but not now. He wanted to be left alone.

While the Hobbs wouldn't talk, the crowd hanging around at the boat landing were more than happy to tell everything they knew and even some things they didn't know. While none of them had ever thought Harold was worth a tinker's damn, they all admitted him crossing the river in that storm was a real accomplishment. None of them would have chanced it and they couldn't believe he'd pulled it off. They all agreed it was a hell of a feat.

Several men brought Boot's name into the conversation with the reporters and said they thought he might have done something like that, but not Harold. When the reporter asked more questions about Boot, the ante was raised. They passed on the rumors that Boot had shot Red Hogan some weeks before and everybody said the people at Shoal Creek had killed him and buried him. While there was no proof that was true, the reporters took it and ran with it.

This led some reporters to concoct the story that a feud existed between the Hobbs and the Hogans. They had no proof to back up their thinking so they couldn't print why they thought this.

The idea of a feud between two families or clans on different sides of the Chattahoochee River was what the readers wanted, and the papers fed it to them. The information was coming from the River Bluff side because no reporter could get into Shoal Creek as there were guards all around. One reporter decided to get a boat at the River Bluff landing and slip in at night. He was caught soon after landing, stripped naked, tied up and covered from head to foot with a mixture of cow shit and axle grease. He was put back in the boat and somehow the boat was found at the River Bluff landing the next morning with him lying naked in the bottom. Nobody else tried this again.

Some of the boat landing crowd told first-hand stories of making the trek to Shoal Creek to buy illegal whiskey and the fights and drunken parties they saw. Some reporters were looking for the motive for the feud, what had started the bad feelings and they felt they had found it. The headlines in the papers the next day declared, "Illegal Whiskey at Shoal Creek Fueled Feud." The fact that none of this was true didn't matter. The whole world knew Shoal Creek was guilty of making illegal whiskey and all the money Red Hogan had paid to be left alone by the law and politicians was forgotten. All these people were suddenly more concerned about their own wellbeing than protecting Red Hogan. Authorities at different levels saw all the negative publicity and regardless of how much money had been paid, they knew they had to do something.

Soon afterwards, the police invaded Shoal Creek. Red Hogan was arrested and led away in handcuffs. His stay in custody was short-lived; he was out on bond in a few hours and back at the farm. He shut down the stills immediately and all whiskey on the farm was carted away. He wanted to get all evidence hidden until the pressure died down. He wasn't worried about the charges against him, his lawyers would take care of them, as they always did. He had too much money available to the right people for them to remain serious about moonshining. Also, the reporters would soon have another murder or disaster to occupy their time and forget all about Shoal Creek. That was the way things had always worked.

His personal life, which he'd always kept tightly controlled, was in disarray. His wife and daughters were in Atlanta and Miss Sara swore she'd never return. Brit had joined them after being released from the hospital, but he had no intention of remaining there. One of Red's main sources of income, whiskey sales, was shut down.

Red raised hell with the guards and everybody else for allowing Hobb to slip on the farm and camp for days under their noses, kill Joe Hyde and wound Brit. The next day he had the magnolia tree cut down.

He knew the publicity would fade in a few days, he'd get the stills back in operation and business would resume as usual. However, he would never again do business with anybody from Alabama.

May Hobb's life was in chaos. Her parents wouldn't leave the house and she was ashamed to be seen in public because of the news in the papers about Harold and her family. Reporters camped outside the house looking for a chance to talk to anybody.

She'd not been to school since the shootings and she didn't see a chance to go anytime soon.

That afternoon someone knocked on the door. They usually ignored anyone knocking, thinking it would be a reporter. May peeped out the window and saw Miss Tinney, her tenth-grade teacher, standing on the steps. She quickly opened the door and let her in. Miss Tinney was her favorite teacher and had always been good to her. She wasn't married because school rules wouldn't allow married women to teach, therefore all women teachers were single. Women teachers lived in the school dormitory, which was owned by the mill.

Miss Tinney voiced her concern for May's situation, especially her missing school, and she offered her the opportunity to come live with her in the dormitory until all the excitement settled down. She knew May's situation with her parents. That relationship had always been bad but had been made worse by the recent news. She made it clear May could come and stay with her so long as she wished. May didn't hesitate in accepting the offer. She wanted to get out of her parents' house and away from the family. Asking them for permission to leave wasn't discussed since they'd never cared what she did. She started packing, then went in, told them she was leaving and walked out. Jack and Rudy didn't comment; they were dealing with their own problems. She went out the door with Miss Tinney, avoiding questions from reporters along the way.

The next morning Miss Tinney escorted May into the classroom. As she looked at the students seated at their desks, her countenance dared them to say a word. No one did. The word that May was back in school made the rounds. Rolley Hill smiled when he heard it.

Rep was concerned as he headed down Back Slough toward Walnut Creek to see Bess. He was in a quandary as what he should do. Brit's wounding and Red's threat to fire him had changed everything. Instead of planning to marry Bess and take her to the cabin, he was worried about his livelihood and a place to live. He didn't see how he could marry Bess with all this uncertainty. He hoped she would understand but he hadn't dealt with her long enough to know how she might react.

He landed and as he got out of the boat, Lick walked down the steps and come toward the landing. "What the hell's goin' on up at Shoal Creek?" he said. "I heard somebody done shot Brit and they got Red in jail." He laughed. "Bastard oughta been in jail long ago."

Rep walked past him. "Where's Bess?"

"She's in the house. You come to get 'er?"

Rep didn't comment. He climbed up the steps and knocked on the door. The door opened and Bess was standing there in her new dress. He was struck by how pretty she looked and knew she expected to go see the preacher. "I need to talk to you," he said. He took her hand and pulled her out on the porch and put his arm around her waist. "You look pretty."

She immediately knew something wasn't right. "Lick say there be trouble at Shoal Creek. Do you be in trouble?"

He shook his head. "I'm not in trouble, but there is trouble." He explained what had happened with Brit and the shooting and Red's reaction toward him. "I just don't see how we can get married till ever thang get settled down. I don't know if we'd have a place to live."

"What do all this mean?"

"I need a few days to see what happens. Then, if ever thang be alright, I be back and git you."

She was quiet, looking in his eyes, questioning. "How long you be?"

He could tell she was worried. Maybe that doubt was questioning his sincerity. He wrapped his arms around her. "I'm comin' back, I promise you that. Maybe a week."

"I wait for you one more week." Without another word she turned and went into the house. Rep went to the boat and headed upriver.

25

When a person drowns, water is inhaled and replaces air in the lungs, making the body heavier and it will sink more easily. When a dead person is thrown into the water, obviously no water is inhaled and while the body will eventually sink, it maintains more buoyancy for a longer time with air in the lungs. How long the body stays down depends on various factors, but all bodies will eventually come to the surface.

Harold Hobb's body sank to the bottom of Shoal Creek, the current carried it downstream into the main river flow and then into Back Slough. A large oak tree had been dislodged from the riverbank upriver and floated downstream, rolling and bouncing off the river bottom. By chance, Harold's body, with the rope still around his neck, became entangled with the tree's limbs. When the tree floated into a raft of logs and debris against the bank on the lower end of Big Island, his body surfaced and remained attached to the tree in the raft.

∾

J ohn Watt cared little for all the excitement that had been going on in town. He was anxious to get away from the reporters and the confusion. He pushed his wooden bateau away from the landing at River Bluff, paddled across the river to Big Island and beached in a small inlet. He tied to a willow tree, grabbed his shotgun and started in a trot down the island. He was running late to his favorite hunting spot. The crisp fall leaves blanketing the ground rustled and cracked as he ran. He reached Back Slough and turned downstream when a bright reflection from the water below caught his eye. Curious, he stopped and peered down at a raft of logs and debris washed up against the bank. The glint caught his eye again, the afternoon sun reflecting from a dead limb in the debris below. But leaning closer, he saw it wasn't a limb but a boot with a shiny silver star on the side, sticking out of the water. He grabbed a tree limb and leaned out for a better look and saw the boot was connected to a leg and the leg to a man's body half-submerged in the water. A rope was tied around his neck. His eyes were open staring toward the sky.

"Good God Almighty," muttered John as he fell back on the steep bank. Leaving his shotgun where it lay, he headed in a gallop across the island toward his boat. When he reached the boat, he had to stop and catch his breath. He was on Big Island, straight across from the River Bluff landing. "I found a dead man," he yelled toward the landing. "It must be Harold Hobb."

That last comment got the attention of those at the landing, including one reporter who had been hanging around, hoping for something to happen. Several of the men jumped in a boat and started across. One of the men on the bank said, "I'll go find Hawke and tell him."

Five men and the reporter followed John down the island to where he'd left his shotgun. The men from River Bluff quickly agreed it was Harold Hobb as they looked down at the body tangled in the tree limbs. "Look," said one, "there's a rope around his neck. Damn, they must have hanged him." That comment changed the situation in their minds from a drowning to a murder.

They all agreed they shouldn't touch the body but wait for the law. They also understood Big Island was in Georgia and Alabama had no jurisdiction. As Alabama people they wanted to stay away from getting involved with Georgia problems. One man volunteered to go across the river to River Bluff, get somebody to call the folks in Shoal County and tell them what happened. The reporter stood to the side scribbling notes and thinking this was the luckiest day of his life.

~

I t took several hours for the Shoal County Sheriff and Coroner to arrive at the scene. When they saw the rope around Harold's neck, they shooed all the spectators away. They said it was a possible murder case and they didn't want anybody tampering with any evidence.

The River Bluff people didn't appreciate being pushed away. They said they'd been there alone for several hours and could have tampered with anything they wished to during that time. As they talked, it was the Shoal County Sheriff they were concerned about. They all knew he'd been allowing Red Hogan to do whatever he wanted to do for years, so they didn't trust him. They also agreed if Harold had shot those men at Shoal Creek as they claimed, then somebody at Shoal Creek had caught him and hanged him. One man pointed out that if Harold had indeed shot and killed one man, he was guilty of murder. If somebody then killed him, a murderer, did that make them guilty of murder? That possibility seemed to muddy the water in their minds but gave them something to talk about.

~

R ep was at the cabin when he heard boats coming down Back Slough. That was unusual so he walked to the pier just as the sheriff and some other men in two boats passed by. He knew something serious was going on if the law was involved, so he got in his boat and followed them. When the sheriff's boat pulled into the bank on Big Island, he turned and landed up the slough from him. He walked down the bank to where the crowd of men were gathered, careful to stay away from the sheriff's group.

The men told him it was Harold Hobb's body in the water and he had a rope around his neck. They'd already decided somebody at Shoal Creek had hanged him. Rep didn't wait to hear any more. He went to his boat and went back upriver. He knew he had to find Mose. He felt like all hell was about to break loose.

He landed and went straight to the barn where he found Mose talking with Red Hogan. They already knew about Hobb's body being found; the sheriff had called as soon as he was notified. They'd already met with the three guards who'd been involved in the hanging and instructed them to stay quiet. Since there were no other witnesses to the hanging, if they didn't talk, nothing could be proved. Red was most upset that the rope had been left around Hobb's neck and cussed the guards out. Otherwise when the body was found they'd have assumed he'd drowned, and nothing further would have been suspected.

Red figured Hobb was a known murderer, guilty of premeditated murder and whether he was drowned or hanged, he got what he deserved. He wasn't sure how the law would view this, but he intended to deny any knowledge of the hanging and continue to point out Hobb had murdered Joe Hyde. The fact he was killed in the search or chase was immaterial as to the cause of his death.

T he sheriff stopped at the landing after taking care of the body and came to see Red at the barn. They had a long conversation about the shooting, the chase and search for Hobb. The rope around his neck complicated the cause of death. The sheriff didn't believe anything Red said about not being involved in the hanging but he had no stomach for pushing the case forward. Since he had no witnesses to what happened, and doubted he would ever get any, he would let it all fade away. Hobb was dead, he deserved to be dead and the sheriff didn't want to deal with a pissed off Red Hogan. Unless somebody else pushed the case, and he didn't know who that might be, he would send Hobb's body to his folks in Alabama and that would be it. He didn't give a damn about Hobb and doubted anybody in Georgia cared about Hobb, so he wouldn't worry about it.

The reporter that had been with the first group on Big Island to find the body filed his story and the next day's edition headlined, "Shoal Creek Shooter Hanged." The story detailed the facts in the case from day one, when Brit Hogan beat up Harold Hobb to finding his body in the river with a rope around his neck. For the first time, this story included the fact that Hobb had committed statutory rape with two underage girls which had led to his beating by Brit Hogan. Nobody knew how the reporter got this information. This news negated any thought that he'd been mistreated at Shoal Creek without cause.

The rope around his neck was a mystery. Several witnesses had seen Hobb escape from the Magnolia tree and go into the woods, but no one came forward. Those that were there said he jumped in the creek. The sheriff said he had to accept that as the fact. He didn't care how the rope got around Hobb's neck. Hobb had committed premeditated murder and got what he deserved. As far as he was concerned, the case was closed.

When asked, the coroner said the body was already starting to decompose and it was difficult to tell if the rope around his neck contributed to his death. As far as he was concerned the cause of death was drowning.

It was obvious that nobody in Georgia cared that Harold Hobb, a murderer, had been found dead in the river and had possibly been hanged. Overwhelming public opinion said he deserved to be punished for his actions and how it happened made no difference to them.

26

Georgians weren't alone in feeling that Harold Hobb got what he deserved; the citizens of River Bluff felt the same way. Regardless of questions being raised about how his death came about, the feeling was that he got justice. The Hobb family had caused enough trouble, the town had been dragged through the mud in the press and now they wanted to forget everything that had happened. Harold's body had been shipped to the local funeral home and plans for his burial were set. Under the circumstances there was no reason to have a church service, there was nothing positive to say about him. Some of the younger crowd remembered Miss Sands comment in the fifth grade, that Harrold was sorrier than gulley dirt. Now he was a murderer, there was no debate about that.

The local Baptist Preacher said Harold was bound for Hell and nothing he or anyone said would change that. He would be buried quietly in a plot on the backside of the local cemetery and hopefully soon forgotten. Jack and Ruby couldn't afford a burial so Mr. Gill said the mill would supply the plot and bear the cost. Everything was decided.

∾

That afternoon Star Hobb came home to River Bluff. Neither the Hobb family nor anyone else in town had heard a word from her since she ran off with a Fort Benning soldier several years before. Both her family and the town's citizens had been glad when she left. Nobody was concerned or cared enough about her whereabouts to look for her. Fort Benning, a huge army base, was located some distance away near Columbus, Georgia. Unbeknownst to anyone, Star had been living all those years in Columbus and working across the Chattahoochee River in Phenix City, Alabama.

Phenix City was the go-to destination for soldiers from Fort Benning. Many were away from home for the first time and were looking for entertainment. Whatever they might want, they could find it in Phenix City – alcohol, gambling and women. The city was wide open, and no law bothered them. A small group of men, like a local mafia, ran the town and tolerated no outside interference. Star worked in one of the higher-class clubs as a stripper and hostess. She was popular and her services were expensive. She looked and dressed in line with her work – bleached hair and tight, low-cut dresses with little left to the imagination.

She'd had no interest in her family for years. Then the recent exploits of her brothers showed up in the local newspapers daily and got her attention. When she heard Harold had been hanged and no charges would be filed, for some unknown reason she decided to get involved. She'd never cared for Harold when she lived at home. She hadn't seen him in years, had no idea what kind of person he was and had no right to be involved in his case.

Mid-afternoon she arrived in River Bluff in a fancy car owned by her current live-in boyfriend, who was one of the group running the city. Her first stop was at the funeral home. There she informed the director she was taking charge of all arrangements for Harold's funeral. The director informed her arrangements had already been made, her parents had agreed to those arrangements and she had no say in the matter. Everything was handled by Mr. John Gill.

After cursing the director soundly, she went to her parents' home on Pot Licker Lane. She told them she was going to take charge of the funeral and John Gill would have no say in the matter. They were surprised by her appearance in their house, were not happy to see her and wondered why she showed up after all these years. She'd never been anything but trouble growing up and they had enough trouble already. They'd lost two sons and they'd had enough. While they were still employed and had a house to live in, they realized both were in jeopardy. They didn't want her to stir up more trouble, especially with John Gill. She ordered them to call the funeral director and rescind their approval of the burial plans. They refused to do so. She cursed them for being the sorry parents they were and left the house, headed for John Gill's office.

She pranced into the mill office and demanded to see John Gill. Mary McCall, the receptionist, took one look her appearance and told her to take a seat. Mary had known Star as a young girl, knew of her checkered past and had no use for her. She had no idea where Star had been or what she'd been doing, but looking at her, she could imagine. John Gill had already been warned by the funeral director she was in town, so he was prepared for her.

Miss McCall showed Star to Mr. Gill's office, walking slowly through the work area so the other ladies at the desks could get a good look at her. Star dealt with men all the time and usually got her way. She stormed into Mr. Gill's office, leaned over his desk and told him she would be handling Harold's funeral arrangements. She told him he had two minutes to call the funeral director and tell him she would be in charge, or he would face a lawsuit.

John Gill wasn't intimidated. He rocked back in his chair and stared at her. "Miss Star," he said, "I don't know you, and based on what I see standing in front of me, I wouldn't want to. All my life I've been taught to be mindful of my manners when talking to women, but you are testing me. The arrangements for Harold's burial have been made and will not be changed. Your parents have agreed to this. You have no say in the matter." He looked sternly at her. "You need to sit down." She started to interrupt but he held up his hand and she sat down.

"Your family has created problems in this town for years with their drunkenness and fighting. Your parents were poor role models for you children and allowed ya'll to grow up with no moral guidance. However hard it is for me to believe; you children have exceeded your parents in sorriness. Sadly, Jack and Ruby have reaped what they sowed, having lost two sons." He paused and nodded as he stared at her. "It would seem that having you as a daughter, with the reputation you had here in town when you were younger and now elsewhere, is also an ongoing burden they must carry. It is obvious by your appearance you are without shame."

Star again started to interrupt but he shook his head and she stopped.

"I understand you are employed at a club in Phenix City, a very shady establishment, with questionable credentials. I don't approve of what you do there but it's not my business. However, I do care what you do here in River Bluff, and it is my business. I don't know why you chose to get involved with Harold's burial at this late hour, when everybody, including your parents, want to put it quietly to rest. That would be best for everybody, including you."

He leaned forward on the desk. "Miss Star, it would seem by your initial statement, you love to intimidate people. That will not work with me. I myself have influence in Montgomery, but I seldom use it." He took a deep breath. "However, I may use it in this situation if you continue this folly. If you want to continue the lifestyle you now lead in Phenix City, as undesirable and sorry as it is, then I urge you to leave town this afternoon. It would be in your best interest to do so." He paused. "Otherwise, you will find yourself getting unwanted outside interference in your life. You don't want that, and I doubt those you work for would want it." He stared at her as he waited for her reply.

Star had dealt with many men through the years; knowing them was how she survived. As she looked in John Gill's eyes, she knew he wasn't bluffing. He held the cards and he had raised her bet. She knew she was beat. She picked up her purse and stood up. "I thank you for your time, sir," she said. "I'll be leaving today."

Mr. Gill held up his hand again and she stopped. "Miss Star, I doubt you really care about this, but we had already decided to allow your parents to remain employed and live in the house where they are. Their sons are gone now, and they have a sad situation. We felt that was the Christian thing to do."

She nodded but didn't reply and walked out the office without speaking to Miss McCall. She got in the car and left town without seeing her parents again.

Harold was buried the next morning as scheduled. Jack and Ruby were there accompanied by John Gill, who had insisted they come. He wanted them to realize what their sins had wrought. He wanted it etched in their memory forever, as sad as it might be.

May Hobb attended with Miss Tinney. Mr. Gill had heard good things about her and wanted her to be there. Hopefully, she would continue to follow a path different from her siblings. Afterward she went back to the dormitory without speaking to her parents. She wasn't aware that her sister had visited River Bluff.

She was sad Harold had died. She knew he wasn't a good person. He was mean and fought and drank whiskey. He'd been taught that lifestyle by her parents and his brother, Boot, who did the same thing. But he was her brother and although he was weak and a follower, she felt sorry for him.

She was out of that parental bondage now. Being around Miss Tinney had shown her how other people lived without meanness and fighting and drinking. Miss Tinney had grown up in a poor family in another town. Her family had little, but her parents were good church-going people who worked and strived to do better. She had gone to college, working at menial jobs to earn her keep until she graduated as a schoolteacher. Now she was teaching in River Bluff.

Miss Tinney attended the Methodist church and taught a Sunday school class. May went with her, the first time she'd ever been inside a church. She didn't understand all that went on in the services, but the people were nice to her and that was good. She felt it was important to be with good people, like the people at the church who were kind to her.

She knew Rolley was avoiding her at school because of what Harold had done. She wouldn't push him and felt with time he would come around. They had a connection that was important to her and she felt in her heart he had the same feeling. She'd seen his face the day she was pressed against him with her arms around his neck. Like her, he would never forget that feeling.

27

With the furor over Joe Hyde's murder and Harold Hobb's body being found slowly fading, life at Shoal Creek came back toward normal. Red Hogan felt like a new man. The threat of jail was gone, the stills were back in operation, Miss Sara was in Atlanta and he no longer saw the need to hide his dalliances. His philandering was well known on the farm and several young ladies had shared his bed through the years. Like his father, he wasn't prejudiced as to color. Miss Sara knew what he did and she had tolerated it if he was somewhat discreet. She was relieved that he left her alone after four children.

While Red was in such a good mood Mose talked to him about Rep and his threat to send him away. He pointed out Brit's's actions in beating the Hobb boy had caused the subsequent actions and not Rep saving the boy. He also pointed out what a great job Rep was doing on the river and since he now planned to marry Bess, he would certainly settle down. He shouldn't be a problem in the future. Red cursed a bit but then relented.

With no concern for what anybody thought, he moved a young lady into his house fulltime. Neither he nor she expected her to be there permanently. This action, the dismissal of propriety which Miss

Sara had done her best to maintain even in the worst of times, was a step backward and the last visage of decorum was gone. The young woman's parents lived on the farm and Mose had warned against this move, feeling it would eventually cause problems. Red had been involved with young women from the farm in the past and it had always ended up badly. As in the past, Red ignored Mose's warning.

To celebrate the resumed sale of whiskey, he decided to have a party that weekend to let people know everything was back to normal. Mose tried to talk him out of it, feeling it was too soon to celebrate and might draw unneeded attention from the authorities. Red was adamant and the party was scheduled. He called Lila and asked her to come and told her to bring Brit with her.

Mose came to the landing and told Rep about the party, including in the details that Lila was coming, and Brit would be with her. Mose recommended he stay at the cabin and not tempt fate by showing up. "Red done settled down bout you, so it be best you don't stir 'im up no more," he said. Rep agreed, especially since he was supposed marry Bess the next day. It probably wouldn't help matters if he got involved with Lila or had a fight with Brit. He would stay at the cabin.

He was restless all afternoon. He'd stayed at the cabin all day, but Lila was on his mind. He knew she would be at the party that evening, and the temptation to see her was getting to him. He finally convinced himself he could go near the barn, stay in the shadows and just see her. Seeing her would be enough, there would be no need to do more and then he would quietly leave.

He took a bath, put on clean clothes and headed to the landing. When he topped the hill at the kitchen, he saw the barn was decorated as usual and a large crowd was milling about. He stayed in the shadows at the edge of the woods to avoid anyone seeing him as he walked down toward the barn. He thought the place in the trees where he'd met Lila the first time would be a good place to stand in the shadows and watch.

When he walked around the last tree to the place in the shadows, he was face to face with her. She had been waiting for him. "I thought if you came, you'd come here, so here I am waiting for you," she said, as she walked to him.

He stared at her, shaking his head. "I didn't mean to see you. I wasn't gonna come at all."

"I'm glad you came, I wanted to see you. I never thought I'd say this, but I was wrong. I should have stayed with you at the cabin and never left. I know that now. Regardless of what I said about disliking living on the farm, I was wrong. I admit it, I have no shame." She moved closer and her perfume engulfed him.

He knew he should turn and run away, but he couldn't. He wasn't strong enough to overcome the temptation to be with her. He stepped back and shook his head. "We already said this ain't a good idea. You wrote in the note how you really felt."

"I know that, I've thought about what I said for days. I'm admitting I was wrong. I'm here and I'm yours tonight to do with as you wish. My pride is gone and I'm not ashamed to admit I want to be with you."

He looked at this beautiful woman, all that any man would ever want, and he hesitated. "I'm supposed to get married tomorrow."

"To Lick's daughter?"

"Yes, to Bess."

"Do you love her?"

He shook his head. "It's hard to explain. She's mighty special."

"You didn't answer my question. Do you love her?"

"Yes, I love her. She's from my kind of people."

"Tell me you don't love me." She was standing face to face, her eyes boring into him.

He shook his head. "I can't say that, but it's different with you. You know that."

"Are you running away from me by marrying her?"

He nodded and smiled. "Yes, I probably am."

"What if I told you I'll marry you tonight?"

It was difficult to see her eyes in the shadows. "Are you teasing me?"

She laughed. "Maybe, but probably not. I'm here and I'm yours right now if you want me. If it takes marriage, then I'm ready to do it."

"This ain't fair. You know what you do to me."

"I'm not trying to be fair. I'm standing here begging you to marry me or at least go to my room with me and talk to me about it. We can talk this out if you'll go with me."

He shook his head. "I can't do that." He knew he couldn't be alone with her. "I'm going to Bess tomorrow. I gotta. I promised her I'd be there."

She moved closer and put her arms around his neck and pressed against him. "You'll go with me tonight though?"

He shook his head. "I can't. It wouldn't be right."

She turned him loose and stepped back. Her face showed the hurt she felt. "If you do this, if you don't go with me, you'll regret it," she said.

He smiled, ruefully. "I already do, but you know it's best. We both know it's best"

She took a step toward the barn and looked back over her shoulder, "Regardless of what you do, you'll never forget me," she said as she walked away.

Rep watched her all the way to the barn. He knew she was right; he would never forget her. Then he turned and faded into the shadows. As he walked to the landing he wondered if he was doing the right thing. The temptation to turn around and go back to her was his companion all the way to the river.

28

Rep was up early the next morning after a long and restless night. The encounter with Lila and her offer of herself and then the offer of marriage had disturbed him. He attempted to focus on being with Bess today, but Lila's image kept getting in the way. Even though he'd decided a life with Lila wasn't possible, she wouldn't go away.

He tried to clean the cabin the best he could. Normally he didn't worry about the mess he made but now he did. He remembered how Lila had reacted when she came. He washed dishes and swept the floor. He went to the well and filled several buckets with water, so they'd have plenty to heat in case Bess wanted a bath. He hung a sheet to create a private space; Lila had thought that important. When he finished, he stood in the door and looked over the cabin. "Damn," he thought, "this ain't much to offer a woman." But he knew Bess was different from Lila and that was what drew him to her. She wasn't accustomed to much, as he'd never been accustomed to much, so maybe she wouldn't be disappointed.

He'd never been to a wedding, so he had no idea what people wore. He had little choice anyway, so he put on the best shirt and trousers he had. He stood at the pier as he was about to leave and looked at the cabin with chickens running in the yard and several pigs lying in the sun. "I hope Bess don't expect much," he muttered. She'd told him she'd never had much, but she'd never seen the cabin, which certainly wasn't much. Finally, he could do no more, so he got in the boat and headed downriver. He had no idea what was about to happen, but he was looking forward to seeing Bess.

When he got to the landing at Walnut Creek, Lick came running from the house toward the landing. He was in such a hurry that it caught Rep's attention since he'd never seen him move fast at all. Rep got out, pulled the boat up on shore and walked up the bank to meet him.

"That crazy bitch done come back," yelled Lick as he approached.

Rep had no idea what he was talking about. He stared blankly at him.

"Bess's mama! Come back two days ago like nothin' never happened, like she never busted my head with that skillet. Wanted to crawl back in my bed."

Rep was amused to see him so upset. "Did you let 'er?"

"Let 'er? Hell, you don't let 'er do nothin', she does what she wants. She crawled in and took over like nothin' never happened."

"Where's she now?"

"She be in the house with Bess. I wanted to let you know fo' you run up on 'er. She's one crazy white woman."

"What does Bess say?"

"She don't say nothin'. She be waitin' for you. You gonna marry her?"

Rep nodded. "That's why I'm here." He started toward the house.

They walked up on the porch and Lick opened the door. Rep didn't see Bess, who he was looking for, but a tall buxom woman stood on the far side of the room staring at him. She walked toward him looking him up and down. "Damn if you ain't one good lookin' scutter," she said as she slapped him on the shoulder. "I don't know bout Bess handlin' you, boy. Maybe I'll just go with you myself and take care of you."

Rep stepped back. "Long as you don't brang yo' skillet."

She laughed. "I'm Matty, Bess's mama. I thank I'm gonna like you." She paused and looked at him. "Bess say she gonna be married and go wit'chu." Her tone was more serious.

"I hope so."

"She be right to git the paper. That make it legal."

Rep didn't comment. He didn't want to get crossed up with this woman.

The bedroom door opened, and Bess walked out. She looked at him and smiled as he walked to her and wrapped his arms around her. He was amazed at how she looked, not the wild-haired girl but a beautiful young woman.

"You come back," she said, wrapping her arms around his neck.

"I told you I was."

"I be glad."

He turned and looked at Matty, who seemed to be in charge. "What now?"

"We be goin' up the creek to Preacher Snow's house," said Bess, and Rep immediately saw she was in charge. That impressed him. She laid out the plan. She and Sassy would ride with Rep. Lick would bring Matty and the other two girls. The preacher lived a mile up the creek near the bridge.

"How do you know this preacher?" Rep asked as they walked toward the boats.

"He has a church by his house, and I been there some," Bess replied. "I feel better when I go there."

"Damn Holy Rollers," interjected Lick, "ever time I see him he gits on me about drankin'. Says I'm gonna go to hell if I don't quit."

"He's right about going to hell," said Matty. "I bout sent you there with that skillet the last time you hit me when you were drankin'."

"Preacher Snow be a good man," Bess replied. "When Sassy be sick, he come and brung her a mustard plaster and prayed over her. Then she got well." She looked at Rep. "I like 'im."

Rep was glad they got to the boats and stopped the discussion. The ride up the creek was quiet. It was a warm day and he could see the first signs of spring in the trees and bushes along the bank. Bess sat in the front of the boat and held Sassy. She kept her eyes on him all the way, like he was something special, causing him to smile. They parked at the bridge and walked up the hill to Preacher Snow's house.

He was standing on the steps waiting, a tall thin man, white-haired and stoop shouldered. Rep was drawn to him immediately and that was unusual. He had a kind face and his voice, while soft, immediately caught his attention. He met Rep's gaze directly, without wavering. He hugged Bess and the girls; it was obvious they responded to him. He turned to Rep.

"What is your name, young man?" he asked as he shook his hand.

"I'm Rep Doe, suh."

"Bess tells me you are to marry her."

"Yes, suh."

"Do you love her?"

Rep was surprised by such a direct question. "Yes suh, I do."

Preacher Snow noted Rep's hesitation. "You may be surprised I ask that, but I want to be sure there is a valid basis for this marriage. Marriage is a long trip, to last many years and many young people these days don't realize what they're getting into."

Rep wasn't sure what all he said meant, but it was said with good meaning. "Yes, suh, I do love Bess."

Preacher Snow nodded. "That's good. Might I ask, are you a church-going man?"

Rep shook his head. "No. suh. I ain't never been to church."

"Then I'll pray for you, that is something you should give thought to." he said. "You're about to be married. God's word can guide you through life's challenges." He smiled. "I can assure you there will be challenges. Who will you call on to help you through those challenges?"

Rep didn't reply. He'd never been asked such a question.

Preacher Snow looked at him for a moment, patted him on the shoulder, then turned to talk to Bess.

For some reason his statement touched Rep, but he didn't understand why. He'd been alone, without anybody to call on when he had challenges. He'd always tried to handle his own problems. He felt this kind man would be a good person to know and felt drawn to him. He felt this way about few people.

Bess came over, took him by the hand and walked with him into the next room where Preacher Snow was standing with Lick, Matty and the girls.

"I'm not going to make this a long service by much talking but will ask the pertinent questions since it seems Bess and Rep intend to go forward with this marriage." He put his hand on Rep's shoulder and looked in his face. "Rep Doe, do you take Bess Shell as your wedded wife and will you love, honor and cherish her as long as you live?"

Rep squeezed Bess' hand. "I will."

Preacher Snow looked at Bess. "Bess Shell, do you take Rep Doe to be your wedded husband and will you love, honor and cherish him as long as you live?"

"I will."

He looked at Rep. "Do you have a ring?"

Rep nodded. "I do." He reached in his pocket and pulled out the ring he'd bought in River Bluff when he'd bought Bess's winter clothes. He'd never told her he had it.

"Place it on her finger."

He took Bess' hand and as he put the ring on her finger, she looked up at him and smiled, "I didn't never know you really had a ring. I didn't thank I'd ever have one."

He smiled. "So you and everbody know you be my wife."

Preacher Snow said, "Now, in front of God and these witnesses, I pronounce you man and wife." He looked at Rep. "You may kiss your bride."

Rep started to bend toward Bess, but she met him halfway and they held on to each other for a long time.

Matty hugged him, he shook hands with Lick and then kissed all three sisters. He felt good.

Preacher Snow led them into another room to his desk and signed the paper certifying they were legally married. Bess took it and hugged it to her breast. "I be so proud," she said, looking up at Rep with tears in her eyes. "I do thank you."

Rep wrapped her in his arms and held her.

With the ceremony over, Preacher Snow got Matty and Lick in the corner to discuss their marital problems. He knew their history. He felt this might be the last time he'd have a chance since they hadn't given any indication that they'd ever attend church services. "It seems Bess has found a fine young man, although he may be as poor as a church mouse and is not a Christian, hopefully they will have a good life. At least they have hope and I will pray for them. Now you have three other young girls under your care and your drinking and fighting sets a terrible example. What are they to think, that this is the way sensible people act?" He turned to Lick. "You, sir, are a reprobate and have little hope as you are now. I've never said that to many people." Then he looked at Matty. "You, as a mother have a special responsibility to teach these girls how to live responsible, and to date you have failed. I pray you will mend your ways. Both of you need to make sure these girls are in church on Sunday. At least you should do that."

Lick and Matty listened respectfully but neither made any promises.

Rep and Bess took the three girls to the boat and waited. Finally Lick and Matty came down the hill, both fussing about Preacher Snow meddling in their business. It was doubtful his talk had any effect on either one. They were still grumbling as they headed back down the creek to the house.

Rep waited at the boat while Bess ran to the house to get her belongings. He kissed the girls, shook hands with Lick and they headed to the house. Matty stayed behind, intending to talk to Rep although he didn't want to talk to her. He had little regard for her or Lick or the way they lived and acted. He didn't want to start this day off with a fuss in front of Bess, so he waited.

"Lick says you ain't got much of a house up on Sallie White, just a log cabin and not much of one."

Rep stared at her for several seconds, resenting her butting in his business. "Bess knows what I got. I told her that plain out to start with. I tried to git her to go see the cabin, but she wouldn't."

"She ain't never been away from home much."

"She'll be with me. She'll be fine."

"She's mighty young."

"She ain't much younger than me."

"She ain't never been with no man."

Rep's patience was about to run out. "She told me that. We'll deal with it."

"She says you don't drink."

"I ain't never."

"That be good. I want to quit myself. Lick oughta quit too."

Rep looked at her. "I grew up with dranking, ain't got no use fir it. Everybody oughta quit it. You and Lick sho' oughta quit, the way ya'll act."

She started toward the house then stopped. "You look after Bess. She's a good girl."

Rep nodded. "I'm gonna look after 'er."

She turned and went to the house. In a few minutes Bess came down the steps carrying two sacks. Rep met her, kissed her, then put her belongings in the boat and they started upriver.

29

B rit returned from Atlanta with Lila to attend the party. That night everyone noticed a difference in how he acted. He was quieter, nobody saw him with a drink during the party and he went to the house early, something entirely out of character for him. The next day several people discussed how he'd seemed different, and some suggested his recent wounding and Joe Hyde's death may have caused this change. The question was, was this behavior, which seemed to be for the better, for real?

He went to the barn early the next morning and asked Red to give him a real job on the farm so he could learn about the business and earn his keep. Red was surprised at his request. Mose was standing against the wall listening and he also was surprised, but suspicious. He decided he'd watch Brit closely in the coming days and make sure he was indeed serious about this sudden change of attitude. He'd known Brit since he was boy and had never seen any sign of one ounce of decency in his bones. The recent events may have changed him, but time would tell.

Red told him that if he was serious about wanting a job, he would think on it and come up with something. Brit thanked him and left.

Red sat quietly for several minutes, his head down in deep thought. He raised up and looked at Mose. "What do you think?" It was obvious Brit's request had surprised him and puzzled him. "You think he's serious?"

Mose shrugged his shoulders. "It be strange. He ain't never acted like he cared befo'. Maybe he growed some, I don't know."

Red nodded. "Maybe so. I'll give him something to do and we'll see how he does."

Mose stepped away from the wall and came to the desk. "You be lucky, Red, not bein' dead or in jail. You done been shot, Brit be shot, and three men dead and we still be here. Them folks cross the river hate you, and they hate all we'uns. Miss Sara and yo' girls gone and you done moved that woman in yo house and everbody knows it. Now we be making whiskey again. This ain't gonna be good." He stopped and waited for Red's reply.

Red smiled and nodded. "Everything you said is right, Mose, and I have been lucky, in several ways. But all this don't matter to me, I'm gonna do what I want. And I want things like they are now. It don't matter what you say. What comes will come."

"I just want you to know I ain't fur what you doin'." He started to walk away and turned around. "I be fraid if everthang keep like it be, somethin' sho nuff bad gonna happen."

Red laughed. "Hell, you didn't have to tell me that." He looked up. "Something else you don't know. Lila come to me yesterday and told me she wanted to marry Rep and move back to the farm. I told her she was crazy as hell, but she said she wanted to anyway." He laughed. "Then she come back last night and said the bastard turned her down. He said he was gonna marry Lick's gal, Bess, cause he'd promised her he would. She said she offered to go to bed with him last night and he wouldn't do that either." He chuckled and shook his head. "All my kids have gone crazy as hell."

Mose nodded. "Rep said he was goin' to Walnut Creek yesterday to marry Bess. He supposed to be back tomorrow."

"He probably done the best thing," said Red. "If he comes back tomorrow, tell him to come see me."

Mose laughed. "He might not come back, if he done got that wild girl in his bed."

30

B ess sat quietly in the front of the boat all the way from Walnut Creek. She'd never been up Back Slough before, and it was all new to her. She never said a word until they arrived at the cabin. Rep parked the boat at the pier. He was concerned as to how she would react to what she saw and watched her response as several chickens ran across the yard toward them. She stood in the boat as her eyes swept across the island and the cabin.

"I told you it ain't much," he said.

She turned and smiled. "It be our home, Rep. I like it, I ain't never had nothin' what be my own before."

Rep walked to her and hugged her. "I'm a lucky man to have you, girl," he said as he helped her onto the pier. He picked up her sacks and they walked to the cabin.

She went in and stood for a minute just looking at everything. Then she walked around and touched each piece of furniture – the table and stove and cabinet. She went to the curtain and looked at the tub. She didn't comment. She was just getting acquainted with her surroundings.

"I fixed that curtain in the back," said Rep, "so you'd have a place what'd be private. We can warm some water later if'un you wanta take a bath."

She walked over to him and kissed him. She kept her arms around him, holding him close, then looked up and smiled. "Mama made me take a bath this mornin' and put on some good smellin' stuff. You heat up a bucket of water and let me wash off some, then I be ready."

Her comment confused him. She saw his puzzlement.

She laughed. "Mama say I ain't really married till you bed me. She say ain't no need to wait till dark, so you git me some water."

"Are you serious?" he asked, as she stood there smiling.

"Lest you don't want to?"

"Damn, girl," he said as he pushed her away and went to the stove and filled a bucket with water. She got a towel, went behind the curtain and started taking off her clothes. In a few minutes he carried the water to the curtain and put it on a table by the tub. Then he went to the bed, crawled in and waited.

She came from behind the curtain wearing the nightgown he'd bought her and walked to the bed and stopped beside him. She looked down at him, seemingly in deep thought. Suddenly she reached down and pulled the nightgown over her head and threw it on the bed. "I don't reckon I need this," she said.

Rep lay there and marveled at her nakedness. He pulled the covers back and she crawled in, nestled against him and wrapped her arms around him. She kissed him and said, "Now tell me what to do."

They held each other till the sun went down, then they held each other in the dark and sometime in the night they went to sleep. She woke up just after daylight, jumped out of bed without a word and cooked breakfast. They ate, then crawled back in bed and lay together, getting to know each other. He told her what he did each day and she asked what she could do to help other than cook and look after the house.

Until now they'd only been together for a few hours, so this was new to them, to have so much time. He was amazed at her questions, her grasp of matters and her maturity at such a young age. The last twenty-four hours with her had been special, so different from the encounters with Tish and Lila. Those too had been special, but brief; what he had with Bess was long-term special. He marveled at how it had all come about. He'd gone to Walnut Creek to pick up a dog and met her. He wondered if their meeting was an accident. He'd never thought about things like that before. For some reason Preacher Snow's words were in his head but he couldn't remember why.

He told her about Mose and mentioned the possibility of her going with him to Shoal Creek and meeting the people there. For the first time in their conversation she had a negative reaction and drew back. He hastened to assure her a visit didn't have to take place any time soon. It could wait till she felt comfortable. She agreed with that.

Later they walked around the island and across the rude bridge to Big Island. She knew how to fish for brim, so they caught several to use for bait that afternoon. She went with him to bait up and fish the set hooks and trotline. When they returned that evening, he heated water and filled the tub where they bathed together. As he held her in the warm water, he reflected on what a lucky man he was.

The next morning, he went to fish the lines and she stayed at the cabin. When he returned, she met him at the door and kissed him. He could tell she had something on her mind. Finally, she spoke. "I want to be here with you all the time and never leave, but maybe some time, I could go and see my sisters. They be down there with Lick and Mama and sometimes they ain't got no sense when they git to drankin' and fightin'. I be worried bout 'em."

He hugged her. "We'll go anytime you want. It's good you worry bout 'em." He led her to the bed, sat down and then pulled her down beside him. "Tomorrow mornin', I have to go to the landing and take fish. You be welcome to go with me if you want." Before he could finish, she shook her head negatively. "You don't have to go but you'll be by yo'self-till I get back." He thought for a minute. "Have you ever shot a gun?"

She cocked her head to the side and looked questioning at him. "Lick showed me how to shoot the shotgun. I kilt squirrels."

He smiled. "That's good. I'll keep a loaded shotgun by the door in

case you need it. I'll show you how to shoot a pistol too. I keep it by
the bed where it's easy to get to. There ain't nothin' to be worried
bout, but I'd feel better if you knowed how."

She nodded. "That be good if you want me to." She put her arm
around him and pulled him back on the bed beside her and kissed
him. "We be on the bed, why don't we just stay for a bit?"

"Girl," he said as he lay down beside her, "I don't know bout me
keepin' up with you."

Later that afternoon he took the pistol outside, showed her how
to load it and practiced firing at targets. He was surprised how well
she took to it and shot. She was pleased he was taking up time with
her. Afterward he took the pistol inside and showed her where he hid
it at the bed.

He knew he'd be going to Shoal Creek after fishing and dressing
fish the next morning, so they went to bed early. He held her close
and thought how lucky he was to have found her. He found himself
wishing he could relive these last two days for some longer but knew
that wasn't possible.

He was up before daylight and while he was dressing, she cooked
eggs and bacon. Lick had told him early on Bess could cook but he'd
not been real interested at the time, but it was true. He kissed her,
went to the boat and started up the slough.

When he got to the landing, Mose was waiting. "You git that gal?"
he asked.

Rep smiling, nodded. "I did."

Rep didn't comment more but look on his face told Mose he was
pleased. "Red wants to see you."

"Anythang going on more than usual?" Rep asked.

Mose didn't reply but as they walked up the hill, he told him
about Brit's's unusual actions in the past days. They discussed this
and both agreed they would wait and see how he acted before they
believed he'd changed. Rep certainly didn't trust Brit at all. Mose
didn't mention what Red had said about Lila asking him to
marry her.

When they walked in the barn, Rep was surprised to see Brit

sitting on the other side of the desk. Red was sitting behind the desk and motioned for him to sit as Mose walked to the wall. Rep sat but didn't look at Brit.

Red looked at Rep and smiled. "Mose tells me you married Lick's gal, Bess."

"I did." Rep intended to say as little about his business as he could.

"Ya'll living at the cabin?"

Rep nodded.

"It ain't very big, is it?"

"It's alright for now, but I plan to add another room sometime."

"Lick give you any trouble, or that crazy wife, Matty?"

Rep laughed. "They weren't no problem."

Suddenly Red changed the subject. "I know you and Brit ain't never got along, not since you been here."

Rep glanced at Brit and then back at Red. He wondered where this was leading.

"Brit has been through a lot lately, what with getting shot and all. He has seen he has been wrong in some of the things he did, and he wants to get straight." He looked at Rep. "He wants to get straight with you."

Rep stared at Red for a moment, glanced again at Brit and back at Red. He was trying to understand exactly what was happening.

"He don't want no more trouble with you," Red said. "He ain't expecting you to be his friend but he don't want to fight you anymore. He's sorry for all the trouble he's caused with you." He looked at Brit. "Ain't that right, Brit?"

Brit nodded his head, not looking at Rep.

Red turned to Rep. "Alright, that's settled. No more trouble."

Rep didn't move. Stone-faced, he stared at Red. "I want to hear him say it."

Red's face mirrored his surprise. "You want what?"

"I want to hear him say he's sorry."

Red shook his head, frustration on his face. "He's already said it."

Rep shook his head. "That ain't enough. He nodded his head at you. He ain't said shit to me."

Rep glanced at Brit for an instant and when their eyes met, he saw the hate. It only lasted for an instant and then disappeared, but it was long enough. He knew Brit wasn't sorry. He didn't mean nothing he said.

Red stood up and yelled at Rep. "Damn it!" he said, his face reddening. "He's trying to settle this." Frustrated he turned to Brit. "Tell him you're sorry."

Brit stared at Red. It was obvious he didn't want to say anything. Finally, he looked at Rep. "I'm sorry." His heart didn't seem to be in the statement.

"Good," said Red. "That settles that. Ya'll get the hell outa here. I got work to do."

Rep went out the door and Mose followed. They started up the hill. "You keep on watchin' that boy," said Mose, "he ain't no better."

"I know that" said Rep, "I saw his eyes."

31

M ay Hobb had never been around another woman she could talk to or confide in. She certainly couldn't talk to her parents and her sister, Star, wasn't a role model for her to follow, even if she'd been there. She was afraid of both her brothers and tried to avoid them. Boot was mean, and Harrold wasn't someone she'd trust. So, she'd grown to this point in her life with no guidance from her family and no one outside to look to for help.

She'd been with Miss Tinney, who she learned was named Alva, for some time now. She'd told May to call her Alva when they were at home. They'd had several heart-to-heart talks. She'd never poured out her personal feelings before, but she trusted Alva. She told her about her feelings for Rolley and the meetings they'd had on the river. She also told her about Rolley holding her and how that made her feel. Now she was disappointed he was avoiding her.

Alva had taught Rolley in school and had great regard for him. She was sure he was under pressure from his parents about being seen with a Hobb, even if she was innocent of any wrongdoing. She was aware the townspeople treated the Hobb family as lepers, as untouchable. She hadn't mentioned it to May, but she'd heard the talk about Star coming to town, how she looked and what her present occupation was. Star's visit hadn't helped to improve everyone's opinion of the Hobb family.

She understood what May was going through, having grown up in a poor family herself. She was more fortunate than May in that her family, although poor, were honest and God-fearing folk. They were uneducated and life was a struggle financially but they worked and persevered. While never wealthy, they were regarded as good contributing citizens in their community. Alva had worked her way through school and, although it took her an extra year, she graduated.

She told May to hold her head high, she wasn't responsible for what her family did, but she was responsible for what she did. As far as Rolley was concerned, she advised May to continue to conduct herself in a way that would show everybody what kind of person she was, regardless of some trying to stigmatize her for being a Hobb. If he had feelings for her, then let him be the one to take the first step.

32

The next several weeks were quiet and peaceful. Rep and Bess settled into a regular schedule. They were still getting used to married life and learning about each other and they were very happy. Bess hadn't been to Shoal Creek, but they were having discussions about a possible visit and she was considering it.

Lick and Matty had made a visit with the sisters. Rep was glad Bess got to see her sisters but was glad when Lick and Matty left; he could only take a little of them at a time. Rep had stayed away from Red as much as possible and hadn't seen Brit at all. Mose told him Brit was working on the south forty trying to get the fields in shape for planting. Rep hoped he stayed there.

Red Hogan seemed to be pleased with the way things were. He did complain about whiskey sales being down in part because of the loss of Alabama business, but felt it would come back in time. He'd only called Rep to the barn twice and nothing important was discussed.

He did have to deal with one domestic problem involving the young lady he'd moved into his house. She got bored being alone and invited another man into her bedroom where Red caught them. He kicked the woman out of the house and then had to face her daddy, who made all sorts of claims about how Red had mistreated his daughter. Money changing hands finally settled everything down as it always had. Mose reminded him he'd warned about moving the woman into his house at the beginning.

~

R iver Bluff was quiet. All the reporters were gone. Jack and Ruby were seldom seen outside the house, except for infrequent visits to the store. Some of the men were grumbling about their whiskey supply being gone with Shoal Creek off-limits, but nobody had dared go over since the last shooting. May remained with Alva and away from her family. She hadn't talked to Rolley in weeks. Since he was avoiding her, she'd made no effort to see him.

Lila had remained in Atlanta. Since Rep had rebuffed her advances, she'd not been back.

On Monday Red and Mose were at the barn when Brit unexpectedly walked in. "What are you doing up here?" asked Red. "I thought you were on the south forty."

"Was, but I wanted to talk to you about something," he said, as he flopped in a chair in front of the desk.

Red shrugged. "What is it?" He'd had little interest in talking to Brit for some weeks now.

"I know you been worried about the loss of whiskey sales."

Red nodded. He was puzzled and waited for another comment.

"Some of that is 'cause them Alabama folks ain't coming here no more."

Red's brow furrowed. "Hell, everybody knows that. What the hell are you talking about?"

Brit smiled, cockily. "If they won't come over here, why don't we take the whiskey to them? We sell it to them over there."

Red shook his head. "Take the whiskey to Alabama? Are you crazy?"

"Wouldn't take it to Alabama. The state line is the riverbank on the other side of the river, so the islands in the river near the

Alabama side are still in Georgia. We stay in Georgia and sell the whiskey and the Alabama law can't touch us."

Red looked at Mose and then back at Brit. "Would that work?"

Brit nodded. "One of the men from Alabama told me the river still runs under the mill and half the mill building is in Georgia. We could walk to the end of the mill and sell if we wanted to. That would make it easier 'cause them folks wouldn't have to come across the river."

Red sat for a minute in thought. He shook his head. "Damn, you might be right."

Mose walked over to the desk. "You might be right but them folks ain't bothering us right now. You wanta git them stirred back up?"

"Just let me try," said Brit. "Let me take a load over and let the people know it's there and see what happens. The last men that came over said everybody wanted whiskey. You know all them regular customers would."

"You might be right," said Red, "but Mose has a point. We oughta just lay low for a bit. Ain't nobody after us right now. There ain't nothing about us in the papers right now. We'll leave it alone and look at it later."

Brit didn't like it. "Just let me try one time and see."

"Damn, boy. You can't go over there. Everybody knows you. They'll be done hung you for sure if they saw you."

Brit got up. "I thought it was a good idea, maybe later," he said as he walked out the door. He had no intention of waiting till later. It was his plan to get a load of whiskey, have a couple of pals go with him and make some extra money. He wasn't afraid of that bunch across the river.

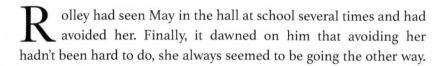

Rolley had seen May in the hall at school several times and had avoided her. Finally, it dawned on him that avoiding her hadn't been hard to do, she always seemed to be going the other way. After thinking about this for several days, he decided she seemed to be avoiding him. He didn't know how to handle that. After several days of no change in her behavior, he went looking for her. He saw her coming out of her second class and started toward her. She saw him coming and turned the other way, making him walk fast to catch up with her.

"May," he called out as he came up behind her.

She walked several steps, turned and waited for him to catch up.

"I wanted to talk to you."

"About what?"

"I know you're staying with Miss Tinney now. Do you go to church with her on Sunday night?"

"I do go to church." She didn't intend to give in to him at all. He would have to come to her. "Why are you asking?"

"I thought I'd come go with you, if you don't mind."

May stared in his eyes for a moment. "Why, after not speaking to me for weeks, you decided to want to be seen with me?"

"I can't explain that. I just want to be with you."

"You know I'm still a Hobb. May Hobb is my name. You know what that means."

Rolley nodded. "I know that. That doesn't matter, I want to be with you."

She decided she'd pushed him far enough. "If that's what you want, then come to the dormitory Sunday night and I'll walk to church with you." She'd decided if he wanted to be with her, he would have to prove it before the entire town. To get to the Methodist Church, they'd have to walk through the middle of town and past the Baptist Church where his folks would be. If he'd do that, then he wanted to be with her.

That afternoon when his daddy came home from work, Rolley was waiting. He knew he had to tell him what was going on. "I need to talk to you, daddy."

His daddy could tell it was something serious by looking at Rolley's face. He sat and waited.

"You remember talking to me about the Hobb family and staying away from May Hobb."

"Yes, I remember that, and I've heard nothing more about it."

"May has moved out of her family's house and is staying with Miss Tinney at the dormitory. She's doing good in school."

His daddy knew he was leading up to something, so he nodded.

"She's a good girl and ain't like her folks."

"You don't say ain't."

"Yes sir, sorry. She isn't like her folks." Rolley continued.

"So, what's your point?"

"I've asked her about me going to church with her Sunday night."

"What did she say?"

"She said yes."

"So, you already have a date with May."

"Yes sir."

"Church is a good place to go to start with. You know how to act, and I never expect your actions to embarrass our family."

"Yes sir."

When Rep returned to the cabin that afternoon, Bess was in the yard feeding the chickens. He walked over, hugged and kissed her as he did every day when he returned. "Bess, you've been here for a while now with just me and ain't seen nobody else since yo' folks come up. What about tomorrow you go with me up to the landin' and meet Mose and see the farm?"

She frowned. "I ain't complainin'."

"I know, but I'd like for you to go with me. I think it's time."

"You want me to go?"

"Yes, I want you to meet some people."

"I don't much want to, but if that be what you want."

He hugged her and lifted her off the ground. "Thank you."

She helped him dress the fish the next morning, then they loaded the boat and headed upstream. When they got to the landing Mose was waiting. Rep cut the motor and drifted into the bank. "There's Mose," he said.

Bess, in the front of the boat, turned and looked at Rep, surprise on her face. "Mose be a colored man."

"Yes, he is. I thought you knew that."

"You ain't never told me."

"I ain't never thought about it."

Rep took her hand and helped her out as Mose walked up. "Mose, this is my wife, Bess."

Mose took off his hat and smiled. "Lordy, Miss Bess, you bout the prettiest thang I ever did see."

Bess smiled and offered her hand. "I be glad to meet you, Mose."

He looked at Rep. "Boy, you done mighty good." Then he looked more serious. "Red was asking about you. I told him you was coming today. He want to see you. He be at the barn."

Rep took Bess by the hand. "This'll give you a chance to meet 'im."

Bess hung back, obviously concerned. "Lick say he ain't no good man."

Rep laughed. "He ain't real sweet, but he's not gonna bother you. I want 'im to meet my wife."

Bess relented and she started up the trail, holding Rep's hand. They stopped at the kitchen and he introduced her to Hattie Mae who took over her as Mose had. "Yo man be about the sweetest one I ever did see, honey. You sho be a lucky girl."

Bess hugged her. "Rep say you made him breakfast ever mornin' fo' I come.

"Sho did, honey. That man sho catch fish and now he dun cotch you."

They all laughed and headed down the trail. To this point Bess seemed to be enjoying meeting the people. As they neared the barn, she tightened her grip on Rep's hand and he knew she was getting nervous. He put his arm around her waist and pulled her to him.

When they walked in the barn Red was sitting at the desk. He stood up and smiled at Bess. "Rep, who you got with you?" His tone was friendlier than Rep was accustomed to.

Rep was surprised by the smile and the use of his name. "This be my wife, Bess."

Red nodded. "It's good to have you with us, Bess. The last time I saw you at Lick's place, you were a little girl, now you're a grown woman. Damn good looking one too."

Bess blushed. "I thank you."

"Rep said he was gonna get married, so I guess ya'll did."

Bess smiled and held up her hand. "We be married. I got a ring and the paper."

Red laughed. "By God, you surely did. Good for you."

Rep was amazed by this banter from Red and Bess's retort. He'd never seen him so relaxed, but times were good so that could account for his better mood. He also knew Red could turn into a bastard at any time if something happened that he didn't like.

Red looked at Rep. "How about ya'll having dinner with me at the house Saturday night. Lila is coming down and I know she'd like to meet Bess, ya'll being good friends and everything."

Rep was surprised by the offer and started to object but Red continued, looking at Bess. "This could be like ya'll's wedding party and all. You make sure he brings you, Bess."

Bess was flustered by Red's sudden attention to her and the question addressed to her. She looked at Rep for help.

Rep put his arm around her. "I'll talk to Bess and let you know about Saturday. We're still tryin' to get settled at the cabin. We thank you for askin' us."

Red nodded. "You let me know now, but we'll be planning on ya'll being there."

There was more small talk and then Rep and Bess left the barn alone. As they walked up the hill, she took his hand.

Rep was flustered by Red's invitation to dinner, especially since he'd said Lila would be there. His mistrust of him was too strong to take the invitation at face value, as a simple wedding dinner. The more he thought of it, he knew Red wouldn't have invited him to dinner at his house, whether he got married or not. That wasn't his way. This had to be Lila's doing, she had cooked this up.

"He weren't so mean as I heared he be," Bess said, looking up at him for his reaction.

"No, he was nice to you."

"You seed him be mean to folks?"

"Yes, I have."

"He be mean to you?"

Rep smiled. "Yes, he has."

"I don't like him for that."

"Don't worry about it."

They walked on in silence. His mind was on Saturday night and why that came up. Red had something in mind, and he didn't trust him, especially if Lila was there.

"You ever been to his house to eat?"

"No, I ain't."

"Why he ask us?"

"He said it was like a weddin' dinner."

They walked on past the kitchen to the landing and then down the slough to the cabin. Bess hadn't said another word. When they got inside, she led him to the table, pushed him to sit in the chair and she sat on his lap with her arm around his neck. "Who is Lila?"

He looked up and her eyes were looking straight in his eyes. He almost smiled but thought he'd better not. "She's Red's daughter that lives in Atlanta."

"She be pretty?"

"Yes, she is."

"She married?"

"No, she's not married."

"How old she be?"

"I don't know. Be in her twenties, maybe."

"He said ya'll be friends."

Rep nodded. "We know each other."

Bess put her hands on each side of his face and turned his head till they were nose to nose. She was staring into his soul. "She come to the cabin?"

"Yes, she's been to the cabin."

"She sleep in the bed?"

"Yes."

"She be in the bed with you?"

"Yes."

She reached down and kissed him, then pulled him out of the chair and led him to the bed. She pushed him down on the bed and lay beside him. "Won't never be no need she ever come to the cabin agin."

"That's right."

"We go to his house for the weddin' dinner?"

"Yes."

33

Jim Hawke had been the constable for River Bluff for thirteen years. The mill paid his salary, so they'd have someone in town with legal authority. His job wasn't usually demanding. Mainly he sat on the bench in front of the gymnasium and represented the presence of the law. Sometimes he'd get on some of the younger boys for smoking or fighting, but usually the town was quiet. He was deputized by the county sheriff and authorized to carry a weapon. He had a .38 caliber Smith and Wesson revolver on his hip but had never fired it.

The only time he'd ever drawn his revolver, was once when Jack Hobb was drunk in the street terrorizing the neighborhood and he'd whacked him upside the head. That one time resulted in ten stitches in Jack's scalp and fueled his intense dislike for the Hobb clan.

The town was normally quiet, except when Jack or one of his offspring decided to create trouble. The last few weeks had been troubling enough, since Boot and Harold decided to get themselves killed and Star came to town and gave the women's missionary union enough gossip to cover their agenda for several years. He also had no use for the Shoal Creek crowd.

Jim had never been an angel himself, especially in his younger years. In those years he'd paddled across the river and imbibed numerous fruit jars of moonshine. He knew what it was to get sot drunk and pay the price the next day with a splitting headache and his mouth tasting like baked cow shit.

He claimed the day he saw the error of his ways was when he woke up on the riverbank, not knowing where he was or who he was. He looked in a tree above his head and saw a little bird sitting on a limb. He said he pointed to his nose and said, "Little bird, come light on my nose." Then he swore the bird came and lit on his nose, scaring the hell out of him. He thought he'd been given supernatural powers. He jumped up and ran to the riverbank and ordered the water to flow in the opposite direction. Thankfully, it didn't obey. He said if alcohol could mess up your mind to that point, he didn't want any more of it, so he quit drinking and stuck to it.

Before becoming constable, he had made a living catfishing, but illegally. He had fished baskets, which was against the law. He made these baskets himself, using heavy-duty chicken wire. A basket, about five feet long shaped like a cylinder, would have one end closed and the other end equipped with a wire funnel with a small hole in the center for the fish to enter and then not be able to find their way out. The basket would be baited with various smelly vegetables and meal cake to attract the fish. It would be anchored with a weight and long rope in the river channel and allowed to stay for several days.

The basket's location wouldn't be marked in any way. This was to keep the Game Wardens or anyone else from finding it. Jim knew generally where it was and would retrieve it using a drag along the river bottom behind the boat. He would have several baskets out in different locations and did very well selling catfish.

Now sixty years old, he'd decided to give up the river life and come to town. Now with the two Hobb boys gone, Star wherever she was and Shoal Creek off-limits, he looked forward to peace and quiet.

~

B rit had enlisted two men who worked on the south forty to join his scheme to sell whiskey on the Alabama side. The promise of easy money was the enticement. The challenge was to get the word to those who would be customers without alerting the law. Luckily, one desperate soul from River Bluff, having severe withdrawal pains from the lack of alcohol, made his way to Shoal Creek looking for relief. He was given a free supply of whiskey and told to spread the word they would be selling whiskey at the end of the mill in two days. He was told to be careful who he told.

∾

J im Hawke sat on the bench in front of the gym each day, usually about half asleep. After years of watching the townspeople, he could tell if something was going on or if everything was normal by watching the comings and goings. He saw Mrs. Watt hurriedly rush to the drugstore and he knew someone was sick at home. By observation he kept his finger on the town's pulse.

The next morning, he was in his customary place when he saw Ed Smith and Huck Walker come out of the general store across the street. They stopped on the porch and talked and then went around back to the post office. Later they came back to the front of the store as Rick Johnson came out of the drugstore. Rick saw them, walked over and they all huddled on the sidewalk. They had an animated conversation for three or four minutes, occasionally one would glance toward Jim and then resume talking. Their actions got Jim's attention. Then they turned and walked together past the Christian Church and turned down Lower Street toward the mill. Neither of the three lived in that direction so Jim suspected something out of the ordinary was going on. He waited until they were out of sight and eased to his car.

∾

Brit and his two accomplices loaded the boat with several boxes of whiskey he'd slipped out of the storage shack. They eased out of Shoal creek and headed to the Alabama shore. They landed on the island upstream of the River Bluff landing near the end of the mill building. The plan was for Brit to stay with the boat since he might be recognized. The two men would carry the merchandise ashore and conduct the sales. Everything seemed to be proceeding as planned.

~

Jim Hawke drove to the hill in front of the mill and parked. He watched several men go around to the back of the mill and walk down the fence line until they were out of sight. He didn't know what was going on, but he knew it wasn't normal. He eased down the hill along the riverbank where he could see the far end of the mill toward the river. He saw two men he didn't recognize come out of the woods carrying boxes. They sat the boxes down and waited. Ed Smith and Huck Walker came into view from the other side of the mill and walked to where the two men with the boxes were waiting. They began talking. The men opened the boxes, pulled out a jar and handed it to Ed. He unscrewed the lid and took a drink, testing the quality. He handed the bottle to Huck and he took a drink. It seemed the whiskey passed the taste test and money changed hands. Soon several other men came walking up and more business was conducted.

Jim didn't know who the men with the whiskey were, but he figured they were from Shoal Creek. He thought it strange they would attempt this on this side of the river, even though he knew they were technically still in Georgia. Bad feelings had simmered down though and he didn't want to do anything to stir them up again. He decided the best thing would be to run these people off and send them from whence they came. He certainly didn't want to arrest anybody from Shoal Creek and get that started again.

He walked around the end of the building, drew his revolver and shouted, "You're on mill property and you're under arrest!" His words were directed toward the two men with the whiskey.

One of the men yelled back, "We're in Georgia! You can't arrest us!"

Jim pointed his revolver at them. "You're on mill property, put your hands in the air!" he yelled, as he raised his pistol and fired two shots straight up.

The two men dropped what they were holding and ran headlong toward the woods and headed for the boat. When Brit heard the shots, he cranked the motor and was about to pull out when they came out of the woods and dove into the boat. He backed around and then headed across the river. "That crazy son'abitch about killed us," said one of the men.

"Where's the boxes?" asked Brit.

"Boxes? Who gives a damn about the boxes? If you want 'em, you go get 'em," yelled one of the men.

Jim walked down to where two or three of the locals were gathered by the fence. "Damn, Jim," Ed Smith said, "you scared the shit out of us."

Jim laughed. "You boys knew better than to do this." Then he pointed to the boxes and bottles scattered on the ground. "Ya'll done made a mess here. Ya'll pick all this stuff up and do something with it." He turned and walked up the hill.

R olley's Sunday night date to go to church with May had turned out well. On the walk back to the dormitory he had taken her hand and she didn't pull away but held his hand until they reached her door. He thanked her for letting him go with her and left.

They made it a point for the next several days to meet somewhere during the school day and talk. It was assumed by their friends that they were now a couple. It seemed since she was living with Miss Tinney, and not with the Hobb family, she wasn't regarded by the young people as untouchable. He asked her to go with him to the movie on Saturday night and she agreed. They met at the theatre and he bought popcorn and cokes. They found seats off to the side out of the crowd and sat very close holding hands.

After the movie they walked slowly to the dormitory, making the time last as long as they could. He put his arm around her waist and held her as they walked. Near the dormitory they passed under a tree overhang and he pulled her into the shadows and kissed her. She fully returned his kiss and they stood there for several minutes. She was soft pressed against him as he held her and they both had feelings and sensations they'd never felt before. The desire to stay there holding each other was strong, almost overpowering. Finally, without wanting to, they turned loose and parted, both knowing their relationship had reached another level. Neither spoke about it as they resumed their walk but they both felt it. The sensations they felt left an ache in places they'd never experienced. At the door he again thanked her for going with him.

R ep was concerned about Saturday night for several reasons. Lila being at the dinner was on top of the list with Red's motive for inviting them being second. He had no idea how either would act or what they might try. His third concern was how Bess would be treated, and how she would handle whatever happened. He couldn't control the first two, but he could talk to Bess.

He brought up the subject that evening. "Bess, I ain't never been to Red's house. I don't know how they do thangs but it ain't like us. One time I ate at a house where they had a cloth on the table and napkins for you to use. I hadn't never seen such and felt about stupid cause I wasn't sure what to do."

"I thought about that too," she replied. "Mama weren't smart about some thangs, but she knowed about some others. She used to have us girls' tea parties, with knives and forks and spoons and napkins. She made us do like them fancy folks done in the movies. You put the napkin in yo' lap. Forks go on the left and knife on the right and then the spoon. She say if there be more than one fork, whatever they feed you first, you eat with the smallest fork, 'cept it be soup. We didn't never eat no whole supper like that, but she taught us how if we ever did. We played havin' tea parties all the time."

Rep looked at her in amazement. "You amaze me, girl. I never knowed none of that." After that talk, he stopped worrying about her and thought about himself. He was concerned about what they would wear. He'd seen Red and Lila at the parties dressed in fancy clothes and he knew Bess had nothing to match what Lila wore. He didn't care about himself, it wouldn't bother him, but he didn't want Bess to be embarrassed and hurt. Regardless, he could do nothing about it; they had what they had. He'd bought Bess two dresses in River Bluff. They were new but plain.

"Them folks what live in that big house, they be rich?" Bess asked as they were dressing.

"I don't know but they got a lot."

"That Lila wear pretty dresses?"

"She did to a party, but mostly regular clothes everday."

Bess didn't say anything else, but he knew all this was on her mind. They headed to the landing.

Lila opened the door after Rep knocked. She was wearing a nice dress but nothing fancy. She ignored Rep; her eyes were on Bess. "I'm Lila," she said as she took both her hands and pulled her into the room, "I'm so glad to meet you. The last time I saw you, you were a little girl. Daddy told me you were grown up and were so pretty and he was right."

"Thank you," replied Bess, surprised by this reception as was Rep, who stood and stared at Lila.

Lila turned her attention to Rep. She walked over, put her hands on his shoulders and kissed him on the cheek. Her familiar perfume surrounded him. She looked back at Bess, took her hand and looked at the ring. "And you married this scoundrel," she said, smiling and hugging Bess.

"I got the paper too," Bess replied.

Lila laughed. "Good for you. You know how men are," she said as she looked at Rep and smiled, "sometimes they'll use you and then leave you." She took Bess' hand and led her down the hallway. "Come with me and we'll freshen up." She turned to Rep and pointed to a chair. "Daddy will be here in a minute. Have a seat." She and Bess went into her room and she handed her a brush. "You rode up here in that boat and that wind, thought you might need a minute to fix your hair."

Bess smiled. "That wind bout blowed me away. I thank you."

Lila stood to the side as Bess worked with her hair and marveled at this young girl, so very young and so pretty. She knew how Bess had grown up with Lick and Matty, having nothing and little if any help. Her situation sounded every much like how Rep grew up, from what he'd told her. Now, they had found each other and seemed to be doing well.

Bess finished her hair, stood up and looked at Lila. "Rep told me you come to the cabin."

Lila was surprised she brought the subject up so directly. "Yes, I've been to the cabin."

"It ain't much," said Bess, "but I like it."

Lila smiled. "I liked it too."

"Rep said you stay with 'im."

"I did stay some. I liked Rep."

"He like you too. I could tell he did."

Lila walked over and hugged Bess. "But he liked you best." She stared in Bess' eyes. "I offered myself to him. I asked him to marry me, but he wouldn't. He said he was going to marry you. And he did."

Bess looked up at Lila. "I ain't never knowed nobody like 'im"

Lila laughed. "I ain't neither. Let's go see where the men are."

Red and Rep were in the den. "I've been talking to Rep about taking over the farming, the livestock and the river. Mose will look after the houses and other things. I told him it's a good opportunity and with a family now, he needs to look at the future."

Bess looked at Rep, a questioning look and some concern on her face.

Rep went over and hugged her. "We'll talk and decide what to do. I thank you for askin' me."

"You'd have a house here on the farm," said Red, "with running water and the bathroom inside. That'd be better than you have at the cabin."

They went into the dining room and everything went fine. Hattie Mae was the cook and she couldn't do enough for them, constantly fussing over Bess. It was also obvious she also had a place in her heart for Lila. She'd fried catfish, had potatoes and coleslaw with cornbread balls called hushpuppies. Rep watched Lila and Bess as they ate and followed their lead with the napkin and forks and such. He was glad Lila and Bess seemed to get along well. They dominated the conversation.

They left the house with a good feeling. All Rep's concerns about the dinner were unfounded. Bess had handled everything well, Lila had been extremely nice, and Red had been quiet most of the time.

It was getting dark when they got back to the cabin. Bess had been quiet since they left the big house, she had a lot to digest. She'd had several first-time experiences and they were still fresh in her mind. "I like Lila," she said as they undressed. She be real nice to me."

"Lila's a nice person."

"She said she wanted to marry you."

Rep laughed. "She said somethin' like that, but I didn't thank she be serious."

Bess shook her head. "She be serious. She be in love with you."

Rep chuckled. "You need to go to sleep and stop talking so much."

She rolled over and kissed him. "I be in love with you too."

They were eating breakfast when Bess mentioned the offer of a job and a house. "He say we come live in a house on the farm and leave the cabin?"

Rep nodded. "That's what he said, if I take that job."

"What you think?" She was watching his face closely.

"I ain't never done nothin' like that."

"You be smart. You can do it if'un you want to."

"I ain't never liked livin' in a bunch of people."

"I ain't never lived in no house with a bathroom inside and water runnin'."

He laughed. "I ain't neither."

"What you thank?"

He shook his head. "We'll talk about it some more later."

She hugged him. "I do what you want. You tell me."

34

Red Hogan and Mose were in the barn when an irate Brit came busting in. "Lila told me you offered that bastard Rep the farm job."

Red leaned back in the chair and stared at his son, standing red-faced in front of the desk. "I did offer him the job."

"Lila said you ate supper with him and Lick's white-trash bitch he's with."

"She's his wife and a damn sight better than the white-trash whores you run with."

"Well. I ain't working for the son'abitch."

"Then you'll have a problem since you work on the south-forty and he'll be in charge of the south-forty."

Brit held up his arms in frustration. "Why didn't I get that job? Hell, I'm yo' son."

Red shook his head. "You are my son and a sorrier one I ain't never seen. You can't look after nothing and ain't got sense to pour piss out a boot." He stood up. "I told you not to go to Alabama with whiskey and you went anyway. Damn near got somebody shot. Now them people across the river are all stirred up again."

Brit shook his head. "I ain't gonna work for the bastard."

Red shrugged. "If you don't work, you can't stay here. Get your ass back to Atlanta and let your mama take care of you."

Brit started to the door and turned back. "That bastard ain't been nothin' but trouble since he got here. I'm gonna fix his ass."

Red laughed. "Damn boy, you are stupid. He's already whipped you more than once."

Brit walked to the door and pointed his finger at Red. "You watch. I'm gonna fix that bastard. You'll see." He walked out, slamming the door.

"You better do some'in wit that boy, Red," said Mose. "He gonna kill somebody or git kilt hisself."

"He's just talking. He's not gonna do anything."

Mose shook his head. "You be wrong, Red. They's too much hate in dat boy. He sho gonna do some'in stupid." When Mose left he knew he had to tell Rep about Brit's threats.

35

B rit's confrontation with Red about offering the farm job to Rep had stoked the flames of hatred already residing in his heart and fueled his desire to act. But the hatred hadn't completely blotted out his common sense. He had no intention of facing Rep in a fair fight. The hurt he'd felt from the other encounters was still fresh in his mind. He intended to hurt Rep, but he'd have to find another way.

It made him mad that his daddy had invited Rep and his white-trash bitch to eat in the big house, and Lila had been there too. That house was to be his, he'd grown up there.

He knew where the cabin on Sallie White was, he'd been past there several times. He also knew Rep fished in the morning and went to the landing later in the morning and sometimes was there for several hours. That afternoon he left the farm, went over the hill behind the big house through the woods to Back Slough and hid in the bushes across from the cabin.

About mid-afternoon Rep returned from the landing and as he tied up, Bess came running from the cabin completely naked. She ran past him across the pier and jumped in the water. Rep laughed and said something to her, then took off his clothes and jumped in with her. They swam around, laughing and playing for several minutes, then swam to the pier, climbed out and went to the cabin.

Brit watched until near dark but didn't see them again and left as the sky darkened. He followed this schedule for the next three days and Rep's return each day was about the same time. He had a good idea how long he'd have once Rep left for the landing in the morning.

～

Star Hobb had never used her real name in Phenix City, she was known as Dee Pretty on stage. She was certain nobody in Phenix City or Columbus could connect her with River Bluff and the Hobb family. The soldier that she left town with years before and had known her as Star Hobb had shipped out long ago.

She was still young, only twenty-four, although she'd had about fifty years of experience. The body, which enabled her to do what she did in her act, was still exceptional. When she chose to, she'd wash off the makeup, dye her hair a soft brunette color and dress as a young professional woman. Even people who knew her would never recognize her. That allowed her to move in any circle she chose.

After her trip to River Bluff and her foolish attempt to take charge of Harold's burial turned out to be a disaster, she returned to Columbus. Her conversation with Mr. Gill in his office and his criticisms of the way she looked and her employment in Phenix City had stung her. His words to her, "Miss Star, I don't know you and based on what I see, I wouldn't want to," coming from a man who everybody admired, had raised questions in her mind. He'd accused her of having no shame. He was right; she'd had none in years.

She'd kept all the newspapers with articles about the killing of Boot and Harold. She'd never liked either one when she was at home and hadn't thought about them in years, but the circumstances of their deaths had her attention and bothered her. As she reviewed the newspaper articles, the Hogan name was always mentioned. Everything that had happened to Boot and Harold was due to the actions of one of the Hogans, either Red or Brit. She decided that the

Hogans should shoulder the responsibility for her brother's deaths. She couldn't explain her feelings about this any more than she could explain her foolish attempt to take over Harold's burial.

Whether her thinking was right or wrong wasn't considered. Morality hadn't played a part in her decisions in years. With her or her acquaintances, there was no moral true north. She decided she would deal with the Hogans and then leave her life in Phenix City. Neither decision had anything to do with her talk with Mr.Gill.

One of the men that ran the rackets in Phenix City was named Marvin Hale. He was older, near fifty and was frequently one of Star's escorts. He was proud to be seen with the young beauty and catered to her wishes. She had used him for years while he thought he was using her. One night they were in bed and she broached the subject, "Do you know a man in Shoal County named Red Hogan?"

"Yeah, I know Red. We buy whiskey from him. He's one mean bastard."

That was what she wanted to hear. "I want you to do me a favor," she said as she rolled against him and kissed him. Marvin was ready to do anything she wanted.

She explained that Red Hogan had hurt a friend of hers and she wanted to get even with him. It wouldn't be anything bad, but she wanted to embarrass him. One of the men at the club had said Shoal Creek was having a party on Saturday night and she wanted him to take her there. He didn't have to do anything else, just let her out and wait for her. She promised she would do something special for him when they got back to her apartment. Marvin was putty in her hands and was happy to agree to anything she wanted.

When Marvin came to her house to pick her up, he hardly recognized her when she walked out. "Damn Dee, you look like you're going to Sunday School in that outfit."

She got in the car and slid up against him. "You just forget everything about what happens tonight when we get back and I'll make you very happy from now on."

Marvin smiled. "I done forgot everything about tonight except what you promised."

They drove up the Georgia side of the Chattahoochee and arrived at Shoal Creek. The party was in full swing. Star told Marvin to let her out away from the party so he wouldn't be seen with her. Then he was to watch for her and if she went to the big house with somebody, he was to have the car ready when she came out and they would leave immediately. He had no idea what she was planning and didn't care. Most everything he was involved in was illegal, so he wasn't concerned about legality. His only concern was remaining connected with Dee.

She'd never been to Shoal Creek before, but it only took a few minutes to get her bearings. The barn was the center of all activity. The bars supplied free whiskey and the band played nonstop loud music. She moved around quietly, not speaking to anyone. She didn't want to be noticed as she looked for Red Hogan. She stayed away from the barn where the largest crowd was gathered.

He wasn't hard to find. He was wearing a large white hat and smoking a big cigar, so he was easy to spot in the middle of a group outside the barn. She moved near the group, staying out of the light, not wanting to be conspicuous. It wasn't long before his wandering eye spotted her. Although her outfit was conservative, her physical attributes were obvious and difficult to hide. When he looked her way, she boldly met his look and moved more into the shadows. He said something to the group, pointed them toward the barn and walked toward her. She met his gaze all the way. "I don't believe I've seen you here before," he said as he came beside her."

"Oh," she said, seeming to be startled by his attention. "This is my first time here. I came with Uncle Marvin."

Very smoothly he took her arm. "I'm Red Hogan, I own Shoal Creek. Let me show you around."

"Oh my," she cooed, "I just love successful men. Uncle Marvin told me about you. He also told me I should be careful around you, because you have a reputation." She smiled as she said this and rubbed against him.

Red smiled. "And are you being careful?"

"I'm always careful till I see something I like and then I do whatever I want to," she said as she brushed against him. "And I certainly like what I see here."

Emboldened, he put his hand on her waist and started leading her toward the barn.

"Is that your big house on the hill?" she asked, still pressing against him. "I just love houses like that."

"Maybe I can show it to you sometime."

"That would be so good," she said, sliding her hand down his back. "If it wasn't too much trouble maybe we could peep at it now. But maybe you're too busy."

He took the bait. "We could do that, other things can wait," he said, as she gently pushed him away from the barn and toward the road. They left the barn and as they walked up the hill toward the house, he had his arm around her and his hands all over her. She didn't seem to mind at all, in fact encouraged him. There was no doubt in his mind they were headed straight to the bedroom and she did nothing to change his mind.

They entered the house and he took her hand as they walked up the stairs. To him they were past the talking stage, he would enjoy this dalliance quickly and get back to the party. He kissed her and led her into his bedroom. She quickly shed her dress and started helping him unbutton his shirt. She told him she needed to make a trip to the ladies' room, and he could undress and wait for her in the bed. He hurriedly did as she asked.

She came out of the bathroom; his eyes were on her. She walked to the bed, set her bag on the floor and leaned over, kissing him as she slipped her hand under the pillow. Then she stood up and took off her remaining clothes very slowly. She'd done this act a thousand times in the club in Phenix City. He was propped up on an elbow watching her the entire time. She lay down beside him and rolled over against him. She allowed his hands to roam over her body as he got comfortable. Then he reached to pull her against him, and she backed away, sliding her hand back under the pillow. She put her hand on his chest and held him away. His look questioned her change in attitude and then he felt the prick on the side of his neck.

"Don't move," she whispered, "this knife is razor sharp."

She could see the surprise in his eyes.

"What the hell are you doing? "he said, still not sure what was happening.

"Do you remember Boot and Harold Hobb?"

His was confused. He hadn't expected a question. But then his eyes changed, and she knew he remembered the names.

"You killed them both."

He shook his head. "I didn't kill them. Why are you doing this?"

"I'm their sister, Star Hobb."

His eyes now showed the panic he felt. "What do you want? I can pay you," he muttered.

She shook her head. "I don't want your money." She moved the knife an inch, slicing through his skin and watching his eyes as the pain hit him. "I wanted to make sure you knew what you did."

"Wait," he said, "we can straighten this out."

She shook her head. "No more talking. I just wanted you to know why you died," she said as the knife slid into his neck and severed his jugular vein. She jumped back as blood spurted all over the white sheets.

She got out of bed, dressed and looked at him lying in a pool of blood. She felt no remorse, no satisfaction. She had done what she came to do. She hurried downstairs and out the front door. Marvin was waiting in the car at the road as she came out. She opened the car door, jumped in and said, "Drive." They left Shoal Creek, and nobody even realized they'd been there.

The next day Dee Pretty came to the club with bleached hair, too much makeup and a dress cut down to her navel.

Mose came to the barn the next morning at daylight. He was surprised Red wasn't already there, but then they'd had the party the night before and he probably was sleeping late. Mose had gone to bed early and missed the party. Red always enjoyed these outings, but Mose never liked them. Too many times they'd ended up causing problems afterward that took time to clean up.

After an hour and still no sign of Red, he decided to go to the kitchen. He left the barn and was stepping on the road when Red's housekeeper, Rosie, came out the front door of the big house screaming. At first he couldn't understand what she was saying, but then he heard it clearly. "Lordy, Mr. Red, he be dead," she screamed over and over.

Mose rushed toward the house and the hysterical Rosie who was still screaming. "Hush up, girl," Mose yelled as he came near her. "Where he be?"

"He be in his bed," she said as she fell crying to her knees.

Mose went through the front door and bounded up the stairs. He rushed in the bedroom and immediately saw Rosie was correct – Red was dead. The bed was covered in blood and a knife was lying on the bed beside him. He stood by the bed shaking his head. "Somebody done kilt him," he thought. "What we gonna do now?" He looked around the room but saw no sign that anyone else had been there. He hurried downstairs and out the door. By this time a crowd had gathered outside.

Mose went to the barn and called the sheriff. When he arrived he took charge of the murder scene. It was obvious Red had been murdered, they had the murder weapon, but nothing else. A search of the room turned up nothing.

They began interviewing those people on the farm who'd been at the party, but it would take days to find and question all the outsiders that had attended. Nobody they interviewed had seen anything of interest. One man said he had been talking to Red with some other people outside the barn and later he thought he saw him talking to a young woman with dark hair. They were standing in the shadows and he wasn't sure about her. After that one time, he never saw Red or her again. This was all they had to go on.

Some of the people mentioned that Red was usually the last person to leave the party but last night it seemed he left early. After the one group had talked to him outside the barn, nobody saw him again.

None of the servants had been at the house, all were working at the party. So the house had been empty, except for Red and whoever killed him.

Rep came up with dressed fish later that morning and found a hysterical Hattie Mae at the kitchen. It took a minute for him to understand Red had been murdered. He was stunned and went to find Mose, who was in shock by what had happened. He and Red weren't only brothers, they had spent every day of most of their life together.

Someone told the sheriff about the woman that Red had recently kicked out of his house, thinking she may have had a reason to kill him, but she'd been checked out and was clear. She'd been shacked up that night with the man who'd gotten her kicked out.

Someone had mentioned Jack Hobb as a possible suspect, since the Hobb family had been involved earlier but the Sheriff called River Bluff and Jack was home and his alibi was good. He couldn't have gotten that close to Red to cut his throat anyway. That eliminated the Hobbs as suspects.

After talking to all the people from the party, the Sherriff had nothing more to go on. He was certain a woman had killed Red, but nobody knew any woman who may have had a reason to kill him. He felt sure Red left the party with a woman but who was she? He had no idea. Under the circumstances he doubted he'd ever find her.

Rep left the landing and went to the cabin. There was nothing he could do at the farm. He told Bess what had happened. She was upset since Red had been so nice to her at the dinner. She also felt sad for Lila losing her daddy. They had been discussing Red's offer for them to move to a house on the farm, but his death put everything on hold. Until things got sorted out, they'd continue to do as they'd done, and wait. He told Bess he'd go back to the farm that afternoon to help Mose with whatever was needed. Lila and her mother were expected in later and there would be much to do. Bess made him promise he'd come back and get her if Lila needed her. Rep told her he would.

~

When Brit arrived at the big house, he was raising hell. The sheriff and Mose had been dealing with the situation the best they could, and he jumped right in, told everybody he was the last Hogan male alive and he was in charge. The Sheriff told him this was a murder investigation and he wasn't in charge of anything. Mose told him Miss Sara and Lila were on their way from Atlanta and he needed to shut his mouth until they arrived.

Brit didn't care that his daddy was dead. When Red had told him that he wasn't in line for any management position at Shoal Creek and Lila would be in charge in the future, he lost all regard for him. That, coupled with Red saying he'd have to work for Rep, cemented his disregard for his daddy. Regardless of what anyone said, he was the last Hogan man, and Shoal Creek was going to be his. He didn't care what he had to do to get it.

Lila and Miss Sara came in that afternoon. Miss Sara told the sheriff to do whatever was necessary about the investigation, he had free rein on Shoal Creek. If anyone gave him trouble, he was to talk to Mose, who was in charge until Lila returned after the funeral. She told Brit they were taking her husband's body to Atlanta for burial and he was going with them. As far as she was concerned, the last several weeks had been pure hell, with the killings and shootings. When she left this time, she never intended to return to Shoal Creek.

Rep was in the barn with Mose when Lila came in. She immediately went to Mose and hugged him. They talked for a few minutes and then she came to Rep. As always, she put her hands on his shoulders and kissed him on the cheek. They stood for several seconds and looked into each other's eyes. They both knew that the love they'd had for each other would never go away. Neither had any intention of pushing it any further right now but it would always be there.

They talked about the plans to take Red's body to Atlanta for burial in the family plot and Miss Sara's determination never to return to Shoal Creek. "I'm sure mother means it," said Lila, "These last months have been hard on her and now with daddy's death, there's no reason for her to be here. She never really liked it here and daddy's reputation for running around with other women finally got to be more than she could stand."

She walked over and put her arm around Mose. "I knew all these years you were daddy's brother and I knew how close you were. Daddy had his faults and I knew you disagreed with much he did, but you stayed with him, looked after him as an older brother the best you could. I appreciated that. All the trouble we've had recently came from selling whiskey. You've been against that and I agree. We should shut it down immediately."

Mose nodded. "That be the best to do."

"When you deal in alcohol you invite unsavory people in. They bring trouble with them. That's what we did and we're paying for it. Daddy was warned about the danger, but he ignored it and now he's dead."

She looked at Rep. "Daddy offered you the job of looking after the farm. He knew you had no experience there, but he knew you were a good man and could do it. That offer still stands and with it you can move in a house here on the farm. That would be nicer than the cabin but that is up to you."

"Bess and I are talkin' about that and I'll let you know fo' long." Rep replied. "She wanted you to know she be sorry about Red. He was nice to her at the supper the other night."

Lila smiled. "He was nice the other night. That was somewhat out of character for him and I was surprised."

Mose spoke up. "Brit is gonna be a sho'nuff problem now. He thank he gonna be in charge. It be best he stay in Atlanta."

Lila shook her head. "Mama don't want him in Atlanta. All he does is cause trouble and she's tired of trouble. He has to stay here."

"He be full of hate. He gonna hurt somebody or git hurt."

Lila couldn't help. "I'm sorry. Ya'll watch him the best you can."

Later that afternoon Lila, Miss Sara and Brit left for Atlanta. Lila promised to return in several days and they'd sit down and get everything ironed out. There were many questions to be answered.

R ed Hogan's death was big news and the reporters descended on Shoal Creek but were frustrated because they couldn't get in and couldn't talk to anyone on the farm. They talked to the sheriff and coroner but that was all they got and there were many unanswered questions. The identity of the young woman with dark hair who somebody said Red Hogan was seen talking to before his death gained some interest but with so little to go on, it went nowhere.

Star read the papers every day and was pleased.

Marvin Hale also read the papers and he knew that Dee killed Red Hogan that night. He broke out in a sweat thinking of the times he'd been in bed with her under the same conditions. He decided he'd stay away from Dee in the future.

One reporter showed up in River Bluff and tried to get something out of the boat landing crowd, but they knew nothing. They agreed Red Hogan's death was justified; they still blamed him for killing Boot and Harold Hobb. They had no idea who might have killed him, but they were certain it wasn't anyone from River Bluff.

W hen Rolley heard about Red Hogan being murdered, he wondered what had happened to the young man with the long brown hair who had come to buy women's clothes. He'd liked him. He thought about visiting him on Back Slough but didn't have the courage.

May was in his thoughts all the time. They spent as much time together as possible. Movie nights were the best time when they could get way off to the side in the dark. They had no interest in the movies but were wrapped up in each other. They were at the heavy-petting stage of kissing and touching that left little else to the imagination. They needed complete privacy to go to the next step. They hadn't talked about it, but they both knew it was coming.

May found Rolley at school the next day. "We need to talk," she said. Then she explained to him that she had special feelings for him, but she wasn't comfortable with what they'd been doing. She'd talked to Miss Tinney about her feelings and what they'd done, and Miss Tinney said those feelings were normal, but needed to be kept under control. May didn't tell Miss Tinney about her sister Star, but she knew what Star had done and how people talked about her, calling her a slut and a whore. She didn't want to end up like Star.

"I've been going to church with Miss Tinney and I'm a Christian and what we're doing ain't right unless we're married," May said. "I care for you and want to be with you but not like we've been. What happens now is up to you," she said as she walked away.

Rolley didn't see May for the next two days. He found her after school. "What you said is right, I know that too. I want to be with you." He smiled. "You will kiss me sometimes, won't you?"

She stared at him for a moment, then turned up her nose. "Maybe," she said, as she walked away.

∽

When Brit returned from his daddy's funeral, he had decided on a plan. He would quit complaining and arguing about the farm and his job and go along with whatever he was told to do. He wouldn't cause trouble of any kind. Then, after giving everybody time to stop worrying about him, he would act. He wasn't in a hurry, he had plenty of time.

∽

J im Hawke had never thought of himself as a smart man, but he understood more than most about human nature. He wasn't surprised when he heard Red Hogan had been murdered. Any man in his business made enemies. His enemies were known and ought to provide a list of possible suspects, but that didn't seem to be the case here. His potential enemies were men and not one woman's name had come up. The men that were checked all had alibis. But somebody wanted him dead and usually people wanted somebody dead for a reason. Who had a reason? Law enforcement was baffled.

Jim chuckled as he pondered all this. Star Hobb had killed Red Hogan for killing her two brothers; she wanted revenge and she got it. The law didn't know she was a Hobb and couldn't tie her to River Bluff. He had no way to prove what he thought, and he had no intention of getting involved, but he knew he was right, He didn't condone murder, but there were some people in the world who ran roughshod over folks, till one day somebody said they'd had enough.

36

Three weeks had passed since Red's death. The funeral and burial were held in Atlanta and Red's will was being probated. There wasn't any question about the will, he had left everything to Miss Sara. She, once the will was probated, had told everyone she was turning Shoal Creek over to Lila, to do with as she wanted. She made it clear she never intended to set foot in Shoal County again.

Lila returned from Atlanta and met with Mose at the barn. He told her the stills along the creek bank had been shut down and all whiskey in storage had been shipped out. For all practical purposes, Shoal Creek was out of the whiskey business. The people that had been involved in that business had been given other jobs on the farm. They were discussing other topics when Brit came in unexpectedly. He had been back on the farm for several days and had gone to the south forty to work upon arrival. Surprisingly, Mose had heard nothing out of him since he returned and was surprised to see him.

"You done shut down all the stills?" he asked, directing the question to Lila.

"Yes," she answered. "All the problems we've had during the past weeks were directly or indirectly caused by the whiskey business." She looked at him. "You were shot, Daddy was shot, Joe was killed and then Daddy was killed. Also, those two Hobb boys from Alabama were killed. That's a terrible price to pay so a bunch of people can get drunk."

Brit nodded. "That's all true but the whiskey business brought in a lot of money. It's gonna be tough to run the farm without it."

Lila was surprised by his tone, normally he would be cursing and raising hell if he disagreed about something. "We've talked about that and feel everything will be fine if we look after our business properly. We're also talking about expanding the cattle business. We have plenty of land to expand."

Brit shrugged. "Maybe you're right. Let me know if there's anything I can do to help." He turned and went out the door.

Lila cut her eyes at Mose, a question on her face.

"That bout beat all," he said. "I done heard that boy cuss his daddy mighty bad and now he be sweet."

"You don't trust him, do you Mose?"

"I sho don't, Miss Lila. I dun seed the devil in 'im. Devil don't turn loose that quick."

"I'm afraid you're right, Mose. We'll both keep an eye on him."

`The next morning Brit was in the bushes on Back Slough across from the cabin. He watched Rep get in the boat and go downstream to fish his hooks and then return. Bess came out of the cabin and helped him dress the fish. Brit knew he could kill them both where they were if he had his rifle, but this wasn't the right time. Then Rep got back in the boat and went toward the landing. The sun was midway toward the trees on Big Island when he returned later in the afternoon. Brit went back to the farm, planning to watch the next two or three days to make sure the schedule remained the same.

The next morning Mose was waiting for Rep at the landing. "Lila want you to come see her at the barn. Miss Sara done give her all the farm and she be in charge now."

"You done shut down the stills?"

Mose nodded. "They be done."

"That's good," said Rep as they walked up the hill toward the kitchen. He was apprehensive as they neared the barn, being around Lila always affected him that way. Even though he loved Bess and she meant everything to him, Lila was very special. Regardless of his best intentions, being around her made him uncomfortable. He knew she knew that and enjoyed seeing him squirm.

She was sitting behind the desk when he walked in. She immediately got up, came around the desk, put her hands on his shoulders and kissed him on the cheek. Her perfume enveloped and surrounded him as it always did. She smiled, her eyes twinkling with mischief. "Is Bess treating you good?"

"Better than anybody ever has," he said, giving it back to her.

She leaned over, her body against him, and whispered, "I don't believe that." She laughed as she walked around the desk and sat down.

Mose had watched all this encounter. He looked down at the floor and shook his head. "Lordy," he thought, "what's gonna happen to this po' boy?"

They talked about various subjects concerning the farm for several minutes, then Lila looked at Rep. "I understand you've been to River Bluff several times and know some of the people."

"Can't say I know many folks, but I met a young boy and a lady at the store."

"When you were there you said there were several men hanging around the landing.

"Yes, they was."

"We want to have peace with those people and stop any trouble. Would you go over there and tell the men at the landing we don't sell whiskey anymore and we won't have any more parties."

Rep was surprised. "You want me to go?"

"Yes, you've had dealings with them before. It would be good to go tomorrow."

Rep had doubts and looked at Mose for guidance.

Mose nodded that he agreed.

Finally, although he had doubts about going into town, Rep said he would go.

When he got to the cabin that evening, he told Bess about going to River Bluff and asked her to go with him. She had doubts about going. The thought of going into the town across the river made her nervous. He told her about the store where he bought her clothes with a movie theatre nearby and streets lined with white houses. She'd never seen anything like that. It sounded mystical and scary but if he wanted her to go, she would.

~

S chool was out and when he wasn't working, Rolley was on the river. He was cleaning out his boat about mid-morning when he saw a boat come out of Shoal Creek and head toward the landing. As it neared, he recognized the young man with long brown hair who he'd met before. He walked up the bank and waited. There was a young woman sitting in the front of the boat. When the man saw Rolley, he waved as he ran the boat up on the shore right at his feet, jumped out and extended his hand.

"I'm Rep," he said, "I met you before."

"I'm Rolley, I remember you. You went to the store and bought clothes."

Rep took Bess' hand and helped her out of the boat. "This is my wife, Bess," he said.

Rolley was surprised when he said she was his wife. She didn't look to be as old as he was but she sure was pretty. "Glad to meet you, Bess," he said.

There were several men up and down the riverbank watching them. He explained to Rolley what his mission was and that he wanted to talk to the men and tell them Shoal Creek was out of the whiskey business. Rolley walked with him over to the men and Rep talked to them for a few minutes. He explained it wasn't a discussion, the stills were already shut down and out of business. Since Red Hogan was dead, the new owner didn't want that business operating.

He answered questions from a few of the men and several were concerned about losing their source for whiskey, but overall, the reception was good.

When they finished talking, Rep told Rolley he wanted to take Bess into town and let her see everything. Rolley volunteered to be their guide and walked with them up the hill. Bess was amazed at the streets lined with white houses that all looked alike. The cotton mill by the river at the bottom of the hill was huge to her, she'd never seen a four-story building. Rolley told her they brought in cotton and made towels and all the people in the town worked in the mill. She couldn't imagine how that was possible.

They went to the general store and met Mrs. Williams, who showed Bess all around. She had never been inside a store and was amazed at all the things to buy. She walked around wide-eyed. Rep told her they could come back anytime she wanted and buy whatever she wanted. He bought a sack of chocolate candy and put it in his pocket for later.

Rolley watched them walk around in amazement. He didn't understand there were people across the river who'd never seen the things he took for granted.

When they walked out of the store, Rolley saw Jim Hawke sitting on his regular perch on the bench in front of the gym. He told Rep that Jim was the constable for the town, and he should tell him about the whiskey sales being stopped. They walked across the street, Rolley introduced Rep to Jim and Rep told him about the whiskey. Jim was pleased with the news and he said it would make his job much easier.

When they got back to the landing Rep and Bess thanked Rolley for his help and invited him to come to their cabin on Back Slough and visit them. "Have you ever heard of a flathead catfish," Rep asked Rolley.

Rolley shook his head.

Rep then explained to him how to catch flatheads with live bait on a set hook and about the places to look for where flatheads fed. When he told him that he was catching them weighing twenty or more pounds, Rolley couldn't believe it. He told Rolley this information was just for him and not for him to tell everybody. Rolley agreed and could hardly wait to try it.

When Rep and Bess got back to the cabin, she was so excited about all she had seen. "I wanta go back and do one thang," she said.

"Whatever you want to do," Rep replied.

"I would sho like to go to a picture show. I ain't never seen one."

"Me neither," replied Rep.

37

M rs. McCall was at her receptionist desk at the mill office when the door opened, and a tall young woman, brunette, well-dressed and strikingly beautiful, walked in. Mrs. Mc Call didn't recognize her, but she quickly got to her feet. Although she hadn't been told someone special was coming today, undoubtedly this young lady was somebody special. She prided herself on being a good judge of people. "Yes mam, can I help you?" she asked.

"Thank you," said the young woman, "I'd like to see Mr. Gill."

"Yes ma'm," she said, "and may I ask who's calling?"

The young lady smiled and leaned over the desk. "You know me, Mrs. McCall, I'm Star Hobb. I used to park with your son, Mike, in the back seat of his car down on the river. You remember that, don't you? He said you fussed at him for being seen with me. How is he? I've often thought about him, we had some good times."

Startled, all the color drained from Mrs. McCall's face as she fell back. "I'm sorry, Star. I didn't recognize you. You certainly look very nice." She jumped up, opened the door and led Star through the work area to Mr. Gill's office, not even looking at the other women sitting at their desks. "Mr. Gill," she said, "Star Hobb to see you." Then she fled back to her cubicle.

Mr. Gill stood up. "Happy to see you again, Miss Star." He smiled and offered his hand. "Quite a transformation has been made in your appearance, I'd say."

Star smiled as she shook his hand. "First, let me apologize for my actions during my last visit. I was out of line and you reminded me of how decent folks conduct themselves. The people I normally run with have no concept of decency and I'm afraid I'd gotten to be just like them."

He shook his head. "No apologies needed. I understood your situation. You'd just lost two brothers and those were trying times for everybody. What can I do for you today?"

"I wanted to tell you I've left Phenix City and the line of work you found so despicable. When I talked to you before and you told me you didn't know me and didn't really care to know me, that hit a nerve in me that had been dead for a long time. It'd been years since I cared what any person thought about me and how they regarded me. You're an honest man and I've known very few of those in my life and I realized I did care what you thought. I wanted you to know that."

"Maybe I was too blunt," replied Mr. Gill.

Star laughed. "I'm a hard woman, Mr. Gill and not a good person. It takes bluntness to reach me. A person must be hard to survive where I've been and what I've done. Don't get the wrong idea about me. The person who came to your office before and acted like an ass, is the same person before you now, just cleaned up a bit. Although I may do better in the future, I have no plans to apply for sainthood."

Mr. Gill smiled. "We can always hope, Miss Star."

Star shook her head. "You have no idea who and what you're dealing with here, Mr. Gill, but I appreciate your good thoughts.

Star picked up her purse. "I came back to see you today because I want to ask you a favor, if you'd be so kind."

"I will if I can."

"I have money, although you may rightly question how I earned it. I wouldn't try to justify the things I've done to get it. I'm about to go leave the area and there are things I want to do before I go. I know you have little respect for my parents, and they deserve no respect for the way they've lived. The deaths of Boot and Harold attest to that. Their deaths was a terrible price to pay for all the years of our family drinking and fighting. You said my parents can keep their jobs and house and I know that's out of the goodness of your heart, and I appreciate that. You said that was the Christian thing to do. I haven't been involved in Christian circles in some years, but your example is what Christians ought to do."

"So, what is it you want me to do?"

"When I get settled where I'm going, I'll send you my address and telephone number. If anything happens that I should know about with my folks, I ask you to let me know. I'd like to give you some money to hold in case my folks get in trouble. I'll not give them any, they'd squander it.

"You'll be the only person in town who knows where I am. I've dealt with some bad, dangerous people in my time and I'm trying to get away from all that. Some don't want me to leave and I'd rather they didn't find me. I'll tell you, if some found me, my life would be in danger."

Mr. Gill nodded. "I can do that. What else?"

"My sister, May, is a good girl and could have a good future. I want to help her. I understand she moved away from my parents and is living with Miss Tinney at the dormitory. That's good. May has two more years in high school and wants to go to college and be a teacher. She'd never be able to do that as her life is now, she wouldn't have the money. I've put money for her college in savings at the bank. I'll tell her about the money, but she can't touch it until she finishes high school. I'll give the bank book to you and you can give it to her when it's time. I realize this is an imposition on you, but I have nobody else to trust." She took the bank book out of her purse and handed it to him.

"I'll be glad to do this," he said as he took the book. "All this is very thoughtful of you."

Star shook her head. "I've done some bad things in my life Mr. Gill, and I can never erase them or change them. I just have to live with them. At first, when I was young, I didn't know any better and later when I was older and did know better, I didn't care. But now I do know better and I do care."

"None of us are perfect, Miss Star. We just do the best we can."

"Thank you for your kindness, Mr. Gill," Star said, as she walked out the door. She smiled at the ladies in the work area and saw Mrs. McCall wasn't sitting at her desk, so she didn't get a chance to ask about her son, Mike.

She left the mill and went to the dormitory. When she knocked, May opened the door and Star could tell she didn't recognize her. That wasn't unexpected, when she'd left home May had only been six years old, so she understood her not knowing her. "May, I'm your sister, Star."

May stood there for several seconds, her mind trying to grasp what she'd heard. "You're Star?"

"Yes. I am," she said and held out her arms. May rushed out and hugged her.

Miss Tinney came out, was introduced and they sat for hours talking. Star brought them up to date about the savings account and told May if she had any questions or problems to go see Mr. Gill. She gave Alva an envelope filled with money to cover May's expenses until she finished high school and thanked her for looking after her so well. She told May she was going to the general store and put money in an account for her. They walked from the dormitory to the store holding hands. Jim Hawkes was sitting on his bench and watched them enter the store.

Mrs. Williams had always been nice to Star as a little girl. She realized what she was facing with her no-account family and how she was treated by the community. She remembered her coming in, standing in front of the candy counter staring at all the goodies without any money. Many days Mrs. Williams would give her a sucker or a bag of candy. Star remembered this kindness and thanked her for it, then paid for May's account. She cautioned her to spend it wisely.

When they walked out of the store, Star saw Jim Hawke sitting on the bench across the street. She remembered the nights he'd come to their house and broke up drunken fights between her parents and the boys. She remembered the nights he'd protected her by letting her stay in his car until peace was restored, sometimes she'd slept there all night. She held May's hand as they walked across the street to where he sat. "I'm Star Hobb, Mr. Hawke."

He smiled. "I know who you are, Star. You've grown up to be a fine-looking woman."

"Thank you. I wanted to thank you for your kindness years ago when I was a little girl. My family gave you a lot of trouble and I've never forgotten you for it."

He laughed. "That be true. Ya'll have had more than your share of sadness lately."

"Yes, we have." She started to leave but turned back. "I'm moving away and will be gone for a while. I'd appreciate it if you'd look in on my folks now and then. Also, May will be here, and she might need a friend."

"I'll do that. Be glad to."

Then something in his eyes caught her attention. She knew he had something else on his mind, but she didn't know what. He motioned for her to come closer. "Might be good you be leaving, Star," he said. "That Red Hogan getting killed has settled down now with no idea who killed him as far as I know. That talk early on about a dark-haired young woman what might be involved seems about all they got to go on. Everybody has lost interest now, but one of these days one of them smart folks across the river might git to studying on that again and recollect that all the Hobb children ain't dead. That might stir up questions again."

Star backed away and smiled. "You be one of them smart people?"

He shook his head. "Not me, all the folks I care about live on this side of the river and I don't judge nobody. I don't know nothing, cept I remember a little girl that grew up rough. If anybody asks me, May is the only Hobb left."

Star reached over and kissed him on the cheek. "Mr. Gill will know how to get in touch with me. If anything gets stirred up and smart people start nosing around, you let me know. Also, there are people from Phenix City who will be looking for me. They will probably come up here asking around."

"I'll take care of everything for you. You take care of yourself, little girl."

On the way back to the dormitory May held tightly to her hand. "What was Mr. Jim talking about?"

"He was talking about friends and old times and what it means to grow up in River Bluff." They walked a bit further. "May, if you ever have a problem, you go talk to Mr. Hawke. You can trust him."

May nodded that she understood. "Why do you have to leave, Star? I wish you would stay."

"I would like to stay but it's best I leave, May. I'll check on you sometimes. I want you to finish school and go to college and be a teacher if that's what you want to do. I wish I'd done that."

"I thank you for doing that, making it so I can go to college." They were both quiet as they walked. "I have a friend that I like," said May.

"Boy or girl?" The way she'd said it caught Star's attention. Her tone indicated it was important.

"It's a boy," May replied and then she told Star about Rolley Hill. How they'd met on the river, how he'd been nice to her when nobody else would and then their dating and the emotions she felt. Finally, she told her what Miss Tinney had said and her last conversation with Rolley.

"Miss Tinney was right," Star said, "These emotions are normal, but they need to be controlled. Sex can have serious consequences that can ruin your life. You don't want that. Decisions you make when you're young can stay with you the rest of your life. I made some bad choices when I was your age and I don't want you to make the same mistake." They walked down the steps to the dormitory. "You like this boy a lot?"

"I do."

"The Hill family are good people. You say he agreed to using good sense and do right when you're together?"

May nodded.

"Then it should be alright." Star thought it strange she was giving this advice to May when she'd never hesitated to climb in bed with any man if it was to her advantage. And, if she was honest, she'd probably do the same in the future although that wasn't her intention at present. Right now, she was trying to help her family, which was out of character for her. She had to admit, after all the years of being a tramp, to say the least, these last few days had felt good. She had no second thoughts about killing Red Hogan. He was a bad person. However, she knew the law wouldn't look at it that way. Also, the people in Phenix City wouldn't care that she was trying to change her ways. All they'd be interested in was getting their money back.

Going forward she would play the cards dealt to her the best she could. At this time the cards were being shuffled and the first one hadn't been dealt. She thought about what Jim Hawke had said. If he could figure out who killed Red Hogan, then other people could too. The people in Phenix City weren't aware she'd left and when they found out, they would be looking for her. It was time she left and went far away. She hugged May and left town.

38

Rep reported back to Lila and Mose after his visit to River Bluff. The reception had been for the most part positive. They thought that stopping whiskey sales should end the conflict with the River Bluff people since there would be no reason for them to come to Shoal Creek.

Rep told them about his trip into River Bluff and his thoughts about that. The nearest town to Shoal Creek on the Georgia side was several miles away while River Bluff was just across the river and had much more to offer. The town had general stores, a drugstore, a doctor and even a movie theatre. There were other towns upriver from River Bluff on the Alabama side that were easily available. It would seem there could be a market for the farm's products in these towns as there had been a market for whiskey, but without the accompanying problems.

Lila was surprised and impressed with Rep's analysis of the situation. Nothing in his background had taught him basic supply and demand economics, but he had diagnosed their situation well. She agreed with what he said.

Rep wanted Mose in the room when he was with Lila. He never wanted to be alone with her. While he was happy with Bess, it'd only been a few weeks since he'd been with Lila at the cabin and that memory refused to leave his mind. Those two days were etched in his mind like in granite. He'd not been able to get it purged, although he'd tried. Every time he saw her, heard her voice or smelled her perfume everything that had happened between them was in his mind. It was driving him crazy.

Mose watched Rep when he was around Lila and knew the pain and confusion he was dealing with. They were walking away from the barn after the meeting when he brought up the subject. "You stay around Lila it ain't never gonna git no better."

Rep shook his head. "She ain't supposed to be here all the time, Mose. She was supposed to be in Atlanta and not be around me."

"It ain't no easier on her, I see that too."

"I'm gonna have to tell her I can't be involved like this. I need to stay on the river with Bess and fish."

Mose nodded. "I thank that be best."

Brit had been completely shut out of any involvement in the farm's operation. He had complained to Lila, but she told him he was partially responsible for all the trouble they'd been through, including Red's death and the best thing for him to do would be to go back to Atlanta and never come back. He had seen Rep at the barn meeting with her and Mose and his hatred for him was white-hot. Her saying he should go to Atlanta set him into a tirade about her relationship with Rep, calling her a white-trash whore. She slapped him hard across his face and if Mose hadn't been in the room, undoubtedly, he would have hurt her. He threatened them both, told them they'd be sorry for the way they'd done him and then left the barn.

The next morning, he was hidden in the bushes on Back Slough in front of the cabin. He watched Rep come to the boat and go downriver to fish the trotlines and limb hooks as he normally did. When Rep came back; Bess came to the pier and they dressed the fish. He loaded the boat, kissed Bess and headed upriver. Bess watched him until he was out of sight and then ran back in the cabin.

Brit waited a few minutes to make sure she was settled in the cabin. He sat his rifle aside and took off his clothes, keeping on his belt with his hunting knife and scabbard. He eased into the water and started across the slough, dogpaddling to avoid making any noise. It didn't take long to reach the pier. He grabbed the ladder and started climbing up.

There were several chickens in a tree on the bank alongside the pier and when he came out of the water and started running across the pier, they were startled and flew across the yard, cackling loudly as they went.

Bess was in the house washing dishes and when she heard the chickens in panic, she thought something was after them. She ran to the door and as she opened it, she saw a half-naked red-headed man running toward the cabin with a large knife in his hand. She screamed and slammed the door, put down the wooden block to lock the door and ran toward the bed.

Brit ran into the door at full speed and burst it open, splintering the frame. He saw Bess running across the cabin and caught her by the dress sleeve, jerked her around and threw her across the room against the wall. Stunned, she fell to the floor and he was on top of her, tearing at her dress.

She somehow remembered what her mama said she was to do if a man ever tried to have his way with her. Brit was directly above her and she jammed her hand in his face and her finger in his eye. He screamed and fell back, swinging the knife at her and cutting her shoulder. She managed to get out from under him and again started toward the bed.

He struggled up, yelling at her and grabbed the back of her dress, ripping part of it away. He grabbed her by the hair, pulled her toward him and as she turned, she kneed him in the stomach. As he fell back, he swung the knife and cut her in the side. The force of the blow knocked her back against the end of the bed. She put both hands on the foot of the bed and as he struggled to get up, she fell back and kicked him in the face with both feet, knocking him to the floor on his butt. With him down, she jumped across the bed, jerked the drawer open and got the pistol. She cocked the hammer as she turned and looked up, he was in the air above her. She pulled the trigger and then she felt the knife slice into her chest.

Lick, Matty and their crew were on Big Island below the cabin and heard Bess scream. Then other screams echoed across the water. Lick ran with Matty and the girls to the boat, cranked the motor and started up the slough. When they got to the pier, they saw the shattered door and knew something was wrong. Lick ran inside and didn't see Bess at first but then he saw she was on the bed with Brit on top of her. They both were covered in blood. He snatched Brit off her and saw the hole in his chest and knew he was dead. Then he heard Bess moan. "She's alive!" he yelled.

Matty quickly took over. She got a bucket and a cloth and washed the blood off Bess so they could see the damage. They knew she'd lost a great deal of blood and the wound in her chest was serious. They knew they had to get her to a doctor if she was going to have a chance to survive. They wrapped her in a blanket and Lick carried her to the boat. Matty held her as they started up the slough, headed for Shoal Creek.

When they got in sight of the landing, Rep was getting in his boat and Mose was standing on the bank. Lick started yelling as he pulled into the landing.

Rep saw Matty holding Bess wrapped in a blanket. He jumped in the boat. "What happened?" he asked, looking at Bess, unconscious and so pale.

Lick quickly told him what they'd found at the cabin, Bess hurt and Brit dead. "She's hurt bad," he said, "we gotta git her to a doctor."

Rep looked at Mose. "They got a doctor at River Bluff. We can get her there quicker." He turned to Lick. "I'll get in my boat, you follow me." He jumped into his boat, cranked up and started across the river with Lick following.

As they neared the Alabama bank Rep could see several men at the River bluff landing and two trucks parked nearby. He started yelling and several men came running to meet him as he ran the boat on shore. He quickly told them what had happened as he helped Lick get Bess out of the boat. One of the men brought a truck over near the boat. Rep climbed in the back with Bess. Lick, Matty and the girls got in with him.

"Be best if we take her to the mill to Miss Neal's office, she's the nurse," said the driver. He turned to the driver of the other truck. "Go get Doctor Floyd and tell him to come to Miss Neal's office." They all loaded in the trucks and headed toward the mill.

~

Mose stood at the landing and watched the two boats head toward River Bluff. "Lordy, Lordy," he thought, "how do I tell Lila all this." With slumped shoulders he headed at a trot up the hill toward the kitchen and then toward the barn.

Lila was sitting at the desk when Mose rushed in. His face showed something was wrong.

"Lord, Miss Lila," he said in a rush, "Brit done stabbed Bess and now she done killed him daid and ......

Lila held up her hand. "Mose, stop. Slow down. What are you saying?" She went around the desk and took him by the arm and looked in his face.

He took a deep breath and then told her what had happened. Brit had busted into the cabin and stabbed Bess. She had shot him, and he was dead, according to Lick. Rep had taken Bess, who was hurt bad, to River Bluff to a doctor.

Lila stepped back and sat on the desk, shaking her head, trying to take in what Mose had said. "This will kill Mama," she said, as tears began streaming down her face. "When does all this stop?" She looked at Mose. "Call the sheriff. Get them over here." Then Lila called Atlanta.

~

The truck raced up the road to Miss Neal's office. Rep carried Bess inside and Miss Neal, with Matty's help, started cleaning her up. Rep and the others waited outside in the waiting room. In a few minutes Dr. Floyd rushed in and went into the back room with Miss Neal. He came out later and asked who was with her. Rep came forward and the doctor explained Bess was in very serious condition. She was in shock, had lost a lot of blood and the knife wound in her chest was extremely serious. She needed to be moved to the hospital, but he was hesitant to move her that far in her weakened condition. He would stay with her throughout the night and if she made it till morning, he would then have her moved. He told Rep there was nothing else to do except pray.

Mr. Gill saw all the activity going on and came to the nurse's office. Dr. Floyd and Miss Neal explained the situation and he instructed them to do what was needed. Some of the men told him Rep was the man who'd found Harold Hobb and brought him to River Bluff.

Rep talked with Lick and Matty and they decided Matty would remain at the mill with Rep and Lick would take the girls home. If Bess survived the night, then they'd do whatever was necessary then. One of the men took Lick and the girls back to the landing and they went downriver. Rep thanked all the men for their help and kindness and then he and Matty settled down for a long night.

∽

The sheriff and the coroner came to Shoal Creek and headed down Back Slough to the cabin with Mose and Lila following in another boat. The scene at the cabin backed up Lick's description of what had happened. The shattered front door, blood stains on the floor, pieces of Bess's torn dress scattered about and the blood-stained bed with Brit's body on it. The pistol with one round fired was lying on the bloody sheets. The black gunpowder residue around the wound on Brit's chest was proof the weapon was fired at close range.

The sheriff and coroner told Lila that based on the evidence they had to conclude Brit had attempted to murder Bess and she had killed him in self-defense. She agreed with their conclusion. She asked them to take Brit's body back and when they were finished with their investigation to have it sent to Atlanta for burial. They agreed to do this.

Lila rode with Mose back to the Shoal Creek landing. "I'll have to go to Atlanta to be with Mama, Mose," she said. "I want you to send some people to the cabin this afternoon and clean up that mess. I don't want Rep to come back to that. Get new sheets and blankets and a new mattress for the bed."

Mose nodded. "I do dat."

"When you find out anything about poor Bess, please let me know." She shook her head. "I feel so sorry for Rep, but I don't know what to do. My brother has hurt his wife. How he must hate all of us for this?"

Mose didn't agree. "He don't hate ya'll, Miss Lila. "That boy be lovin you. This ain't yo' fault."

His words didn't console her. "Regardless, you let me know what's happening. I'll be here for two or three days. You have somebody watch at the landing and see if anybody comes from Alabama with news."

It was a long night for Rep. He sat by the bed holding Bess's hand. She never moved nor made a sound during all the hours. Her breathing was labored, and he hurt with every breath she took. He was still trying to deal with what had happened. All the trouble he'd had with Brit had ended up with Bess being hurt. He felt it was his fault, he should've watched after her better.

The doctor checked on her every hour. Afterward, when Rep would look at him, he would frown and shake his head.

It was almost daylight. Rep had dozed off when suddenly Bess moaned. Rep woke up as she raised her head for a moment, her eyes opened and then she fell back and was still. The doctor jumped up and ran to the bed, leaned over and listened for a moment. Then he looked up at Rep and shook his head. "I'm sorry, son. She's gone. She was hurt too bad."

Rep sat with his head down, still holding Bess's hand. Matty stood by the bed sobbing. After some time, Dr. Floyd walked over and sat by Rep. He didn't speak, sat quietly with his hand on his shoulder. Finally, he spoke. "Ya'll take as long as you need with her and then I'll get the funeral home folks to come get her."

His statement awoke Rep from wherever his mind was. He stood up, looked at the doctor and shook his head. He looked at Matty. "Me and her mama will take her home," he said. "We ain't got no money to do all that funeral stuff. We need somebody to take us to the landing."

"Son, that's highly irregular," replied Dr. Floyd.

"Don't matter what you say. We gonna take her home and look after her."

The doctor rushed upstairs and told Mr. Gill what was going on. Mr. Gill came down to the nurse's office and talked to Rep and Matty. He offered his sympathy and then offered to help any way he could. He realized they were shocked by what happened and had no idea what to do. "You have had a terrible shock," he said, "and are worn out. It's been a long day. I know you're concerned about Miss Bess and I understand that. Please let me handle this for you?"

Rep looked at him. "What do you mean?"

"Let our folks take her and take care of her. Don't you worry about any cost. Miss Williams at the store where you bought her dresses, has a dress for her. The folks will see after her and tomorrow she'll be delivered to Walnut Creek or wherever you want her to be. Our folks will stay down there with you as long as you need them." He paused and looked at Rep. "Ya'll talk it over and let me know, but I hope you'll let us help you."

Rep looked at Matty. "Bess be yo wife," she said, "so it's up to you but she loved that little church and Preacher Snow. Them folks can brang her home."

Rep nodded and turned to Mr. Gill. "I thank you, suh, for yo' kindness. You do what you thank be best. Me and Matty will go home, if you can have somebody take us to the landin'."

~

L ila saw Mose at the barn. "We got word that Bess died this morning. Rep will be coming back today so you go to the landing and see what you can do."

Mose nodded. "I go wait for 'im. This sho'nuff be a bad day." He turned and left the barn headed toward the landing.

Lila stood at the door and watched him walk up the road. She knew she had to go to Atlanta, but her thoughts were with Rep.

When Rep turned up the river toward Back Slough and the Shoal Creek landing, he saw Mose waiting at the shed. He slowed down and stopped in the water in front of the landing.

"I be sorry bout Bess" said Mose.

Rep nodded; he couldn't say anything else. "I'm taking Matty home."

"I be to Walnut Creek tomorrow."

Rep nodded, cranked the motor and started down Back Slough.

Mose watched them go and went up the hill toward the kitchen.

~

R ep passed the cabin and didn't look that way, just kept on going down the slough. He didn't know how he could handle coming back. He turned up in Walnut Creek and let Matty out, backed away from the landing and headed back upriver.

He tied up at the pier and sat in the boat for an hour, images running through his mind of Bess. When he came back every day she would run out of the cabin and greet him, sometimes running buck-naked past the pier and jumping in the river. There was no way he could come back to this cabin every day and her not be here.

He finally got out, walked up to the cabin and pushed the door open. The inside was cleaner than it had ever been without any sign of the struggle that had taken place. He walked to the back, picked up his pack, just as it had been since he arrived at Shoal Creek. He walked out, went across the bridge to Big Island and made camp on top of the ridge. That's where he stayed the night, never sleeping.

At daylight he broke camp and took his pack to the boat. He went to the cabin, gathered up the new sheets and blankets off the bed, put them in a sack and carried them to the boat. Lastly, he went in the cabin for the final time and gathered all of Bess's clothes and put them with the other sacks. He cranked up and went downriver. He was acting without thinking, grief was his only companion.

At Walnut Creek he carried the bedclothes and Bess's clothes to the house. He told Matty he thought they could use the sheets and blankets and the girls would be big enough before long to wear Bess's clothes. Matty was concerned and asked him what he would use on the bed at the cabin that night. He didn't answer, just looked at her for a moment and walked away.

Matty had made the arrangements at the cemetery and with Preacher Snow for the service that afternoon. Mose and Hattie Mae arrived before lunch. Several of the women from the church brought food but no one had any appetite. Hattie Mae stayed with Matty and the girls and Mose sat at the landing with Rep. Very little was said.

The hearse arrived and took Bess to the church. They all loaded up in the boats, went up the creek to the bridge, then up the hill to the church. They all stood at graveside, some of the church women sang a song, Preacher Snow said some words and then it was over. Rep stood with his head down, deep in his thoughts. They went back to the bridge and down to the landing.

Mose and Hattie Mae said goodbye to Lick, Matty and the girls and they went to the house. Mose and Rep went off to the side. "I'll be leaving today, Mose," said Rep.

"Where you goin'? You know you can stay."

Rep shook his head. "I can't stay now. I gotta get away for a while and have time to say goodbye to Bess. On the road is a good place to be with her."

"Lila said to tell you she be sorry about everthang."

"I know she is. Everybody's been hurt, Lila too." He walked to the boat with Mose. "I'll bring the boat to the landin' as soon as I say goodbye down here."

"I'll wait for you at the landin'." Mose and Hattie Mae loaded up went back toward Shoal Creek.

Rep walked to the house and called for everybody to come outside. He couldn't make himself go inside the house again. He shook hands with Lick, hugged Matty and told her he was leaving. Then he kissed and hugged the three girls. As he started walking toward the boat, Sassy ran and took his hand. He looked down at her, wondering what she wanted."

"When I git older, I'll come and be yo wife like Bess did, if you want me to."

Rep reached down and picked her up and hugged her. "I would like that, Sassy. When you git older." He smiled for the first time in a while, as he put her down.

He got in the boat, headed down the creek and up the river to Back Slough. He tied up at the cabin and sat for a few minutes, memories running through his mind. Then he walked up to the cabin with a can of gasoline, poured some in the doorway and struck a match. He stood for a moment and watched the flames crawl up the logs. He turned and walked to the pier, got in the boat and headed up the slough. He never looked back.

Mose was waiting at the landing. Rep tied up and as he got out Mose handed him an envelope. Rep immediately thought of another time when Mose gave him another envelope. He looked at his name and knew it was from Lila. He walked over to the bench at the shed and sat down. As he had before, he held it for a while, staring into space. Then he tore it open.

D ear Rep,
      I'm so sorry about Bess. She was a sweet person and she loved you so much as you did her. I'm sorry my family was involved in

causing this heartache for you and Bess's family. I wish so many things had been different.

I was never going to tell you one other thing. I was just going to go away and handle it myself. I wouldn't be telling you now if everything had stayed as it was. But everything has changed, for all of us and I think you deserve to know the truth. I am pregnant. I am carrying your child. This happened during the two days we spent at your cabin. I'm not asking you to do anything, you have enough to deal with now and that is what I want you to do. I'll handle this myself. But I will have this baby and if it's a girl, I'll name her Bess. She'll be Bess Doe. You'll be on the birth certificate as her father.

I know now you must deal with your sorrow in your way. I know how you are. You will be in my heart and mind as you work this out. But I want you to know I'll be here at Shoal Creek in the future, I plan to live here and run the farm. We'll both be here, waiting.

I love you, Lila

M ose had been watching as he sat and read the note. When Rep put the note in the envelope and tucked it in his pocket and got up, he walked over and waited. They both saw the black smoke down the slough at the same time.

"I set the cabin on fire," said Rep.

Mose nodded. "Spected you would."

"I couldn't stay there, and I don't want nobody else to be there."

Mose could hear the pain in his voice. He didn't know anything to say.

They walked on up the hill to the kitchen. Rep called Hattie Mae to come out, thanked her for everything, hugged her and walked on toward the barn with Mose alongside.

"I thank you for everything you did for me," Rep said as they walked.

"I be sorry ever thang be so bad."

"Like I told you, I can't stay here now, but I'll see you sometime. You've been a good friend." He started to shake Mose's hand, but instead reached out, hugged him and held on. He finally stepped back, nodded and started walking up the road toward the gate.

Rep was about halfway to the gate when the barn door opened, and Lila walked out. She stood beside Mose on the porch and watched Rep walk away. "Did he read the note?" she asked.

"He read it." Mose pointed to the smoke over the trees toward the river. "He done burnt the cabin down."

She looked at the smoke. "He would do that. That was a special place for him." She sighed. "A special place for me too."

"He say he gotta have some time to be with Miss Bess. He say on the road he can do that."

Lila smiled. "That's his place where he's at peace, alone with himself. One thing I've learned with Rep, he's a man of his word." She looked at Mose. "He'll be back, he has a reason to come back."

Mose nodded. "You be right bout that, Miss Lila. He sho'nuff be coming back."

The End

Thanks for reading Shoal Creek.
If you enjoyed it please consider leaving a review on Amazon.com
This will help the author and also help others to find books they will enjoy reading.

Made in the USA
Middletown, DE
31 March 2021